NOTHING
KNEW

D1073323

NOTHING KNEW

REDEMPTION GRAY SERIES

BOOK 2 OF 3

S. WESTLEY KING

REDEMPTION
PRESS

Copyright © 2021, S. Westley King. All rights reserved.
Published by Redemption Press, PO Box 427, Enumclaw, WA 98022.
Toll-Free (844) 2REDEEM (273-3336)

Redemption Press is honored to present this title in partnership with the author. Redemption Press provides our imprint seal representing design excellence, creative content, and high quality production.

Scripture used on pages 100–106 are from The Holy Bible, English Standard Version. ESV® Text Edition: 2016. © 2001 by Crossway Bibles, a publishing ministry of Good News Publishers.

Scripture used beginning on page 194 is from The Holy Bible, New International Version®, NIV® ©1973, 1978, 1984, 2011 by Biblica, Inc.® Used by permission. All rights reserved worldwide.

Lyrics from "Scars," written by Matthew Hein, Jon McConnell, Ethan Hulse, and Matthew Armstrong, are used by permission of I Am They Publishing (BMI) / Be Essential Songs (BMI) / EGH Music Publishing (BMI) / admin at EssentialMusicPublishing.com. All rights reserved.

This book is a work of fiction. Names, characters, places, and incidents are products of the author's imagination or are used fictitiously. Any resemblance to actual events or locales or persons, living or dead, is entirely coincidental.

No part of this publication may be reproduced, stored in a retrieval system, or transmitted in any way by any means—electronic, mechanical, photocopy, recording, or otherwise—without the prior permission of the copyright holder, except as provided by USA copyright law.

ISBN: 978-1-64645-377-1 (Paperback)
978-1-64645-379-5 (ePub)
978-1-64645-378-8 (Mobi)

LCCN: 2021915341

CONTENTS

INTRODUCTION

Never jump on the back of a motorcycle with the devil just because you think he's Jesus. I'm not saying he was the actual devil in bodily form, but I'm not entirely sure, either. Actually, I'm not sure about a lot of things, so I'm going to slow it down a little and try to figure out what I am sure of.

I *am* sure that last Friday morning I was at school in Dallas, just a few weeks away from graduation. My granddad died the day before, and I was a total wreck on the inside. I guess that's what made me walk out of English class and drive fifteen hundred miles north after Mr. Adams told me I couldn't find happiness under a rock in Montana.

I am sure Mr. Adams was wrong about that. I did find happiness under a rock in Montana, but it probably had more to do with being alone in a car for two days than anything else. Driving away from the noise of the city, stripping away all my usual distractions, and then wrestling with the thoughts and emotions that were left—it wasn't easy. Silence and aloneness were completely new to me, but it turned out good. I learned a lot.

I *am* sure Mr. Adams was right when he talked about meaning being everywhere. Everything is a metaphor if you think about it, if you look for it. I'm still working on that, though. This thinking thing is new to me. I've been taught to memorize facts and repeat what teachers say. I'm not an awful student in school, but I've got a long way to go to be a good student of life.

I'm also sure that truth exists, just as surely as the bedrock of earth, and it is covered with (and sometimes hiding under) layers of history, plants, animals, humans, roads, and cities. I *know* I sat on that mountainside and, just for a minute, everything made sense and I was happy. I know there are a lot of views out there about every topic, and not all of them can be right—but there is something bigger that is true. There's *truth*.

I am sure that there is something "native" in all of us. I'm not sure what it is, but it's something more than our stories, our histories, our identities. It's like the way I've been thinking about the struggle between Native Americans and the settlers who conquered their world. It's too simple; the wrong enemy's too easy to blame. The fight going on inside us and around us is not so black and white, and it's easy to confuse what is native with what feels natural. History books make things sound so clear cut, but I'm learning it takes a lot more to sort out what really happened and how it still plays out around us.

And that's why I'm sure now that evil exists and that there really are people out there who don't care if their actions hurt other people. But good exists too. I've seen it. I think there's a war going on between them. It's not usually a war you can see—not like two armies facing off in a Kansas field. No, it's more like . . .

What is it like? It's the invisible forces and the things that look good outside but, on the inside, are rotten. Like a perfect apple with a worm inside. Or maybe the wolf, dressed in Granny's clothes, trying to coax Red Riding Hood closer and closer so it could eat her. If you know to look carefully, you might see it's not right, but you don't look. You assume it's good or it means well. And you trust it until, too late, you realize it's dangerous, and you've been deceived.

It's like Longstoryshort, who you'll learn more about as I write. Just enough truth to make a lie sound believable. Just enough reason to make you feel crazy. Just enough power to make you feel powerless. Just the right questions to make you doubt everything.

So much has happened in a week. So much to think about, to try to figure out.

What I can tell you for sure is that, as I was making the turn from running away to coming home, I ran into an elk— or maybe it ran into me. Either way, it totaled my parents' car and left me stuck on the side of the road. I had just found God, had just cried out my belief in Him, and had given Him my life. So it was natural— wasn't it?—that I thought it was Jesus when, right after the wreck, Longstoryshort pulled up on his motorcycle and said, "Need a ride?" I thought, *God will provide. God will protect me. God has sent someone to save me.*

But I was wrong. And now I'm confused. I need a better understanding of what is true after having been betrayed so badly. What I don't understand is, why would God allow such evil right after I found Him? And I'm still not home, where I've never wanted more to be.

So now, I think I need to slow down and go back to last Sunday night, to the foothills of the Crazy Mountains in Montana, and remember what happened and how it happened. Because I'm sure I have a chance at a new life. A better life. I don't want to just react to everything anymore. I want to live on purpose, to use my life for what is good and true.

I'm pretty sure that's going to take a lot more wisdom than I have right now though. And I'm going to need a lot more courage too . . . to not freeze or wait for someone else to do it for me. I can't be afraid of the fire.

CHAPTER 1

SUNDAY NIGHT: MONTANA

8:45 p.m.

I had just spent the first day of my new life going to church, writing out the details of my drive from Texas to Montana, and basking in the good feeling of a true mountaintop experience. I was on my way home. Things were going to be okay. I had just prayed my life over to God and told Him I was ready for whatever was next.

Running into an elk first thing was not what I expected. But Longstoryshort pulling up on his motorcycle right after it happened seemed like it could be a God-thing. The car was undrivable, and I was shaken up. And before it could register that I didn't have a way home, I had a way home. Wasn't that God, showing me He would provide?

There he is on a motorcycle, taking off his matte-black helmet, strong and calm. I shake my head to stop the spinning and try to focus on him. He's clean and groomed. Has a short gray beard and a long, thick, braided ponytail, a gentle smile, and strong, silver eyes.

"Need a ride?"

"All the way to Texas?" I ask from my dizzy stupor.

He shrugs. "I can get you to Denver in a few days."

My new faith has no experience, no wisdom, no foresight. Faith is supposed to be blind, right? I give my life to God, and everything works out, right? Without consciously thinking any of this, it just happens. "Okay."

"Hop on," he says, gesturing me forward. "People call me Longstoryshort."

I stagger toward him, finding my feet under me and trying to stay upright. I look back at the car, then at the firm man of a man on the motorcycle. It's surreal. This is where I should feel some kind of wariness of strangers on the highway at night, but no fear registers. That's faith, right? Anyway, up until now in my safe and sheltered life, I've never had a reason not to trust people. I'm shaken and dizzy, and somehow, I *know* this is God saving His new believer.

"Are you Jesus?" I ask sheepishly.

The look in his silvery gaze deepens to eternity, and a half smile widens across his face. "Well, I guess I am your savior of sorts," he says.

Then he reaches into a saddlebag that hangs at the back of the long, straight seat. He hands me a white, open-faced helmet. I pull it on, and it fits snug over my head and ears. The tightness immediately helps my pounding temples.

"Fasten the chin strap," he says. The helmet must've muffled his voice, because it takes me a second to understand what he said. I reach up and fumble with the ends of the strap until I figure out how it works. I got it. No problem.

The hard helmet evokes a courage to abandon the wreck and put my life in someone else's hands.

Still straddling the bike, Longstoryshort bends over and pushes something down on both sides of the machine. Then he straightens up and leans forward. "Get on. There's pegs to put your feet on."

Somehow, I manage to get one leg over the bike. I settle gingerly onto the seat and look down. My feet find the pegs. I'm surprised that the saddlebags aren't in my way. They looked like they would be.

There isn't much seat behind me. It'd probably be easy to slip off. I shift and look for something to hold on to.

"Don't touch any of those pipes," Longstoryshort says. "They'll burn the skin right off you." Then he smooths back some loose wisps of hair and pulls on his helmet. He looks back at me before he lowers the visor. "Hang on tight."

The engine starts with the roar of a lion, and before I can hang on tight—to what?—the throttle is open and we swerve onto the dark road. I grab Longstoryshort around the stomach, hard. He slaps my arm to remind me to think of him and his ability to breathe. I loosen up and dare to look ahead.

I can't help but laugh at the first sign the headlight illuminates: "Watch for Wildlife," big and yellow with a few dozen reflective dots around the perimeter.

Riding on the back of a motorcycle is different than riding in a car. The first thing you notice is the immediacy of death. You're on two wheels, and the wind is hitting your skin, clothes, and face as fast as you hit it, stinging with cold friction and reminding you of how much more friction there would be if you hit the hard paved ground. Being a wet patch of leaves or a bighorn sheep away from death really makes you come to terms with your own mortality in ways that most people don't think about. And when you're gliding through time with the constant awareness that your life could be over at any moment, you start to appreciate life, and the things that don't matter blow off with the wind.

Maybe that's why people love motorcycles so much—it brings out something native in them, something free. It makes me glad I've already died, and I feel born again as we pass over death with a forward momentum toward a new life.

The wind and the air pushing against you also reminds you that you're not in control. Not in control of the music, not in control of the temperature. You're not in a safe room with wheels where you get to set the temperature and silence the sounds as you sit back and watch the scenery pass by like a peaceful commercial for antidepressants (while some disembodied voice nonchalantly reads all the warnings, side effects, and possible death).

On a motorcycle, you don't get to enjoy the scenery; you are a part of it. You're no longer a passive observer; you're physically *in* it—as much as the bugs that smack against your forehead or the owls that prey on the scurrying field mouse. The owl. *The owl of Minerva only flies at nightfall.* That owl was supposed to mean something. Wisdom. Nightfall. Wisdom comes too late? I hope that's not true.

I find a comfortable clench on Longstoryshort's firm and unmovable sides and let the forehead of my helmet rest against the top of his leathered back, avoiding the violence of the wind. "I'm riding on the back of a motorcycle with Jesus," I assure myself. "It's okay, I'm safe. I'm going home. God's taking care of me."

I've heard people say, "Trust in Jesus," but it always seemed like one of those empty phrases Christians use to gloss over the hard realities of life. But when you're on the back of a motorcycle going down the highway at night, you learn real quick what trust is. If I move to the right or the left, I risk tilting the balance, so I've got no choice but to sit still and trust. He's in control of the speed. He's in control of avoiding elk and bighorn rams, keeping upright as the occasional RV blows by with a punch of wind. My life is in his hands, and he's in control of aiming us in the direction we are going.

The direction we are going is home. *Swing low, sweet motorbike, coming for to carry me home.* A song from childhood. I can't see much in the darkness, but we swing low into a valley as the general elevation rises. I look out at a canopy of twinkling heavenly lights, interspersed with enough glowing house lights to show the contour of the earth. It's like a starry blanket has come down to tuck in the mountains of truth for the night.

I don't know if we're going to stop to sleep or if we're going to drive through the night, but I've found rest on this thinly padded seat, holding tight to a statue against the whirlwind of air around us. Even with the lingering shock of pain in my body, I am aware of my soul, and I am at peace.

Sitting behind Longstoryshort with no windows or visor, I can't focus much on the scenery, so I close my eyes and admire Longstoryshort. I don't know anything about him other than his kindness to help out a stranger, his motorcycle, and this freedom he is sharing with me. He's older, but not aged. A timeless vitality matches his strong but gentle manliness. In history class, Mr. Homer taught us about the "rugged individualism" of the American West with a romantic tone and dreamy look in his eyes. Mr. Homer is about the same age as Longstoryshort, but with a button-up shirt tight around his marriage belly (as he calls it), wrinkled khakis, and slightly hunched teacher posture. Longstoryshort is who Mr. Homer dreams of being. I picture myself at fifty riding a motorcycle across America, doing what I want, when I want, and helping people along the way.

I turn my head to the right and lean gently again into my rescuer. A green town sign quickly reflects "Pray," with an arrow pointing to the east. I think of Lame Deer, the town I stopped in to stretch my legs and get a snack and my cross. "Our ways are through prayer," the sign said. "Help our people, pray for everyone." So I pray for them. I pray for my mom and dad. I pray for Skip and Tom and the Custers and Natives of this world. I pray for my classmates, my girlfriend, my teachers. And as simply as it started, the prayer spirals outward and upward in a constant unraveling, like the opening of an endless gift. It feels good deep in my bones to be thinking of others, lifting them up with a new knowing and belief in a Creator who loves and cares for us.

A subtle slowing of the motorcycle shifts me out of my well of prayer and back to the cold wind, milky black sky, and now hollow black valley. We turn off the highway, through a sparse mountain neighborhood's streets and occasional intersections, then back and forth, back and forth, up a steep, climbing road. He knows where he's going, slowing and leaning at every turn, higher and higher. The pavement turns to rough rock. The popping of rocks and cutting through gravel becomes louder than the quieting engine. The gravel road empties into hard but flat ground. Small plants whip at my feet on both sides. After a few minutes of no road, Longstoryshort throttles down to a stop, and I am poured out onto a football field of flat land near the top of a mountain.

A deer freezes in the headlight, then runs. It doesn't know if we mean it harm. How can it tell if we do or not? We don't, but fear is natural.

The headlight turns off with the engine. Cliffs of shadow point upward all around us to a living night sky. There are so many stars, it's like we're inside something much bigger than ourselves. The universe's nervous system flickers around us with heavenly thoughts and reflexes.

"This way," Longstoryshort says from a few dozen steps away as he smooths back his hair. I didn't even notice us getting off the motorcycle and him starting to walk. I'm spellbound as I follow, still looking up at the heavens I can almost touch. "We'll sleep here."

I trip over a rock and look to the ground and around, finding my eyes have adjusted as a billion separate light waves end their night's journey with us here. The rock I stumbled on is one of many organized in a circle around where Longstoryshort is unrolling a sleeping bag.

"Have you been here before?" I ask, not knowing what else to say.

"It's a place I know well," Longstoryshort answers as he tosses me a thin wool blanket. "Paradise. The area we just drove through is known as Paradise Valley."

"I can see why. It's beautiful."

"Beauty's got nothing to do with it. In Hebrew, 'paradise' means 'walled place.' That valley is protected on all sides from the world speeding on around it. I call this spot Paradise because of the cliffs all around us. We can sleep safe."

"So is this like Eden?"

"No. Eden had water." He says it like he was there, but now I think I'm just looking for reasons to prove he's Jesus. But he's smart; he knows Hebrew; he saved me; he's kind and generous. Who am I to say God wouldn't send Jesus in the form of Longstoryshort to take me home? He's God. He can do anything, right?

"The Blackfoot camped here hundreds of years ago, before the civilizers came and taught them they were poor and didn't know God. This is where they'd retire for the day, under these same stars. Then they'd tell stories to the children around the campfire before tucking them in, in their tepees." He was sitting up on his sleeping bag, gaze fixed on another time, voice cool and philosophical. "The next day, they'd wake up with the morning mist, climb to a high point, and scan the flats below for herds of buffalo that didn't know they were entering a narrow place. I suppose in that way, the Blackfoot were like the buffalo. . ." He continues and I want to listen, but my mind has drifted to the campfire we don't have.

I become aware of how cold I am. My fingers, arms, and shivering core await a pause in his telling to ask if he wants me to gather firewood. ". . . and Great Turnip, who grew near where Spider-Man lived. . ."

Wait a second, I missed something. Turnips and Spider-Man? Mr. Adams would always get upset when we raised our hands to ask a question while he was on one of his tangents. He'd say, "You can't be thinking of what you want to say and listen at the same time." I guess he was right.

"Long story short, Poya became a star that follows Venus in the morning. You can't see it yet, but he's always chasing something . . . and the sun and the moon . . ." I know I should be paying attention, but my ears are ice and a fire would be nice, and I'm waiting for a break to ask if I can help get that started. ". . . the sky country becomes their home . . ." This is a long story. It just keeps going. I'm not sure he even remembers I'm here. ". . . and it makes me realize"—the tone of his voice changes and catches my attention—"I've got nothing for a name for you."

Oh, the story is over. He's looking at me.

"Oh, um," I stutter as I almost say "Red" out of habit, but want to claim my real name, the name I wrote on that cross yesterday on the mountainside. "Redemption," I say and straighten my posture.

"Did you just make that up?"

"No sir. It's my given name."

"You must've had a hard time growing up with a name like that." I did.

"Your parents really did a number on you, didn't they?" He laughs. "That's a heavy name; you must hate it."

I did, but I appreciate it now, knowing what it means. I'm going to try to live up to it. I can't answer out loud for some reason. My eyes are again transfixed by the ocean of stars above us.

"I see you keep looking up at that sky country, all wide eyed and small. Look at them. In the morning, you'll be able to see the mountain you're on and the ranges for hundreds of miles. And those are small compared to the big world they're on, and even smaller held up to the universe." He pauses; I listen. "If you think about it, you're nothing, really. A little speck of life on a speck of a planet in the great big universe. So many people forget that. Start thinking they're bigger than they are. Make themselves gods of sorts. Not much good happens when people think they're something. I once knew a guy full of energy and big ideas. Wanted to save the world. Things got tough—world didn't want changing, big machine that it is. You see, this world is like that motorcycle over there, each part made with a purpose. You mess with one part, and the whole thing won't work." He shrugs. "Long story short, the guy ended up dying alone . . ." Long*story*long would be more like it.

No, if this is Jesus, I should be paying more attention.

I guess that's what I do to my teachers in school too. They've got something to teach me, make my life better, brain smarter, but I space out and assume they're wasting my time because I don't want to focus. I guess I really am selfish. Longstoryshort slaps his knee, and I jump.

"I think I'll call you 'Nothing,'" he proclaims. "To remind you to stay humble and to remind me you're just a kid passing through. Dallas, huh?"

I don't like the idea of being called "Nothing," but I guess it makes a little sense, considering what he was saying. Anyway, God's been guiding me this far. Who am I to question? No one. *Exactly.*

"Yeah, I left school Friday morning. Drove up the Great Plains, through the Black Hills, and to Montana. I was on my way back when I hit that elk, and that's when you showed up. Right when I was in trouble." Between the cold on my ears and fingers and this throbbing burn all inside my chest . . . it's a wonder I can concentrate at all. I wonder if I have a cracked rib from the airbag or whiplash or something.

Before he can start another monologue, I ask, "Should I get wood for a fire?"

"No," he answers quickly. "With the wind and dry ground, we'd be liable to start a blaze we can't control." After a pause, he asks, "You have a phone?"

"No, I threw it out the window in Nebraska."

"Good for you, kid. Those things are a tool for the devil."

I stand awkwardly for a moment while Longstoryshort sits. It's like he's in his own living room and I'm a guest in his house. I sit on the blanket he gave me, wondering for a moment if this is all I'll have to sleep with, but then I chastise myself again for being selfish. He didn't know he'd be picking me up, and he was kind enough to give me this at his own expense.

I find a spot with only a few rocks and weeds, tuck myself under the blanket, and rest my head on my backpack. Longstoryshort stays still, like a statue, timeless, a part of the world.

As tired as I am, my brain is as awake as the night sky. Coyotes bark and howl, reminding me there's a world beyond this paradise. Sly and carnivorous. Are we safe here? Crickets vibrate the air with a humming pulse, but they're not singing at the same pitch as the ones in Texas. Shooting star. No, not a star. How often do we misname things or misunderstand what they are because of our perspective? Longstoryshort stirs, slides into his sleeping bag. No cars, trains, or power lines. Alone. Just me and God.

And the coyotes and crickets.

And the stars. There are so many I can't make out any constellations. Like all of it is the Milky Way. I'm in awe, remembering our solar system is *in* the Milky Way. I am *in* beauty. I am looking up at a part of it. Some of these stars I am seeing supposedly burned out billions of years ago, but the light is just now getting to me. I am seeing the memory of stars. Lying in the memory of Native Americans.

I picture the tepees that were once set up in this circle, the families who lived in them. They had the food, shelter, and clothing they needed. Until someone told them they were naked. They had each other. I imagine the father calling the children in around the fire to follow the flicker of floating embers to the foundation of the stories of the stars. I see his arms talk and the children laugh as he tells them a story of the deer. I see a group of stars that looks like a deer.

They had what they needed. They were rich because they hadn't been told they were lacking. They had nothing to run away from, no need to escape, nowhere better than where they were. They had love and belonging. They depended on each other.

Or am I romanticizing the past? Did the hunters hunt to get away from their yelling wives? Did they argue and throw things like my parents do? Did the young ones ever take their father's horse and run away? As much as I needed to get away from the home I knew, now I long for family, even if it's mine. As imperfect as they are, I love them and . . . and I belong with them. It can be better. I was named Redemption for a reason. Maybe this is it.

For the first time in my life, I want to be home. And a part of it.

The moon is setting, and for being dark, it's remarkably light here. Now I can see the cracks and crevices in the cliffs, the trees taking root in them, the tufts of grass, and even the parts that make up the motorcycle. Has it gotten brighter, or have my eyes adjusted more? Out of habit, I tap my pocket for my cell phone. If I had it and pulled it out, I wouldn't be able to see anything but the screen. No stars, no cliffs. I wouldn't be here. I'd be in a place that only exists in an artificial, digital world. My eyes were designed by the same God that made *this* world, *this* universe. My eyes were made for *this*.

A satellite passes overhead in its orbit. Cell phones? Spying? Google Earth? *Progress.* It's amazing what we humans are capable of. I wonder what would come of investing the same resources to explore the inner universe—the advancement of our souls, the understanding of God, the search for truth. Or would that be like the guy Longstoryshort was talking about who tried messing with the machine and ended up dead and alone?

My thoughts are clearer than they've ever been, even though I feel like I don't know anything. I'm in awe at the world I live on—in—but never knew existed. Was this what the forty years in the wilderness was like? Less of a trial and more of a re-centering—a stripping away of everything I am not, a reminding of who made me, how He made me, and where He made me? Who am I? Who am I going to be? Nothing? I guess that's where it starts.

A coyote barks at another across the way. A river of icy air flows over me, and I feel a touch of uncertainty. I curl under the blanket. But this is the same wind that blew over me in the car. The same wind that made the fields of grain look like an ocean. The same wind

I gave happiness to under the big Montana sun. I just had that happiness. Where did it go, and how did it go so fast?

So cold. I breathe deep and slow, trying to ignore the coyotes and other animals my imagination puts on the tops of the cliffs, looking down on us, making plans for their hunt. The people. The tepees, fire, and kids. They knew it was a temporary stay. This is just a temporary stay. I pull the blanket over my ears and curl my knees to my chest. The dirt beneath me takes on the warmth of my body, and slowly, I drift into darkness.

CHAPTER 2

EARLY MONDAY MORNING: PARADISE VALLEY

I **awake with a quick breath,** tangled in the blanket. My skin is as crisp as the air, but my blood is warmed by the coals that still radiate inside my ribs. The scenery is calm and quiet. The crickets have gone to sleep, and the coyotes are in their dens. But the silence of nature still isn't silent. A bird sings, and the breeze whispers. The sky is changing colors against the gray rock, and distant purple mountains rise beyond the window we drove in from.

Longstoryshort shoots upright with a gasp and quickly collects himself. Does Jesus have bad dreams? He wipes beads of sweat from his forehead, then carefully rolls his bed into a seat, his defined forearms flexing with ease. Power and grace, even in age. That's what I'd like to be like. He pours water from his canteen into a cup, picks up a handful of dirt, and mixes it in with the water. His granite eyes see me looking at him; he sits and awaits my words.

"I dreamed about fire," I say instead of a kiddish "good morning."

No response. I take it he's listening.

"I was in the fire. My dad was on fire, my mom was screaming. I ran out of the house, and the neighborhood was in flames. I got in the car, drove through the fire, but it wasn't hot. The school was blackening in a slow dancing explosion; my friends were panicking inside. I sped onto the melting highway. The city was burning, and I followed the same northbound highways I just drove. Except the plains were a sea of burning orange and yellow, and plumes of smoke took over the sky. Somehow, I ended up here with you. The fire passed over both of us, and afterward there was only a baby. I think it was me. There were people, if they were people, looking down from these cliffs. It was weird. I don't dream much. Especially not this clear. Do you think it was Satan trying to scare me?"

Longstoryshort seems to be gazing into eternity. Maybe he's thinking about it. I don't want to feel like a child, but I do. What can I say that would be more mature? My mind races from girlfriends to Native Americans to metal fishing boats to books I didn't read for class but should have.

After a long, awkward stillness, I interrupt the chatty birds. "What's your favorite part of the Bible?" The question seems to come from nowhere, but it has been circling my mind. I don't know much about the Bible, really, other than the things I picked up here and there as a kid. Father Abraham had many sons, Moses and the Red Sea, David and Goliath, and some guys who stood in a fire but weren't burned. I've never really thought about the Bible, but the sermon yesterday wasn't a kid story. It felt like wisdom. I want more, but don't know where to start.

I'm starting to question if he's listening, but he answers, "He will command his angels concerning you, and they will lift you up in their hands, so that you will not strike your foot against a stone. It's from . . . uh . . . Psalm 91."

Oh. Maybe that's who Longstoryshort is. Maybe he's an angel. I feel safe in his hands.

"Mine's Ecclesiastes," I say. It's the only part I've read. Money, power, fame—it's all meaningless. Chasing the wind. That's all high school is. It put into words what I already felt, and it made me not feel so crazy for feeling that way. It's what I needed to hear.

"Doesn't that book say that the only thing worthwhile is to fear God?" Longstoryshort says, half as a question, half as a statement.

After a pause and with the same tone, he asks, "Why would God make a creation whose only purpose is to fear Him?"

My eyebrows knit at the idea as my brain hits a wall. I do remember reading that. But I guess I didn't think about it that way. Why would He?

A thin grayness wisps over the cliffs and thickens between us and the bluing morning sky.

"Maybe it was God who gave you the dream to make you afraid," Longstoryshort adds, almost as a distracted afterthought, studying the sky above. "Must be a fire somewhere. We'd better get out of this oven."

He rerolls the blanket I already rolled and handed him, then loads everything into the saddlebags. He walks around the bike and kneels to fidget with some parts near what looks like the engine. I admire the bike as I wait. It's got to be an old one, just by its shape—it isn't as fancy as the ones people drive around Dallas—but he must take really good care of it. It's as clean and shiny as if it were brand new.

"Do you know much about motorcycles?" he asks.

"No," I say honestly, "but it's a beautiful machine."

"It's a glorious idea made of a thousand ugly parts, and one of them is making a noise that it shouldn't. There's a station down the mountain that should have what I need. We'll fill up, fine-tune, and get ready for a long day of riding."

I look around at the cliffs, disappointed we didn't get to climb and see the views he was talking about last night. It doesn't smell like fire, but he knows nature better than I do. And Native American history. And motorcycles. He leans over and sprays something along the side of the bike. I try to figure out what he's doing, but that would take actually knowing how the thing works. My dad always takes the car to the shop and lets a mechanic fix it. There's something manly and *practical* about being able to fix your own problems on the go.

"Nothing," Longstoryshort says, and it takes me a second to remember that that is my name, "I don't know you that well, but you seem to be a good kid. When we're around other people, follow the rules. Don't be a bother, and don't cause a scene."

"What are the rules?" I ask, thinking there were specifics.

"Don't be a bother, and don't cause a scene. We're in other peoples' everyday world, and we're just passing through. They don't think highly of tourists, always being a bother and causing a scene. We don't want to do that. You ready to go?" He drinks the rest of his cup, puts it away, and straddles the motorcycle as I climb on behind him. Without hesitation, the engine announces our presence and departure.

The zigzagging down the mountain seems quicker than our ascent last night, and it's not long before we're at a station in a town named Emigrant.

At the gas pump, I stand and look up at the mountain we were just on top of and around at the others that make this Paradise Valley.

Without the sun or a phone or a watch, I realize I don't know what time it is. I've always known what time it is, religiously looking at my phone or the clock, metering out the timeline of events of daily life—classes, practice, bedtime, and favorite shows. Even on this trip, the awareness of time has helped me remember sights, thoughts, and sounds. I feel a sort of freedom in *not* knowing now, but I check my pocket for my phone anyway, knowing it's not there. I look at Longstoryshort's wrists as he tops off the gas, and he's not wearing a watch. That doesn't surprise me.

A sleek, new motorcycle is pulling up from the south, and Longstoryshort waits for him to exchange niceties.

"How's the weather down the road?" he asks the leather-clad biker, probably in his sixties, as he dismounts and settles at the pump opposite us.

"Air's got a chill, but it's nice. Lots of mansnails out, though. Mind their wind."

"Any sign of fire?" Longstoryshort questions.

"Just whatcha see above us. Could be Yellowstone, could be California."

"Passable through the south?"

"Freshly plowed." He glances at me and back at Longstoryshort. "Chilly though."

Freshly plowed? Chilly? I hope the gas station has coats.

Longstoryshort nods consideringly. "Thanks."

As we walk to the station store, I ask, "Mansnails?"

"RVs, motor homes. People want to get away but take their homes with them. No regard for the danger they are to bikers or much else outside their walls. We just hold on a little tighter when they're coming our way."

"Good morning!" The cashier I can't see announces, "No checks, and the bathroom's out."

Glad for the warmth inside the store, I think about what I need. Water. Snacks. Beef jerky, honey sticks. They have sweatshirts. That'll be nice. Deodorant. Longstoryshort is filling up with coffee, and I unload my arms onto the counter and hand the cashier my card.

"Comes to seventy-one eighty-two. Credit or debit?"

"Credit," I say automatically. I'm not really sure what the difference is, but it always works.

"Card's declined. Got another way to pay?"

My parents must have canceled the card or reported it stolen. I kind of figured they would. I'll call them down the road and see how bad it is. Let them know I'm okay. Do they know about the car already? I swallow, and a lump drops into my stomach.

"Got another way to pay?" she repeats. I'm paralyzed.

"How much?" Longstoryshort has come to save me again.

"Seventy-one dollars and eighty-two cents," the cashier repeats, almost annoyed that we're being a bother.

"Put the sweatshirt back," Longstoryshort instructs me, "and the snacks." I hear him apologize for me as I'm putting the $50 tourist sweatshirt back, and the cashier recalculates the cost. I feel a little shame but thankfulness at the same time. Walking back, I see Longstoryshort peel a $100 bill off a wad from his jacket pocket and stand peacefully waiting for his change.

He hands me my bag with water, jerky, honey sticks, and deodorant. "Thanks," I say, to both him and the attendant, then lead the way out with my tail between my legs.

"Your card!" she hollers. Longstoryshort turns back to grab it as I hold the door for the biker we met outside.

"Good morning," I hear her tell him. "No checks, and the restroom's out."

Longstoryshort wipes my card off with the bottom of his shirt and holds it by the edges as we make our way back to the pumps. "Clean the headlamp while I check the tappers," he instructs.

I don't know what tappers are, but I know how to clean a headlamp. I'm following now, a few steps behind. He doesn't notice me notice him put my card in a saddlebag on the other motorcycle. Why would he do that? I guess it doesn't matter—it doesn't work anyway. I get the squeegee and a few paper towels and start at the hardened bug parts on the bulb. There is no windshield on this motorcycle, and I can't see anything else to do but watch.

"Don't go faster than your spirit," the other motorcyclist says, entering our scene briefly before he mounts, revs, and speeds away.

I want to ask Longstoryshort about the card, but I've already broken the rules by being a bother and causing a scene, and I already feel like a helpless kid. I wonder if he has any kids, what they would look like and how they'd act. What would they do to make him proud? "What do you do for a living?" I ask instead.

"I live," Longstoryshort answers, loosening the screws that hold the license plate in place. "I live for a living. In absolute freedom."

"I mean, what do you do for work?" I ask, not because I'm trying to pry, but more because I'd like to live this kind of life.

"I don't work," he replies with pride. "Work is what you do when you're a slave."

"Well, how do you make money?" I really need to quit asking questions, or he'll regret picking me up.

"I know what you're getting at, kid," he says smoothly and (thankfully) without a hint of annoyance. "People need me. They need what I can do, what I know, and sometimes they just need me around. And they pay for it, and pay well."

"What skills? How can I live free?"

"You sure ask a lot of questions," he answers, tightening the last screw after replacing the license plate.

Too many. Some teachers get annoyed with me because I ask too many questions and don't listen for the answers. Some get annoyed because I don't ask enough questions. There are "right" questions, but I never seem to have them at the right time.

Mr. Adams said asking questions was okay, stopping at them was the problem. "So many answers to the questions you ask are right at the tips of your fingers," he'd tell the class, "but the good ones are the ones you can't find on your phone." He grew up coding and always talks about the time before search engines. He said now it's not much different. The internet's right there with answers, but they might as well be in a book in an archive on the third floor of a dusty library on the other side of the moon. He says all the internet's used for now is what he calls "social media syndrome" and porn.

I don't know. I appreciate that there is so much information out there. But sometimes, there's so much it's hard to sort through it. Mr. Homer, my history teacher, talked about us being in the age of information, but it feels more like the age of *too much* information. And it's near impossible to figure out what's good information and what's going to count off points if you use it as a source on a paper.

Plus, the answers might be at our fingertips, but so are all the distractions. It's like we have phones so we can have easy access to truth, but they're designed to do everything in their power to keep us from getting to it.

"Sorry," I say, feeling it. The burning in my chest gets lower. I don't think it's a bone or muscle thing.

"No need. You're young. Haven't got much life experience." He's right.

"Nothing," I say with a smile. I don't have any life experience, but I'm thankful I'm getting some.

He stands, smiles back, honks the horn with his thumb, and says, "Now, let's find out what's making that sound."

I watch him kneel on the oil-stained concrete and proceed in a ritual he must have done more times than I've brushed my teeth. When's the last time I brushed my teeth? He checks one part, rubs off the grime, puts it back. Checks another part, rubs off the grime, puts it back. I'm not sure if a part is the problem or the grime or if he's narrowing down the possibilities. I couldn't even hear anything wrong with the engine in the first place. I guess you have to be around the right sound for a long time to notice when there is something wrong. He finishes that stage of maintenance and begins another.

"Routine maintenance," he begins like a wise teacher. "Oil the chain, check the plugs, adjust the tappers, inflate the tires. It's all part of life. If you don't do routine maintenance, especially on an old bike like this, you're waiting for something to break. Then you're on the side of the road walking with a big bill coming your way. Most people don't understand how their cars work, their fridges, microwaves, computers, or even their own brains and bodies. Same thing applies. Let someone else fix their problem. Work extra hours to pay the repair bills—and even more if you buy a new one. And all the while, the kids are at home wondering where their dad is." He's hitting home. I've sat at the dinner table more than a few times alone with

Mom while Dad was out picking up extra work to pay for the new transmission, new washer . . . the new(ish) car I wrecked last night.

". . . but you can't buy a new body, can't buy a new brain. Those things were made to wear out, and all the devil needs to do is keep a smart person busy keeping track of all the things that need fixing, and he ends up at the end of his life a fool." *At the end of your life.* Just like Grandpa said in his journal. Live life from the perspective of the end. He's speaking truth, and I'm not listening to the answers to the questions I didn't know to ask. Instead, I want to dig in my backpack for Grandpa's journal and reread what I read a few nights ago in the hotel.

". . . long story short, all of society is like this 1964 Honda Superhawk—every level, no matter how you slice it . . ." I picture Custer on a motorcycle riding through Native American camps with a blast of a gun, a "Yee-haw!" and someone taking his picture for the newspapers in DC. I think of the ancient tent circle we slept in last night and accidentally interrupt Longstoryshort's long story short with another question instead of paying attention.

"Don't you think it's wrong?"

Stunned out of his philosophic treatise, he kindly reorients. "Do I think *what* is wrong?"

"Sleeping in the old tent circle? Naming cities and towns for Native tribes after taking the land and running them out? Shops selling Native jewelry and clothing to rich White people so they can remember the history while the actual Native Americans are struggling in towns and places that are not their home?" I surprise myself at the ability to put things into words. Before this trip, I wasn't able to put anything into words, much less have thoughts and feelings about people outside my immediate world.

"We're always living in consequence. That's about all history is. Like I said, it's like this motorcycle," Longstoryshort continues. He finishes tinkering with the bike and wipes his hands on the rag. I try

31

my best not to get distracted. "The Natives had their machine, and here comes the settlers building a newer, larger, more powerful one. The land was a part of the old Indian machine, but the new mechanics needed it, a lot of it. The new mechanics didn't stop building, and they couldn't share it. That would be like joining two motorcycles going different directions at the engine. Wouldn't work for either of them. So the machine goes to the one with the most power. That's the way it's been since the dawn of creation. We might as well enjoy it; we can't change it."

Trying to not sound like an emotional kid, I reason out the question as a problem of logic. "But what about the Natives?"

Longstoryshort seems to be aware that the argument lacked compassion and adds, "I feel for them. I hope they still get to go visit that tepee circle or that they've made some new ones of their own. But there are a few that have done well for themselves, hopping on the new machine. And there are a lot that are finding ways to be a useful part of it. It's the ones living in the past that have a hard time. They can't go back to those days. You can't go back to Eden. It's just the way it is." He picks up his helmet and straddles the bike, then adds, "But you can get a little closer to home if we get on the road."

We get on the road.

CHAPTER 3

MONDAY MORNING: YELLOWSTONE

I bought water, but didn't think to drink it before we left. Now we're moving at a pace a little slower than the cars that pass, and I don't dare let go of Longstoryshort for anything. He's at the wheel. He's watching the cars. I'm just trying not to think about that sweatshirt as the cold air moves like dull razors over my exposed skin. It's hard to pay attention when you're moving fast on a two-wheeled vehicle on a little gray road between towering mountains under a hazy sky that suggests fire.

An RV passes, and a wall of wind tries to push us off the road. Longstoryshort is ready and makes the appropriate adjustments, turning slightly into the burst and opening the throttle just enough to tell the wall we're not going to be pushed around. I don't know if my life has ever so completely depended on someone else. There is something holy about it, giving your life over to God.

A river rushes beside us in the opposite direction. Part of me can relate. I close my eyes against the whipping wind and measure time with deep breaths.

Finally, we slow in a town where tourists are stopping their cars, getting out with their phones, and leaving their doors open. A large elk with small, uneven antlers is weaving down the center stripe with a look on his face like he's thinking, "What are you and where did you come from?" He isn't interested in taking pictures or having pictures taken of him.

Longstoryshort steers the motorcycle between the open doors and cell-phone-wielding gawkers, making his way to a line of cars, mansnails, and SUVs waiting their turn to go through the entrance gate to Yellowstone National Park.

We're about fifteen vehicles back. At the ranger station, one person is working the gate, and another is walking around each car looking in the windows. Longstoryshort is fidgety, and that makes me anxious to get going too. He has me hop off while he rummages through a bag for something. I'm happy to do so—my backside is killing me. I wonder if being a bike passenger always hurts this bad or if it's from my accident. I walk beside the motorcycle when the line moves and sit on the bristly grass when it stops. The RVs take longer, as the inspecting ranger has to go inside. Is this normal?

One man in a motor-home won't let the ranger in. He gets out and flails his arms, red-faced and yelling at the calm ranger. I wonder what they're looking for. I wonder what this guy has to hide. Maybe he's a private-property Texan still mad about the Civil War. The man in the BMW in front of us sticks his upper body out the window, shouting and shaking his fist toward the driver. As if that would help.

I picture the motor-home man, seeing the BMW man upbraiding him, turn to the ranger and say, "I'm sorry for my ugliness. That guy back there yelling at me made me realize I'm in the wrong. I have two unregistered guns and a tranquilized baby bear in the back. Let me pull out of the way and wait for the police." But then again, if yelling worked, the ranger would have already let him through. Is that what it means that you can't fight fire with fire?

The fire burns out, and the man lets the ranger in. Maybe it was all the honking behind him that made him aware he's not the only one in the world wanting to get past the gates and enjoy life. The gates lift, and the RV passes through. I wonder if he's going to enjoy life now.

When it's finally our turn, I'm back on the bike, and Longstory-short lifts his visor to the ranger at the station who already has her hand out. Before she can ask or say anything, Longstoryshort gives her a few twenties and his ID and park pass or something.

"Sorry for the holdup. There's been a kidnapping, and we're required to check everyone. Standard policy." She counts the money and hands the cards back to Longstoryshort.

"We understand," he says politely. "Thank you." He puts his visor down as the gate goes up, and we roll through.

[Animals are dangerous. Never approach or feed.]

[Fire Danger: HIGH]

Longstoryshort opens the throttle, and I hold on as I'm jerked backward, almost off the seat. Something from science class clicks. *Inertia.*

It's still cold, but with all the slower cars and curves, the wind isn't as cutting as it was on the straight highway. As we leave the congested area, I rest against Longstoryshort's back, trying to stay as still as possible. I see the river, mountains, and trees only enough to appreciate them.

Driving in the car, the scene was outside the glass windows. Earlier on the motorcycle, I felt like part of the scene. Now, with Longstoryshort speeding around sightseeing cars and leaning into the curves, I feel like we *are* the scene. The mountains and trees are just extras.

I felt so safe before and could find a relaxed grip and look around, but since we passed the gates, Longstoryshort seems to be in a hurry. I have no choice but to trust him, even in my discomfort. And I don't want to tell him he's scaring me.

[Mammoth Hot Springs]

We get stuck in a congested entrance to a parking lot. On the right, beyond the cars and people with phones, there is a white, steaming formation trickling with water. It's like an artistic rounded staircase made of frozen white waterfalls. It looks like icicles at first, but it's steaming hot springs, so it can't be. Oh, stalactites, hanging from themselves above ground as water trickles into the steps below. I want to stop and look closer at the white-and-orange phenomenon like everyone else, not to take a picture but to consider things I've never seen. Things I never imagined existed. A break in the ordinary. A glimpse of what's possible. Things we haven't seen at all. Maybe that's what draws so many people.

Inertia. We jump into movement between cars again. Was he driving slow through fast America and now driving fast through slow Yellowstone, or does it just feel that way on a motorcycle? Whatever it is, I'm not liking being afraid in such a protected and beautiful place. Why would God want us to fear Him? Is it to remind us He's in control? But could he go slower? We could appreciate what He made. But we're not supposed to be tourists in life. We're on a mission. What's my mission? To go home. How is that a mission for God? Aren't I supposed to make the world a better place with my new life or something? I guess I can't do that on the back of a motorcycle or gaping at nature on vacation.

Climbing a mountain, we drive through a young forest that looks like a dense Christmas tree farm. It doesn't take many miles to turn into an old, tall forest of the same type of trees. No one cut down and decorated these. We drive through another forest that must have burned in the past year. The life cycle of trees. The burned-up trees make the ground fertile for the next generation. I guess that's why they let these forests burn—because they need to for the new life to grow. The seeds are activated by fire. Funny how I keep remembering that. I thought about it in Montana too, except it means something different this time. I wonder what it'll mean the next time I remember it.

New life grows, and we're back on the winding path between mountains and towering trees. Dallas seems like such a far-removed world.

I close my eyes and try to go with the flow. I measure time by the leans into curves as we snake into higher elevation.

After what feels like an hour, we stop again, this time pulling into a half-full parking lot. We park, and I stretch off the bike. Longstoryshort takes off his glove and gauges the heat from the engine.

"We'll let it cool off a bit," he says, standing over the machine and setting his helmet on the seat. "Don't go too far."

I look around to see what phenomenon might be a reason for the parking lot and find a meadow to the right with some buffalo grazing on green grass with patches of snow. To the left, a thin wall of trees veils a mysterious mist rising from the ground. Longstoryshort walks toward the field with the buffalo and a few groups of people taking selfies.

I am drawn beyond the tree line and find a raised wooden path that leads out into the fog. But it's not fog. The bleached ground beneath the raised walkway steams like I've never seen before. Or I have, but it wasn't rock steam. In science class, we got to do some experiments with dry ice; that's what this looks like. But it's warm, and I am thankful. Large and small ponds look cool and refreshing nestled in the fragile ground, but steam is coming from them as well. I could stay here and thaw or soak in the ponds, but there are signs everywhere to stay on the path.

[Dangerous Ground]

[Stay on Designated Path]

I feel like they're talking to me. Where does this path lead? Where will it take me? Home? The sun is out. I feel good walking on the designated path above dangerous smoking ground.

Stopping to get a drink of water from the bottle I bought this morning, I hear, "Don't go too far," in my head. I scan the smoldering yet uncharred scorched earth. How far have I gone? I turn and walk briskly back past a couple a little older than me, both wearing backpacks and holding hands. They seem like they're in love. They walk slowly, and time slows as I walk past them—like a force field. They look out at the scenery and back at each other like they're thinking, "Which is more beautiful, this or you?" I'd like that.

Once they're a few paces away, time speeds back up, and I turn again and race back, past a few more tourists on their phones. I make it to the tree line and parking lot and look for Longstoryshort.

He's over on the sidewalk talking with a group of kids who are about my age. I pass them on my way to the restroom and hear him telling them a long story short about buffalo.

When I come back out, relieved, the kids are walking and leaping through the tall meadow grass toward the buffalo, having a good time. Longstoryshort is by the motorcycle, putting on his helmet and gloves.

I step up to the motorcycle and look back toward the kids. They're right next to a dozen buffalo now. I put on my helmet as Longstory-short starts the engine. I'm fastening the chinstrap and climbing onto the seat behind him when I swear I hear someone scream. I turn my head and see a kid flying through the air!

I jump and start to say something, but Longstoryshort's voice sounds impatient. "C'mon," he says, his voice raised to be heard over the engine. "Let's go." My body follows the instruction, and I settle on the seat. He's already pushing the bike backward, but I'm craning my neck, trying to see, as if my eyes could do any good. I want to scream, but my voice is steam. Longstoryshort feels my clutch and launches back onto the road.

What in the world just happened? The sign at the park entrance clearly stated: "Animals are dangerous." *What just happened?* Did Longstoryshort see that and drive off? They could be hurt! Or dying! And we're just speeding away. My eyes are bigger than my sockets, my heart thumps out of my chest. Did I just see someone die? *Dear God, be with those kids.* Is that how prayer works? Just talk to Him?

Smoke is coming out of the ground along the sides of the road. In fact, the whole forest seems to be planted in a ground that is not ground but a low, thick, gray, whispering cloud. It's like everything is smoldering, everything is on fire, but nothing is consumed. Even the water is on fire. But there's no flame. And it smells like sulfur. I didn't pay much attention in chemistry class, but sulfur is one of those things that, once you smell it, you know it. It's more than remembering knowledge or connecting vocabulary words with physical properties. It's like a deep knowing that's with you even when you aren't around it. You learn the smell of sulfur quickly and permanently, like it is in our DNA to recognize and avoid it. I'm starting to understand why Longstoryshort is ready to get out of here.

After a while, the shock of the buffalo attacking those kids wears off, and the more distance there is between us, the more I accept I can't do anything about it. But I'm still unsettled. Unsettled. Uncolonized? No, I don't feel like thinking. The sun is warm on my skin, and the burning sensation has returned to my chest.

Traffic slows every mile or so for a scenic pull-off so people can take pictures of the smoking mountainside, open plains with spouts of steam, fields of miniature volcano-looking mounds, and themselves.

[Construction. May take 30 minutes. Turn off engine.]

Longstoryshort turns off his engine. We sit in silence for a few minutes. Why didn't he help those kids? Jesus would have helped them. Healed them. Wouldn't He?

We're stuck in a long line of stopped cars. A lot of people are getting out of their vehicles, frustrated and impatient. We're resting at a place where the trees break into a view of a pristine little lake reflecting the mountains and trees, noon sun and blue sky. There is no up or down, just where they meet. Except one is the real mountains and sky. The other, underneath the glass mirror, could boil you slowly. Or freeze you.

"Why didn't we stay and help those kids?" I ask as Longstoryshort finally takes off his helmet.

"What kids?"

"The ones being attacked by the buffalo."

His face shows concern. "I didn't see that."

"You were looking right at them when that one flew through the air!" I raise my voice like a kid accusing their parent of not seeing the ice-cream truck.

"Are you sure?" he asks.

I guess it is wrong of me to accuse him of seeing something I'm not really sure he saw. And now I'm not even really sure of what I saw. Was it a kid in the air? The scream could have been the motorcycle or another car or maybe a gas jet screaming from the rock.

"If *you* saw it," he says, "why didn't *you* do anything? I would have turned around in a heartbeat."

He's right. I saw it. At least I think I did. Why didn't I do anything? I froze. I was waiting for someone else to do something. I didn't know what to do. I still don't know what to do. I feel awful—guilty and ashamed.

"Surely they wouldn't have tried to get that close to the buffalo," he says with a concerned brow. "There are signs everywhere telling them to beware." He sees my shame and reassures me. "It's not your fault. A lot of people ignore warning signs and get hurt. That's humans for you."

Around us, people are getting back in their cars and, one by one, starting their engines down the line. Longstoryshort smooths back the long, loose hairs on the top of his head and puts his helmet back on. I feel small next to such a big character. I don't know if I want to be a big character or if I just don't want to feel so small, but I don't feel like I'm a new and better person anymore, even after dying and giving my life to God. We move slow for a long time.

We pull over again, this time at a scenic overview with no other vehicles. We are at a high place looking at the sides of mountains to the west. The steam makes it look like there are a dozen forest fires on the steep inclines, and below us are hundreds of the little volcanoes that look like giant white molehills, spread densely across a valley meadow. To the southeast, one giant plume of steam rises high above the treetops. Is that Old Faithful?

"Do you think we can stop and see Old Faithful?" I ask, not knowing exactly where it is or how long it would take to get there in this increasingly expansive park we've been driving through for a few hours now.

"People pay big money to see water come out of the ground. You're looking at it for free," he says, standing up from inspecting the motorcycle and pointing toward the steam vent to our southeast. "Old Faithful isn't even as faithful as it used to be. We don't have time to stop and see all the sights like the tourists." I feel like a burden. He shoots a serious question. "Do you know what's going on down there?"

Down where—the mountain or under the geyser? I know the geyser has something to do with water being heated underground, but I'm not sure that's what he's asking. "No," I reply, waiting for the long story short.

"Water is being heated from underneath, and pressure builds up until it spews. You know what's heating that water underground?"

I know it has something to do with magma and thin layers of crust or something. "Not really," I say, not knowing how to put it into words.

"Sometimes the layers between the world we live in and the end of that world are soft and thin. We're on top of a giant caldera where those two worlds are only a few miles apart. Right now, we're sitting in the middle of an apocalyptic volcano that could erupt at any moment and wipe out life as we know it. And people flock to it to take selfies and watch little geysers spit out of the ground. Freaks me out." That's it. He goes silent, checking gauges and temperatures again.

I wouldn't have pictured Longstoryshort being afraid of anything, and he's afraid of a volcano that doesn't seem like it's going to erupt for a long time. The news would be all over that. The park would be closed. We would know about something that big, wouldn't we?

I think I'm afraid of a lot of things, mainly things that can hurt me, which is a lot. But I'm not afraid here. And I don't feel afraid of God. Do I have it backward? Does Longstoryshort have it right?

After spraying the chain with oil again, he asks, "Are you ready to get out of this hell hole?"

I am. All I need to do now is hold on and relax. He's taking me home. Old Faithful spits a hot stream into the air down the mountain from us, and we join the traffic heading toward it. A mist is taking over the sky again, hiding the sun and its radiant warmth.

[Old Faithful >]

[West Thumb ^]

All the cars in our lane follow the exit directing them to Old Faithful. We follow the forward arrow pointing toward West Thumb on a now-vacant road. I can't tell how high we are or if we're in a valley. I don't know what time it is, and I guess I don't need to. I can't even tell what direction we're driving. I know I'm headed home, but there's a feeling I'm also going away from something I'm supposed to be going toward.

I'm just holding on.

I'm in a thickening haze like the trees and sky, and leaning into the alternating curves is rocking me, not to sleep, but into a sort of hypnosis. Time doesn't exist for a while, and it feels again like I am the scene the rocks and pines are studying.

The fog or smoke or whatever it is gets so thick that I can only see the first line of trees, and we travel in this otherworldly dome of limited vision without another car passing. We could be anywhere, marked in time only by our clothes and the motorcycle. I'm not asleep, but I'm definitely not alert either. Succumbed. And cold.

My eyes close.

Trust. I can't do anything else.

Breathe.

I open my eyes again, and the green blur of trees has been replaced by ten-foot walls of snow on both sides. We've entered another world, a world of whites and grays. Gray sky, white walls, gray road. The road rolls beneath us, the walls run past us. It's otherworldly. Again.

Longstoryshort swims right and left in our lane on the now-straightened road. The burning in my chest fills my arms and neck as the motor vibrates my legs and lower back. My body is not my own. I should be freezing. I should be in school. But I'm here, no place. No time. Nobody. Who am I supposed to be? And when will I become him? Will I know how to fix a motorcycle? The hypnosis sways back over me.

A sudden slowing shakes me alert, and we crawl down the road behind an AmeriCruise motor home taking in the sights we can't see.

[Lewis Falls]

Can't see them.

The walls of snow shrink into patches on green grass, and the decline in the road puts us below the fog at the same time it is rising. The road takes a long curve to the right, and I can make out that we are driving along the top edge of a cliff. People are staggered on the side of the road, outside their cars, standing with their mouths open and eyes gaping behind us into the gorge. I can't turn to see what they're looking at. Has the Yellowstone caldera finally blown? No, they'd be afraid. Maybe it's Lewis Falls pouring from the cloud. No one is taking pictures. What would be so beautiful and awe inspiring that it would overpower the habitual urge to take a picture? Whatever it is, we're driving away from it.

On a long, straight decline, we find an opportunity to pass the mansnail. The rush of speed feels like freedom, and I can feel relief through Longstoryshort's leather jacket. It's contagious. There is less snow, less tension, no steaming ground.

It's not long before we see a sign announcing the south entrance ranger station, but before we get there, Longstoryshort turns left into

Snake River Picnic Area.

We pull through thin, towering pines on a narrow round path circling an empty picnic area. We dismount at a table overlooking a river rushing through a wide snowy floodplain. The quickness of the river contrasts with the permanence of the mountains beyond. The sky is still gray, the air still cold, but I'm surprisingly comfortable in my short sleeves. Maybe I'm acclimating. Maybe I'm getting tougher. Maybe that's why Longstoryshort made me put back the sweatshirt—because it's what is good for me. Or maybe because it was fifty dollars.

I expect Longstoryshort to tinker with the motorcycle, but he walks straight up to the roaring riverbank. I don't want to follow him like a puppy, so I take in the scenery and stretch my stiff body. I check my pocket for my phone, knowing it's not there. Funny, I never noticed how much I had it when I had it, but now that I don't (and don't want it), my habits tell how much I turn to it. What would I do with it? Check the time. Check the messages. Take a picture. I don't need to know what time it is. It's now. I don't need to check the messages and spend ten minutes saying nothing back and forth. I don't need to take a picture.

I just need to soak it in.

Longstoryshort seems to be soaking it in as well. Why this place? Why here and not at Mammoth Hot Springs or Old Faithful? It's beautiful but . . . *ordinary* compared to some of the views we sped by. I walk up and stand beside him to see if I can catch it.

This close to it, the power of the water is undeniable. The river in Livingston, meandering through the scenery at Sacajawea Park, was calm enough to wade in, swim in, or be baptized in. This one, if you took six steps out, you'd be swept away. It's not rough, but it's fast.

It's like life. I haven't even lived that long, but just a short time ago I was a kid, and I haven't done anything but be carried by the current through school, friendships of convenience, and a string of relationships that were no more than someone to hold on to.

Longstoryshort's voice joins that of the water. "If I die, my ashes are going to be scattered on this river." His face shows emotion like he's visiting an old friend he hasn't seen in a long time. "This river has been carving its path since before humans were here. It carved Hell's Canyon out of the Seven Devil Mountain Range thousands of years ago, deeper than the Grand Canyon but without all the glory."

"Sounds evil."

He shrugs. "Americans have always had a hard time understanding the difference between power and evil. Natives always respected this river, lived their lives around it. Lewis and Clark tried braving it but learned quick enough that man has little control once they've entered its powerful current. They were lucky to get out alive. Others weren't so fortunate. White trappers and hunters couldn't cross it. When the settlers came, and especially when they found out there was gold beyond it, they were determined to conquer it and find ways to cross. The first expedition capsized in Snake Canyon, and a lot of the early ferries got swept downriver. Some even got plunged down Shoshone Falls, which is higher and more beautiful than Niagara Falls but without all the glory."

I'm trying to pay attention, but my mind feels like a small, overflowing bowl of gravel, and I'm trying to keep it all but also make room for more pebbles of truth.

". . . and now you got kids rafting the rapids for fun . . . deaths every year . . ."

Power and evil aren't the same thing. God is powerful. So is the devil. Crossing the river to get to gold. Respect. Fear. It's like I'm holding a mine full of thoughts but can't tell the skipping stone from the gold.

Longstoryshort's voice goes quiet. I wait for a "long story short," but it doesn't come. What comes instead washes away any walls I had toward this mysterious man of the road.

"When I was eleven, I had my father bring me here to be baptized, but I wouldn't get in. I wasn't afraid, I just wasn't dumb. My father was dumb. He walked out waist deep in the summer flow, telling me how refreshing the water was, fighting to keep his footing. He didn't even have a chance to scream. And just like that, he was gone." The river's roar swallows any words he has left, if he had any words left, and the rushing *hushhh* becomes the silence.

What? His dad *died* here?! I try but can't imagine watching my dad being grabbed and pulled by the strong flow, dragged, fighting and gasping until the water swallowed him. I can't imagine an eleven-year-old Longstoryshort watching him go. Did he scream? Run after him? How long did he wait there before someone else showed up?

I guess that explains why Longstoryshort is a man of the road, a man of the wild, a man on the roam. Cities and office jobs are for people trying to make their parents proud. Make something of themselves, prove they can survive on their own without having to survive on their own. Longstoryshort has had to survive on his own. Fully human. My heart hurts for him.

I wonder how that affected him when he got to be my age. I wonder how it would have affected me.

"Long story short, this river represents something more powerful than man. Something angelic, worthy of respect and being smarter than dumb."

He picks up a rock and hurls it sidearm across the flow. It bounces, skims, skims, and is swallowed by the hungry water. He does it again.

I try, but the excited surface swallows my rock.

"The magic's in the wrist," he says. "Give it a flick with some speed."

I try again. And again. Longstoryshort skips his perfectly. I try again, against the troubled waters. And again. I finally get a big bounce! I look at him for approval or to share the achievement or something.

"Good job, kid."

"I want to do better." The words fall out of my mouth. I'm not sure why. "I want to be better at life. I don't want to just be a normal person who graduates, goes to college, gets a job, gets married, has kids, and never makes the world a better place. I want to make a difference."

Longstoryshort takes a thoughtful breath and stands pensive for a moment before picking up another smooth stone. "See this rock?"

"Yes."

"Watch it."

He hurls it sidearm again across the dancing surface. Bounce, skip, skim, and the river swallows another. It's gone.

"Did you see those ripples?"

For a brief moment. "Yes."

"Now you do it. Watch the ripples."

It takes two hops before it disappears below the surface.

"What happens?"

Not knowing quite what I'm supposed to get, I say what I saw. "They bounce and make a few ripples."

"Then what?"

"It goes back to normal."

"In a sense," he says. "Have you studied physics?"

"A little." Suddenly, I'm wishing I'd paid more attention. I never thought I'd need it.

"Physics can tell you a lot about how the physical world was made and maybe a little about the One who made it," Longstoryshort says in a matter-of-fact tone. "The rocks cause a brief displacement in the preformed pattern of the flow. But ultimately, the effect of the energy from the disturbance is absorbed back into the river, and it returns to its natural equilibrium."

I think about it. It makes much more sense applying it to actual nature instead of working a math problem on paper in a sterile room with flickering lights.

"See, that's the way our lives are. We want to make a big difference, but the river is too strong, too ancient. I know you want to change the world—everyone does—but God started this river. He started the momentum and determined its path. The machine works. Who are you to tear it apart and play God rebuilding it? To say it needs to be different?"

Nothing.

A smell of fire turns Longstoryshort's eyes to the thickening sky. A raindrop hits my forehead. I exhale more than I inhale. The fire in my constricted chest flickers to embers, and I feel a little ashen. The cold sets in again.

[Leaving Yellowstone National Park]

CHAPTER 4

MONDAY AFTERNOON: INTO JACKSON HOLE

As soon as we pass the ranger station marking the south edge of Yellowstone National Park, we're entering another. A wooden sign with mountains etched white hangs from a frame of cut pine trunks.

[Grand Teton National Park].

I pray it's not as winding, car crowded, and eternally long as Yellowstone.

The road is fairly straight, between tall pines that look dry and scraped of all their needles and bark, like kindling. I can see how quick a fire could get dangerous out here and can appreciate Longstoryshort's fear of fire.

We progress at highway speed, meeting only a few cars and mansnails coming the opposite way through a thin fog. Longstoryshort readies the bike for each RV's wall of wind as if second nature. If I were driving, I would probably get in a road daze; forget; be blown into the Snake River, which slithers in and out of sight; and end up crushed on the rocks at Shoshone Falls.

I can't believe Longstoryshort watched his dad die. Was he an adult from that point on? His own father? I imagine him being my father, taking me on this trip, teaching me how to be a man. He might not be Jesus, but he's a good man.

We spill out of the trees into a green scrubland that must be the flood plain of the river. I keep seeing signs for Teton Point Turnout, but no Tetons turn out through the churning gray soup above us. Longstoryshort could teach me how to build a motorcycle, how to know what's safe and what's dangerous, how to survive in nature, how to live on the road. What else could he teach me? The road inclines toward the fog, and a steep cliff develops to our right as we climb. Soon we get an overhead view of the river below.

The engine growls a long howl up the mountainside, and Longstoryshort leans happily back and forth in our lane on our way back down, mirroring the river to which we return. I don't feel afraid. I feel like I'm in good hands. I smile. The sun peeks out briefly to remind me it's there, touching my arms and revealing an outline of towering mountains to the west. Truth is always on the other side of the river? But I'm on this side of the river, and it's too dangerous to cross. And I don't need gold or power. Just enough to survive and to trust in the one driving. I nod into a dreary, dry shade of almost-sleep.

It's only about an hour before the path beside the road is populated with walkers and cyclists, people with their phones and binoculars. I turn my head to the right and see the snow-capped peaks. I look over Longstoryshort's shoulder and see a sign with a silhouette of a person in a cowboy hat pointing to a welcome sign.

[Howdy stranger—this is Jackson Hole—the last of the Old West]

Longstoryshort points to a clump of houses and buildings huddled at the base of a mountain. I'm so ready to be somewhere. I don't know why my life seems to be drained out of me. I've been on the road a lot in the past few days, died to be born again, was in a wreck, and have been hanging on for my life on the back of this vibrating motorcycle since the break of day. And now it must be after noon. That could be it. I'm ready for what's next. And I'm hungry.

The streets are lined with cars as we inch through the clogged veins leading to the heart of the town I was expecting to be a city. It has an intentional Old West feel. Longstoryshort seems relaxed and cautious around the cars that my imagination turns into cattle being shuffled through corrals.

We make it to a stoplight at what must be the town square. New-old facades welcome incoming customers who meet satisfied ones exiting with brown paper bags hanging from both arms. Cars make hard negotiations over who gets to turn while bag carriers dart between them with just enough confidence to make it across.

The center of the square is a park, and giant archways built out of antlers are at each corner. Thousands of antlers. People shuffle like ants. Cars moan like cows. We turn right at the next block and join the prowling cougars pouncing on potential parking spaces.

We park on a side street at the edge of the hunting ground. Sensing we're done with the highway and national parks for the day, I could kiss the ground. I yawn instead, stretching to the sky, then fold into a standing slouch. Longstoryshort senses my weariness. I want to ask about food but don't want to be a burden.

"We've got some time to kill before we can properly surprise some old friends," Longstoryshort explains.

"Is there a good place to eat?" I ask without meaning to. Fully aware of my dependence on Longstoryshort, I consciously add, "That doesn't cost much?"

"Plenty of good places to eat here, none that don't cost much," he answers. "You've got jerky in your backpack."

He's right. I put the pack on my chest and try rummaging for the jerky while jogging a few steps to catch up as he crosses the street. And not get hit by a cow cougar.

We're under a shaded storefront eave, walking on an old, raised wooden sidewalk. The hard wood makes a different sound than any sidewalk I've ever walked on, and I try to picture a hundred years ago, a man walking with his son on this creaking path. Horses tied to every hitch, the smell of hides, hay, and dirt. I bite into the salted jerky.

"I'll take care of you," Longstoryshort interrupts my time travel. "What's your favorite food?"

"Mexican," is my quick and true answer. Enchiladas, quesadillas, nachos, charro beans, all-you-can-eat chips and salsa. My mouth waters, stomach purrs.

"Okay, I know a great place."

I put the jerky back, excited at the prospect of golden cheese melted on top of a mountain of fajita beef, beans, red sauce, and chips.

We dodge our way through the herds and walk another block to a little building on the corner with patio tables and brightly painted walls.

It's well past the lunch hour, and there are only a few people chatting over empty plates in a booth. Still, it takes a few minutes for someone to notice we're standing here waiting to be noticed.

"Inside or outside?" the hostess asks.

Longstoryshort looks at me and lets me decide.

"Outside, please."

"Follow me," she says in a tired voice, and she guides us to a table under a multicolored umbrella. Dropping a couple menus on the table, she asks, "Water? Beer? Margarita?"

"Waters," Longstoryshort answers and sits across from me, back to the street.

Looking over the menu, it's not the Mexican food I was expecting. It's not Taco John's tater tots either, but I don't see what I'm used to.

"Boy, they've gotten greedy. That's okay; it's the way of the world. Order what you want," Longstoryshort offers and gives me a boost. "You're worth it."

I recognize the tension between Longstoryshort's awareness of spending and his willingness to spend money on me, and I'm thankful he thinks I'm worth it. I want the most expensive thing because it has the most food and I could eat a horse, but don't want to make him regret the offer.

"What's good?" I ask. "I've had Mexican food all my life, but I've never heard of any of these. I guess there are different kinds of Mexican food."

"All food is pretty much the same." Longstoryshort leans back and eases into a new lesson on reality. "Meat, cheese, bread, fruit, and vegetables. Different things grow in different areas. In Jalisco, cilantro grows like grass, and they put it in everything. In Chihuahua, you get cactus on your plate with beans and whatever else is shelf stable in the desert. Jalapeños grow everywhere. The Mexican food you get in America depends on the immigration routes from the gardens of the great-grandparents, the demands of local tastebuds, what's available in the new location."

Tortas are on the menu, described as a "Grande Mexican sandwich with tomato, avocado, beans, onions, lettuce, and mayonnaise." I've never had mayo with Mexican food, but I can almost smell the homemade bread steaming as it comes out of the oven and read more about the options. The Cubana has fried beef, shredded ham, and sliced turkey franks. Turkey franks? Like hot dogs? Surely not.

". . . long story short, food is like religion," Longstoryshort continues. "It's all basically the same ingredients, and how it's put together depends on the soil, geography, history of the people putting it in the pot, and history of the people the pot is feeding." It makes sense, and it explains the Mexi-tots on the Oregon Trail.

But wait. Is he saying—

"Ready to order?" The waitress appears, tapping her pen on the order pad.

Longstoryshort gestures his open hand toward me, and I'm in the panic you get in when it's your turn to order and you haven't really looked at the menu even though you've been looking at it for ten minutes. "Cubana Torta, please."

She tilts her head to Longstoryshort, tapping her pen on the order pad.

"Don't worry about me," he says. "I've got some errands to run. I'll be back to take care of the check."

She does the math for the tip in her head, purses her lips, then with a deep breath and an "Okay" walks back into the building.

Longstoryshort smiles at her sass and says before getting up from his seat with a wink, "No chips and salsa? Now *that's* a sin."

He turns his back to me and strides away, leaving me with an empty table and two waters. No chips and hot sauce. He walks back across the street under the wooden shingled eave supported by logs that look fresh off the tree.

All the buildings look like the Old West, but also look brand new. It's a style. The style says something about who the town is. I've never been big on styles, never really fit in with any of them. At school, the athletes wear athletic clothes, popular kids wear whatever is trending and expensive, the skaters wear worn T-shirts with their favorite bands, bought new with holes in them. If Jackson Hole showed up at school, it would be wearing fancy new cowboy boots, starched denim jeans, a tucked-in rodeo button-up shirt, a clean felt cowboy hat, and empty holsters because the metal detectors would light up with the six-shooters. It'd probably be chewing on the end of a stalk of hay too. Me, I'm the kid you don't notice, the one you pass and your brain subconsciously checks the "other" box. I'd be a town in Kansas.

I think the waitress forgot about me.

I slurp the water dripping from the slow melting ice and notice the close mountains above a new-old log cabin motel with a neon No Vacancy sign. I forgot about the mountains with all the Western architecture and flashy signage, traffic, and scurrying shopping-bag fillers. It's like the mountains are the reason people come here, but once they're here, the town does as much as it can to draw you in and make you forget about the surrounding nature.

Mountains. Truth. Distraction. I'm on a thought. But my food is finally here.

"Here ya go," the waitress says as she puts a large, round, steaming sandwich in front of my wolf eyes. I forget to ask for more water, and she forgets to notice. The bread is heavenly. I could live on this bread alone. The flavors of meat and beans, avocado and lettuce with a creamy mayo melt together in my mouth and dance their way to my brain. I moan in culinary ecstasy. It's hard to distinguish one flavor from another. Except the turkey frank. A cut-up hot dog stands out in a sandwich otherwise made in heaven's kitchen.

It's gone. I lick my fingers. I meant to enjoy it more. I don't have napkins. I don't have water.

I glance around for the waitress, then look over at Longstory-short's water. Would he be upset if I drank it? I'm too thirsty to care. She'll be by to refill it anyway.

I reflect on the Mexican sandwich I'd never heard of before and wonder how many variations of Mexican food there are between Texas and California, between the US and Central America, and around the world. They really are pretty much the same thing, yet with different flavors and styles based on available ingredients, history, and local demand.

Was he saying all religions are the same too? I've never really thought about different religions. I know the Muslims believe in Allah, the Jews don't believe in Jesus, and Hindus don't eat cows. I was raised around Christianity, and I just prayed my life over to God at my cross on the mountainside in Montana. But are they all the same god? Is Buddha the Jesus of Asia? My stomach drops a little at my lack of knowledge. I know God has been talking to me. I know I died on that mountainside and found a new life.

At least I thought I was found, but now I'm lost.

I know there's such a thing as truth, but how do I know Christianity is right? If it is, does that mean all the rest are false? Or are they really *all* right, made of the same basic ingredients, just served on different plates?

"Here's your ticket," the waitress announces out of nowhere and walks off.

But I can't pay what I owe. I have nothing. I *am* nothing. Where is Longstoryshort?

I sit tapping my foot nervously for a while, trying to think thoughts about what is true, but the overwhelming presence of my unpaid tab bothers me. I need to use the restroom, but I'm aware that if the waitress comes, it'll look like I ran off.

She finally comes back, and I explain. "My friend will be back soon. I'll stay here. He's going to pay."

I wait.

And wait. What time is it? It must be close to five. The endorphins released from the sandwich lasted as long as my thoughts, and I'm out of them. Have I been abandoned? What are my options?

I could stay here. If Longstoryshort really has abandoned me, I'll know it eventually. If he hasn't, he'll be back. I could walk away and figure something else out. What? But if he's coming back, I'd be gone and he'd leave too. I could pray. I haven't really prayed since Montana, but I haven't prayed much all my life. Am I even praying to the right God, or just praying to the air in hopes that something's there? But something *was* there. Something *is* there. If there is a God, then He's the God of everything, every being He created. There can't be a thousand different creator gods that created a thousand different people in a thousand different regions that all happen to look, think, act, and cook about the same. There has to be one God. But all the religions don't believe that, do they? So there must be some that have it wrong.

But telling people they're wrong is prejudiced, isn't it? I'm so confused.

I start to pray out loud. "God, Creator of everything—"

"Nothing! I hope you didn't forget about me!" The familiar voice hollers down the planked sidewalk. I'm so relieved. He hasn't abandoned me, and he's here to pay what I owe.

"Here. I hope this fits." He pulls a plain black, hooded sweatshirt out of a Walmart bag. I catch myself slipping into a critical mind because it's from Walmart and it's a size too small, but then I chastise myself for "being an ingrate," as my dad puts it. It didn't kill me to sleep under a blanket on the ground last night, and I got used to the chill on the road in my short sleeves. I didn't starve even though I was hungry, and nothing bad has happened to me yet. It's "character building," my granddad would say about being uncomfortable. It's better than what I have on now, even if it is a little small.

"It'll be perfect," I say. "Thank you."

"I know you've been cold and uncomfortable," Longstoryshort explains, "but you have to think about it from my side. I wasn't looking to have another soul on my bike this trip. You were a surprise. Being kind to people is a tricky thing. I knew a guy once, nicest guy you'd ever meet. He'd give you the shirt right off his back. Trouble is, he was always shirtless. All his neighbors and all his friends always seemed to be having an emergency. Car trouble here, sick mom there, girlfriend ran off with the checkbook on bill day—he even gave a guy $100 both times his grandma died. He thought he was sinning if he didn't say yes. Never got to retire, never got to get his fishing boat . . . and he ended up dying because he couldn't pay for the medicine. Lots of people at his funeral, but what's that worth in the end?"

I stand up to stretch and wait for the absent waitress.

"Another guy I knew never gave a dime to anyone. Held on to every cent he earned. He actually rolled his change and kept it in his basement. Never helped a neighbor, never gave at church, always walked right past the Santa at the grocery store . . . and when he fell and broke his hip, no one was there to check on him, and no one missed him. Starved to death. And after he died, it turned out he had over a million dollars rolled in his basement, about the same in his savings account—but he'd refused to make a will, so Uncle Sam ended up with all of it. Didn't even have a funeral.

"Long story short, it turns out you've been a gift to me. I got ahold of a friend who can take you from Little America all the way back to Dallas. He's going that way anyway."

Wait. Ride with someone else? I don't know how to feel about this. Have I gotten attached to Longstoryshort? I haven't thought about how briefly our paths would cross. I like him. I trust him. I feel like I've got a lot to learn from him. Where's Little America?

He must see the emotions on my face. "Another reason Nothing's a good name for you, kid," he says gruffly. "Can't get attached on the road. Plus, Ghost drives a nice van. Takes it all over the US. It'll be more comfortable, and he'll get you where you need to be. We've got some time to rest before our pavement meets. Let's get you a haircut."

We're standing outside an antiquated barber shop with a rotating red-and-white pole in a protective plastic cylinder. Did we pay for lunch? I don't even remember walking over here. But I've got a way home. And if it's a friend of Longstoryshort, I can trust him, right? Even if his name is Ghost. The Holy Ghost? I've always heard the saying, *God works in mysterious ways*. He sure does.

Haircuts are one of the most relaxing things to me. I just close my eyes and let them work. This barber works quick with skilled hands. There's a TV on the wall in the waiting area blaring Fox News, and a lady is griping and complaining about it to a young female worker behind the cash register.

"Fine," the employee says and changes the channel to another news outlet. A man gets up and starts giving the employee and the other woman a piece of his mind.

"Fine," the employee says again, only this time the TV goes silent. Now both the woman *and* the man are letting the worker have it. She takes the remote and walks to the back, muttering, "Stupid people. Sheesh. . ."

Before I know it, the barber is brushing my neck and forehead with his soft brush and holding up a mirror so I can see the back and give my approval. The back of my head is as unfamiliar as the front. I don't like looking in mirrors. Why not? I see the guy in the mirror, but that's just a body. What do other people see? What do I see? I think back to the lake reflecting the sky. What's underneath? Which is the real one? I feel like something more than my skin, face, and new haircut. Something more eternal. A soul in a body with a haircut. I feel fresh and itchy. At least from the neck up. I could really use some new underwear.

"Looks good. Thanks," I tell the barber and walk out to Longstoryshort, who's in the waiting area reading a table copy of *Fortune 500*. The man and woman who were arguing about the news stations are glued to their phones.

I don't know that I fit in more now with a haircut, but I don't stand out as much. As if people were paying attention. It's a Monday afternoon, and there are hundreds of people exploring the streets and storefronts like they're searching for something.

"Why are there so many people here on a Monday in May?" I ask Longstoryshort, assuming most people in the world go through school, go to college, and get jobs that they work Monday through Friday.

"It's a tourist town. The smart tourists travel during the week and right before and after the real tourist seasons."

"You mean it gets busier than this? I feel like I could get lost in it."

"I think that's the point," Longstoryshort answers. It seems like he's enjoying himself. We walk by a store with a sign hanging: Bad Habits. We clop down the wooden sidewalk, casually heading toward the park at the square, passing paintings of cowboys on bucking horses, stores selling Native American jewelry, Western clothes, leather goods, cowboy hats, and boots. Cars honk, speed up aggressively, and brake the same way.

Longstoryshort stops suddenly. "Wait here," he says, then enters a jewelry store called Pandora's Box. Wasn't that the lady in Greek mythology who opened the box out of curiosity and let out all the evil into the world? I guess I did learn something in English class. Everything got out of the box except hope. That was the only thing that didn't make it out. It's kind of a depressing story, isn't it? Why would someone name their store that?

I look around. One of the antler arches is across the corner from me, and the Western storefronts compete for attention. A saloon is open and busy. A high-end fashion store advertises a brand of something called Envy in its window. Maybe it's not a brand. Maybe it's a directive. Someone is smoking a cigar. I don't envy him. People are taking selfies next to a stuffed buffalo. I hope those kids are okay. I can't believe I witnessed that. And didn't do anything. What could I have done? I could have sworn I saw Longstoryshort see it too. A man sitting across the street watches as two women in high heels and low-cut tops walk by and stop at the corner to talk. He's just staring, like he's undressing them in his mind. Do I do that? Is that what it looks like?

A man bumps into me.

"Excushe me," he slurs. The whiff of whiskey lingers as he walks toward the chatty ladies on the corner. He bumps into them too. And leers back at their rears as he passes. Where is the hope? Is it still in the box? Is that what Longstoryshort is in there to find?

I turn at the same time he's coming out of the store. I don't see a bag, but he taps his pocket and says, "Let's get out of here." I can't agree more.

We make our way back to the motorcycle, work our way through Pandora's zoo, and drive a few blocks past the thick downtown into a quiet neighborhood.

We pull into the driveway of a long, tan house with an open garage. Inside, there's a man sitting on a couch. A sidewalk connects the driveway to a few concrete steps that lead to a red front door. It's not a fancy house like I'd expect in this town, but it's not poor either. It would fit in any middle-class neighborhood in any town in America.

The man raises a bottle as a welcome but doesn't get up from the couch. Longstoryshort takes off his helmet and looks to the right as the front door opens. A woman about his age steps through the red door and stands on the small stoop with her hands on her hips. She holds a half smile, but her eyes are beaming. Longstoryshort gets off his horse nonchalantly and stands like a cowboy, home from the range. Is this his wife? Girlfriend? Who is the guy on the couch?

CHAPTER 5

MONDAY NIGHT: GRACE'S GARAGE

"**H**ello, Grace," Longstoryshort says in a manly voice, without having to try to sound manly.

"Longstory," she answers back, then skips down the steps and leaps into his arms, lifting her legs behind and wrapping them around him. He holds her in a longing embrace. I've never had a girlfriend who was that happy to see me. I guess I've never been anything worth being happy to see. I'm just a town in Kansas. I *was* just a town in Kansas. What will I become? I don't want to be a tourist attraction. I want to be a good town. A safe town surrounded by beauty but not forgetting it. I want to be home.

Longstoryshort sets Grace back on her feet, and she props her hands back on her hips, furrows her brow, and demands, "What took you so long?"

Longstoryshort pulls a narrow black box from his jacket pocket and takes off the top. Grace melts back into adoration as she lifts out a sparkling necklace and gasps. "It's beautiful! Put it on!" She hands it back, turns around, and lifts her hair off her long peach-colored neck.

When he's done, she twirls back around to me. "And who's this handsome fellow?" she asks, flipping her highlighted brown hair over her shoulder and smiling at me with her red lips and carefully lined green eyes. The necklace glimmers. I consciously try not to look at what she's wearing, but she's barefoot in an off-white blouse and stylish blue jeans. She's old enough to be my mom, but she looks more like one of the popular girls at school. I feel a weird mix of nerves—the awkwardness I feel around an attractive girl and the self-conscious nervousness of meeting a respectable adult.

I expect Longstoryshort to introduce me as "Nothing," but instead he surprises me with my real name. "This is Redemption," he says. It's like Grace has a power over him.

"You give them the cutest names," she responds, slapping his arm lightly. Then she reaches out her hand to me. "Well, hello, Redemption," she says. "I'm Grace. Welcome to my humble home."

I shake her hand like Grandpa taught me: firm enough to be respectable, but gentle enough to show respect. I want to continue the conversation, but I'm tongue-tied. My brain is busy analyzing internal and external information. All this time I've been on the motorcycle, and that has been my world. Now I'm entering someone else's world, and whatever's between Longstoryshort and Grace is a new type of landscape. And who is that guy in the garage? I feel like I'm jumping into a book two-thirds of the way in. *You give them the cutest names*, she said. Them? How do I fit in this story?

Grace and Longstoryshort continue a catch-up conversation as they walk arm in arm past me toward the garage. I'm still by the motorcycle with my helmet on. I can't see the mountains.

"It's good to see you still here, Mike," Longstoryshort says to the man on the couch. "Right where I left you."

"I haven't budged," Mike laughs in response, holding up his beer for a lone toast. "Who ya got with you this time?"

"Redemption," Grace answers. "Isn't that a great name?"

I walk in awkwardly and stand with my hands in my pockets, sheepishly looking for cues.

"What's your story?" Mike asks me, to the point but not unwelcoming. He's a gruff man, but I sense a jolliness behind the thick skin and gray mustache. He's strong in the bones but soft in the belly. He's relaxed but means business as he leans back on the couch in his untucked button-up and stretches his arms across the top cushions. His jeans are well worn but not holey, and his broken-in work boots suggest he's not lazy. My tongue is still stuck to my mouth.

Longstoryshort answers before I find words. "He was in a wreck in Montana last night. I happened to be riding by and couldn't help but offer him a ride. He's trying to make his way back home to Texas."

Mike testifies for Longstoryshort's kindness. "Always helping people out. Last year," he says, "this guy rides in here with a young lady who was on a bridge trying to muster the courage to jump off into a canyon and kill herself. Longstoryshort talked her out of it and"—Mike turns to Longstoryshort—"whatever happened to her?"

"I took her to some folks I know who would look after her. Give her a job and some purpose. That's all a kid really needs, isn't it?"

Purpose. Yeah.

"And another year, you had that twelve-year-old runaway you were taking home." Mike looks with admiration at Longstoryshort. "You got a ministry on that road, dontcha?"

"Just a small part in a big machine," Longstoryshort answers. "I do what I can."

Mike turns to me. "Phone off and in the bag," he instructs, pointing to a purple Crown Royal bag hanging from a nail in the wall. "It's a rule here. Be where you are. No distractions." He takes another swig from his brown bottle.

"What's Joe up to?" Longstoryshort asks. "Is Lewis still coming around? Anyone else join the mix?"

"Joe'll be here after he gets off work and runs to the store," Mike says. "He'll be excited to see you. Lewis has counseling sessions on Monday nights. He'll show up all hot and bothered, but after a few beers, he'll tell us all about it. Got a new guy who's been showing up most nights. He's some sort of writer." Grace is clearing off another couch and recliner. He turns to her. "Grace, what's his name?"

"West."

"Yeah, West." Mike continues in his deep, croaky voice. "He can't talk. Got no tongue. Can't tell by lookin' at him. He carries a notebook with him, and if he has something to say, he writes it out. Mostly he just sits over there though"—he points to the blue couch Grace just fluffed—"writing in that journal. Maybe he's writing a book about us. Not sure where he came from or why, but he keeps showing up. Guess it's the same for all of us—we just need a little Grace in our lives."

"Aww," Grace says, flattered.

Longstoryshort claims the recliner like it's a throne that was waiting for his return. Grace plops herself down in his lap and crosses her legs over the arm. Then she takes a long blink and a short but deep breath. An old, boxy Oldsmobile pulls up, a rapping country singer blaring on the radio. The music stops with the engine, and a gangly man in his late twenties or early thirties gets out, wearing a black shirt with a colorful feather on it, hat on backward. He raises both hands and shouts, "Whazzap!" He opens the trunk and pulls out two cases of beer, then walks into the garage like he's carrying the party. "Longssstoryshort! Good to see you, man!"

"Hey, Joe," Longstoryshort replies, still sitting, petting Grace's thigh.

Joe unloads the few dozen new bottles of beer into an already half-full fridge between Mike's couch and a door leading into the house, then plops dramatically onto the cushion next to Mike and submits himself to a headlock welcome. These are grown-ups! I feel like I'm at a friend's garage and we're avoiding the adults inside the house. I don't get the impression that anyone's a bad person, just that there are some kid souls still doing what kids do, but in their grown-up bodies.

Mike introduces me to Joe while Joe downs a beer. "Good to meet you, Red," he says. He opens a second beer and takes a swig. "Welcome to the garage."

Grace grabs a beer from the fridge for Longstoryshort and hands me a root beer. The syrupy sweet sates me, and holding a brown bottle makes me feel like I fit in a little more in this place I don't fit in with these people I don't know.

"How are the wife and kids?" Longstoryshort asks toward Mike and Joe.

Mike answers, "Good."

Joe finishes his second beer, then admits his wife left him.

They banter back and forth a while about what's new in town, where Longstoryshort has been, politics, and people I don't know. The sugar makes my head heavy, and my attention gets sluggish as they bounce from topic to topic.

"You a virgin?" Mike asks. I look up and see he's looking at me.

"Mike," Grace scolds sweetly. "I don't think he wants to talk about that."

"He's a boy. It's a valid question. How old are you?"

"I'm eighteen. Well, almost eighteen."

"Even more valid," Mike argues. "I've got a boy coming up on fourteen, and he's asking questions. I don't know what to say. Maybe you can give me some insight."

I don't want to answer, but I also don't want to screw up their first impression of me. I don't want to be a wimpy, timid kid. What would eighteen-year-old Longstoryshort do? I don't know. I can talk with my friends about sex stuff, but we all pretend like we've done more than we have. It'd be weird to talk about it with my parents or teachers. It's such an awkward subject. Maybe talking with Mike and everyone will help.

"Yes," I answer.

"Yes, you can give me some insight, or yes, you're a virgin?"

"Yes, I'm a virgin," I say with a blush.

"I know some girls that can help with that." Joe laughs and pulls out his phone.

"In the bag!" Mike and Longstoryshort command at the same time.

Joe walks his phone over to the bag and grabs another round of beers for everyone. All eyes are on me.

"You haven't had the chance, or you got a strong will over your urges?" Mike asks.

"Or you take care of it yourself." Joe laughs like he's thirteen, which makes me even more uncomfortable.

"I don't know." I decide to be honest and give a try at putting it to words. "I guess it's fear more than anything."

"What do you mean?" Mike leans in. "Like you're afraid you won't know what to do, or afraid you'll get her pregnant?"

"Yeah, I mean no," I stutter. "I think I'm most afraid of catching some disease."

They're all listening. I guess I have to explain. "There was this presentation in school where they showed how one person with an STD can turn into over half the school having it in just a couple of months. And you don't know who has it until *you* have it, and then you might have already spread it too. After that, I was messing around with this girl, but I knew she'd had a boyfriend the week before, and I knew he had a few girlfriends and—" I shrug. "And the presentation kind of came to life, and it freaked me out. If she would mess around with me, who else would she mess around with? She didn't care and said she was safe, but I don't want pus coming out of places or crabs crawling around or sores or anything."

"Dang," Mike says. "When I was young, all you had to worry about was getting a girl knocked up, and there were ways around that."

"Yeah, like you can't get pregnant if it's a full moon," Joe cackles.

"Or maybe like wearing a white shirt?" Huh? That makes no sense.

"So, you're a teenage boy—what do you do about your urges?" Mike asks, point-blank.

I don't want to answer any more questions like this about me. I feel shame for being a teenager with raging hormones. I feel defensive, angry, shy, sad, and mainly confused. What *do* you do about your urges?

"You don't have to answer his questions, Redemption." Grace saves me. "Mike, what are you getting at?"

"I mean, in Bible times, they got married when they were fourteen and got to make babies with their raging hormones. When I was a kid, we had to make it to sixteen or eighteen before it was socially acceptable. Now we expect 'em to graduate high school, be good through college, and come out in their midtwenties pure and marry someone else who was able to make it all the way through the baby-making heyday without giving in as well? Seems like an impossible task! What are the options? The impossible task—take care of it yourself, or go on and have sex but don't get no disease or get a girl pregnant?"

"Number two," Joe says. "Keeps the hormones at bay and the diseases away." He seems proud of himself.

"Joe," Grace says, "you have a daughter. You want some boy thinking of your daughter that way?"

"Better thinkin' than doin'," Joe answers. "Anyways, they won't be thinkin' of her. They got all kinds of porn we didn't have growin' up."

"And those are someone's daughters, too, Joe," Grace adds.

"What do you think?" Mike asks to Longstoryshort, who has been sitting silent, enjoying the uncomfortable conversation as a spectator.

"I don't know," he ponders. "God made us sexual beings. Why would He give us something so good and treat it so bad?"

Everyone thinks about it. Why would He? It's like we're thrown into a losing battle. Sex is everywhere. Images, advertisements, pop-ups, movies, social pressure, expectation. It's everywhere. It's like God made candy, told us to resist it until it's "right" to enjoy it, and then piles a mountain of it on top of us. But that doesn't seem right either. I know what's right and wrong. I can feel it. But it's like there are two sides of me. And they're battling.

Someone new steps through the doorway, and Joe cackles. "Sounds like a question for a minister," he says.

This guy walks through the garage shaking his head, lost in his own mental world, on his way to the fridge. He grabs a beer, pops off the lid, and settles in next to Joe on the three-cushioned couch. After a long draw, he comes to.

"Oh, hey, Longstory," he says unenthusiastically. He looks at me and introduces himself. "I'm Lewis."

"This is Redemption." Mike completes the introduction.

"You sure give them good names," Lewis says to Longstoryshort and turns back to me. "Welcome to the garage."

It *is* my name.

"Good counseling session?" Mike asks. "Who was it, the McIntyre kids?"

"I'm not at liberty to say. And no. I hate that I have to do these counseling sessions for free. Over and over—premarital counseling, marriage counseling, divorce counseling—all for the same couple! They're all the same! If they had to pay, if it hurt their bank account, maybe they'd pay attention." He tilts the bottle high. "And it kills me that I have to do their weddings for free, too, knowing where it's going to end up."

"I've been thinking about that, Lewis," Mike says. "You've been complaining about the same thing for years. What if you have them sign a contract for the wedding. Charge a ten-thousand-dollar wedding fee, but waive it unless they get divorced. Then, when they get divorced, at least you're compensated for trying!"

"I'd be a rich man," Lewis contemplates, waiting for the beer to calm his nerves.

"Ask him the sex question." Joe bounces on the cushion.

Lewis rolls his eyes and finishes off his beer. Joe gets him another, and Mike starts in.

"Okay, my fourteen-year-old kid is asking me about sex stuff. I don't know what to tell him."

"What kind of sex stuff?" Lewis asks like a counselor.

"Well, he says his friends have been watching porn since they were ten, and he was asking if it was wrong to watch it."

"Yes." Lewis tells it like a minister.

"Right," Mike continues. "So my kid asks, 'Isn't it a better outlet than sex?'"

Lewis thinks, drinks, and thinks.

"I mean, Redemption was talking about all the diseases"—I wish he wouldn't have brought me into it—"and you wouldn't have that or pregnancy to worry about, but it doesn't feel right to give the go-ahead, and it doesn't seem realistic to just tell him to take a cold shower like my old man told me."

Lewis thinks, drinks, and thinks.

Longstoryshort chimes in. "It's an old, old dilemma. Take Jackson Hole, for example. Trappers and hunters were the first ones here. Men's men, you know. *Manly* men. They had enough to keep them busy tracking and hunting and exploring. It wasn't an easy life, and the elements can be damning. Every once in a while, things'd slow down, and the nights would be filled with drinking and fighting. If a girl happened to be around, she wasn't safe from all that built-up urge to mate, all that need to feel good for a minute or two. Wasn't a place for a girl or a woman. Just a sniff of 'em, and the animal would come out in the men.

"As the camp grew into a settlement, someone realized there was money to be made off the situation. They'd bring in girls willing to trade services for a price and in a more controlled environment. The madams made sure the ladies were healthy and taken care of, and at the same time, they'd make sure the men didn't do them any harm. Kept the little girls and wives of the families moving in safe. Kept sort of a balance."

Mike's brow shows concern, but he's listening. Joe looks like a kid at story time. Lewis is pretending not to listen, and Grace is squirming uncomfortably like she wants to say something.

". . . more people moving in . . . the trapper's paradise didn't take long to turn into a full-blown town. Supply stores, places to eat, blacksmiths, dentists, candy shops, whorehouses, and churches . . ."

So it grew up with the town. Why couldn't the men just control their urges or something?

". . . long story short, it's just always been there, right alongside everything else that makes Jackson Hole Jackson Hole, right alongside everything else that makes the world the world. Ever since the dawn of crea—"

Mike interrupts with a laugh of disbelief. "Wait. Are you telling me to take my kid to a whorehouse?!"

"Is that worse than him taking advantage of an innocent girl when his pent-up hormones have nowhere else to go?" Longstoryshort asks back. "Then you could take him to church to keep the universe in balance." I can't tell if he's serious. It doesn't seem like it, but then again, it does.

"I am *not* taking my kid to a whorehouse," Mike responds. "Next idea."

I'm glad at Mike's resolve, and as uncomfortable as the conversation is, it seems to be getting at a deeper issue that never gets touched in school.

"Tell us more about the whorehouses!" Joe redirects, bouncing on his cushion, spilling his beer.

"You'd think if the churches were doing their job," Grace interjects, "they'd've shut the whorehouses down."

"If the churches were doing their job," Longstoryshort snorts, "the *churches* would get shut down." Flipping a beer cap, he continues. "Both would deny it, but the church and the whorehouse are just different sides of the same coin. They both had the opportunity to take the bleakness out of life for a short time, but the church couldn't answer for a man's sex drive, and the whorehouse couldn't appease a man's need for grace."

It makes sense, but something about it doesn't sound right. But he's still talking.

". . . they had an unspoken pact. The whorehouse keeps it quiet and in the dark, and the church doesn't burn it down."

Joe chimes in. "Yeah, but now we don't have to go to a whorehouse. We got it brought to us in the convenience of, well, anywhere we got a phone! And for free!"

"Difference is," Lewis speaks, ignoring Joe, "the whorehouses aren't keeping silent, and the churches aren't burning them down."

"And the church isn't taking the bleakness out of life anymore either." Longstoryshort leers at Lewis. "All I'm saying is, lust has been a part of society since the beginning. And in the grand mechanics of the universe, does it really even matter what we do? King David killed a man to sleep with Bathsheba, and he's still revered as a man 'after God's own heart,' isn't he? Seems to me, God must have some unresolved lust in *His* heart."

He looks over at me, and I can't hide the confusion on my face. That doesn't sound like something Jesus would say. "I'm playing devil's advocate here, kid," he says.

"Of course it matters what we do," Lewis answers, then thinks, drinks, and thinks some more.

"I thought I was going to get a simple answer, not a philosophy lesson," Mike complains. "I just need to know what to tell the kid."

He probably just wants you to be there with him instead of here drinking, I think. But I don't say it aloud.

"It's a tough subject." Lewis squirms with another swig. "I don't know that it has a simple answer. Kids are being raised on porn now, getting into relationships early, trying everything they see and then getting sucked deeper and deeper into it. I'd hate to say it, but Joe's right."

Joe spills his beer again with victory.

Lewis continues. "These phones bring the whorehouse to you. In good houses, at school, everywhere. It's not just easily accessible, it's free and anonymous. And I'd get fired in a Sunday minute if I talked about it in church. I don't know that the church even has a dog in the fight anymore." He thinks over his bottle; everyone waits for his conclusion.

"I wouldn't say watching porn is good for him. I wouldn't say porn was ever innocent, but what's out there nowadays sure makes what it used to be look that way. I watched a TED talk about it the other day, and what they were saying blew my mind. Said now it's all about choking, raping, incest . . . anything to push the limit, like the old limits lost their kicks. Made me sick. If there's a sick idea out there, it's on the front page, and these kids' ten-year-old brains are being warped from it. Then they come to me as adults and want me to fix their marriage without burning down what's full grown in their hearts."

"So porn ain't safe either." Mike gets another beer for everyone. "So the cold shower?"

Lewis shakes his head. "With all the kids parents send to me, I'd assume he's already neck deep in addiction with it."

"So I should send him to you?"

"No. Talk to him about it."

"That's what I'm asking," Mike roars. "What do I say?!" He realizes he's yelling and sits down with a heavy exhale. "What would *you* say, preacher?"

"I'd tell him it's the devil trying to get his claws in deep, that life's about more than pleasure." Lewis takes another drink. "And I'd tell him sexuality is something made for good and must be dealt with delicately."

"And that women don't like being treated like prostitutes," Grace adds. "Even a woman caught up in that world is being used. It's evil. Maybe teach him to control those urges from the beginning, and the whorehouse in his heart will never have to be built. But make sure he knows love and sexuality should *never* involve violence—being thrown around, choked, or slapped." Her expression retreats into itself like she's thinking of something personal. I hope she was never treated like that.

Longstoryshort slaps her thigh, and she snaps out of it, stands up, and slaps him back—not exactly gently—on the shoulder. She pops back into a conversational posture. "I feel like I was duped by the sexual revolution. It was all about women being allowed to be sexualized and free, like men. I mean, a woman wants to feel good, too, and I think she should, but it seems like the girls now are . . . I don't know. What am I trying to say? Like they're becoming kinky slaves for perverted men because they're told it's freedom and equality of the sexes. Since when do women have to become animals to prove they're equal?"

Longstoryshort slaps her on the rear this time, and Grace gets red in the face, obviously trying to keep from getting angry. She sets down her beer, briskly tells everyone good night, and stomps into the house.

I expect we'll all leave, too, seeing that it's her house. But the conversation picks back up.

"So that's all I need to say? That life's about more than pleasure, sex is delicate, and he should treat a woman with respect?" Mike asks it like we're talking about a spark plug that needs replacing.

"That's what *he'd* say," Longstoryshort points a long finger at Lewis, "but Lewis, you're a forty-year-old single guy who's never been married. How do you deal with the pent-up lust in yourself?"

Lewis's face sours, not liking the same question I got earlier. I can relate to his discomfort, but he's a minister. I watch his reaction closely.

"I try to always make the next right choice," he says. It's a good thought, but—

"That doesn't answer the question," Longstoryshort points out. "It's easy to talk theory, but Mike's interested in reality. *Does* it really matter what we do?"

Another guy appears in the doorway of the garage. "Hey, West!" Joe blurts and jumps up. "Come join the fun! Grace stomped off, and we're talking about sex!"

Longstoryshort uses the diversion to slink into the house, I guess to make things right with Grace.

West gives Joe a thumbs-up and a forced smile, grabs a beer, and sits next to me. He gives me a personal wave of his hand and starts writing in his notebook.

Mike introduces West in bullet-point style. "This is West. He's a writer. Can't talk, though. Lost his tongue to cancer. Dippin'. You don't dip no more, do you, West?"

West shakes his head no and tips his notebook toward me.

Don't buy anything these guys say, just pay attention.

I nod, as if I can't speak too.

Joe is getting more excited the more he drinks. "Yeah, West wrote this great book, got it published, and won some awards, but he can't sell any because he can't give no speeches. Kinda messed up, ain't it?"

West shakes his head and starts scribbling notes to show he's not listening.

Mike claps back. "Aw, Joe, that ain't right. First of all, when's the last time you read a book? Second, no one's making millions writing books anymore. I heard on the radio the other day that more than a million books are being published every year just in the US. At the same time, people are reading less and less."

"Of making many books there is no end . . ." Lewis says with a sigh. I just read that somewhere. It's on the tip of my brain.

"What is that from?" I ask.

"Ecclesiastes," Lewis says. I knew it. "Everything is meaningless" comes out of his mouth, and he finishes another beer and closes his eyes.

Even lust? Even trying to do the next right thing?

"Except the fear of God," I say. "What does that mean, anyway?" I could use a preacher's insight.

"It means you'd better watch out and do the right thing, or God's going to strike you down!" Joe explains.

"You're still here, Joe?" Mike laughs. "Explain that one."

Lewis speaks up. "I don't know that it means to be afraid of God. I think it means more of a respect. Like you would your father."

"I don't respect my dad," Joe argues. "But I am afraid of him. He was a deadbeat. Always drunk and beating on us. I'd never hit my kids." His kids that his wife took from him?

I think of my father. I'm not afraid of him, and I respect that he provides for the family and that he doesn't hit us or anything. I don't like it when he gets angry, so I try not to make him angry. Is that what Lewis is saying?

"I take it like this," Mike says. "I work with electricity. Electricity does a lot of good. Lights, microwaves, refrigerators, computers. But it can also kill you. I'm afraid of it when I'm wiring up a new breaker, so I take the proper precautions."

That makes sense, but there's still something off. Can it be the power of God that is charging the phone that ten-year-old kids are watching porn on?

"All I know—" Lewis pauses, and we wait while he visits the fridge. "All I know is, if we had a little more fear of God, my job would be a lot easier." I think he's close to drunk.

"Here we go," Joe whispers to Mike. "What do you mean?" he asks Lewis.

"If more people feared God, then I wouldn't have to spend so much time counseling people who want God to change so they don't have to."

"You talking about the McIntyres?" Mike prods.

"Yeah. We go into premarital counseling for twenty weeks, holding hands and mushy eyed. Neither one reads the book they're supposed to read, like their decision to stop having sex during the engagement is going to be enough. I do their wedding, and now they want a divorce. She had a fairy tale in her head where he was going to turn into Prince Charming, folding the sheets and all, and he thought he was going to have a porn star in the bedroom. They don't want me to save their marriage; they want me to pat 'em on the back and tell 'em God loves them and that they've done nothing wrong."

"What'd you tell them?" Mike asks.

"I gave 'em another book, but I might as well have thrown it in the fire. I tell you, people won't read a book to save their marriage. They won't read a book to save their kids. They won't read a book to save their own lives!"

"D'you think that's because they don't think it'll work," Mike asks, "or because they don't want to be fixed?"

"They don't want to change," Lewis answers quickly. "The path of least resistance."

"Why aren't you married?" Joe has no tact.

"Path of least resistance?" Mike chuckles.

"I'm so sick of that question. You know, Paul says it's better for a man to not be married, and from what I've seen, I think he's right. All these churches want a married preacher with a perfect family. But as soon as someone stubs their toe, they want their preacher to leave the perfect dinner table and console them. I don't know that a preacher can be a shepherd for his own family and be on call all the time too." What would happen if someone called him now? "And the pressure on the kids. There's a reason for the preacher-kid stereotype.

Kid gets put second chair to the church, and when they act out, they get stomped on instead of talked to and loved on, because they're supposed to be perfect too."

"Sorry, Lewis," Mike says. "We don't want to get you worked up; we're here to unwind. Let's change the subject. Hey, Redemption, what's on your mind?"

Me? A lot. Not much. Mountains, truth. Fire, smoke, fear. Tourists. Natives.

"I've been trying to work something out in my head," I begin.

"Let's hear it," Mike says.

"Well, there's this opposition in my head between civilization and Native Americans. I just drove up the Great Plains, and the history is everywhere. Towns, roads, and highways are named after tribes, tepees decorate buildings and gas stations, and Indians are the mascot in a lot of places, but the Native way of life is pretty much gone. It's all houses and farms, train tracks, and power lines. One way of life took over another. And I ended up in a Native town in Montana called Lame Deer, and there was a sign—'Help our people—Pray for everyone.' I can't help but feel like that's a metaphor for something going on inside us too. Like, there's something native in us, but the outside world comes in and takes over."

"You mean like good versus evil?" Mike asks.

"No, good and evil would be saying the Natives are evil. And I don't think Americans are evil, either."

"Civilized and uncivilized?" Lewis asks.

"Not really. The Natives were civilized, in their own way. Different."

Joe is making gun sounds and looks like he's having a shootout with himself on his chest.

"I can see that," Lewis says. "There are good aspects in both of them, but they can't live their different ways in the same space."

"Longstoryshort said it's like they were both building motorcycles, and land was the engine or something. They couldn't both have it, so the strongest one got it."

Joe shouldn't speak, but he does. "Them Indians're always wantin' something. They losht. They should get over it. Now they's all on welfare spending their money on booze."

"Joe," Mike points out, "aren't you wearing a Native American shirt?"

Joe looks down at the colorful feather and says proudly, "My grandma shaid her grandma was an Indian princess. That makesh me part Indian. Not enough to go to college or anythin', but I got hair-a-tage."

Even West has stopped what he's doing to join Mike and Lewis in cocking their heads at Joe in confusion.

"I think Joe makes a good point," Lewis says.

"I did?" Joe asks with excitement.

"It comes down to identity. Both the Natives and Americans are having an identity crisis. We don't know who we are or where we come from. Natives are trying to Americanize and are turning to gangs and alcohol to replace their identity. Americans are like Joe over here, cherishing an idea—like the idea you're talking about, Redemption—but not understanding their own history."

"Now don't go bashing America, Lewis," Mike says defensively. "The Natives weren't all peace loving and innocent, either."

"I'm not bashing America, Mike. And you're right. Both sides're proud to point out their good traits and quick to forget their shins."

"My *shins*!" Joe shouts and doubles over in laughter. He hugs his knees and says, "I forgot about you!"

"So," I ask, "is there always going to be a battle between the idea of modern America and the idea of Native Americans?"

"We can't change the pasht"—Lewis's scholarly tone is getting slurred too—"but we can change the futcher."

"Treaties," Mike states confidently. "Treaties are the answer."

"Treaties?" Lewis asks.

"Yeah," Mike says. "It sounded right. So I said it."

This conversation is going nowhere. I wonder if in their minds the alcohol makes them feel smarter, when in reality, it's making them less so. I think I'm more disappointed in Lewis, because he was actually saying some good things, and he *is* supposed to be a preacher. I could really use a guide in life right now. I guess that's the pressure to be perfect he was talking about.

The dead conversation lingers. It's dark outside, and I wonder how long we're going to be here. At least Longstoryshort didn't drink that much. He can drive. Or are we staying here?

"What's up with Longstoryshort and Grace?" I ask.

"Oh, they've been together longer than any of us have been coming around," Mike says.

"So are they married or just a couple?"

"I would say both and neither," Lewis answers. "It's more like Grace is married to Longstoryshort, and they're a couple when he's passing through, which is only a few days a year. I'm not sure any woman could hold him down, and who knows, he might have Graces all over."

Lewis doesn't sound like he thinks too highly of Longstoryshort. It doesn't sound very fair either.

"We don't know that, Lewis," Mike says. "We don't know much about him."

"If Jesus was on the earth today," I ask, "wouldn't He be about the same, roaming around, being with women, and drinking with sinners?"

Mike laughs. "You callin' us sinners?"

"Shinners!" Joe hugs his shins again. I *know* he's drunk.

"You got a point," Lewis considers. "But I don't think Jesus would have sex with the women who were with Him."

"Unless Longstoryshort had a point," Mike adds, "about God having that hidden lustful side and churches and whorehouses hav-

81

ing that secret pact."

No. I don't care about logic. That one doesn't make *any* sense. It's missing something. I need to believe in a God that is good all the way through.

"So Grace hangs around waiting for him all year, and he just shows up for a few days of romance? Why would she put up with that?"

"She's just like any other woman," Mike says. "She wants to be loved."

"Grace without truth allows all shorts of evil to flourish in the world." Lewis washes the thought down with the last of the bottle. "And truth without grace is Mike."

"Hey!" Mike mockingly protests. "I don't understand what that means, but I'm offended!"

Truth. Grace. I get the feeling that they're supposed to be married but they're not. Where is truth in all this? All these perspectives, all these ideas. Is anyone right? Is everyone? Can they all be wrong? I still feel like the debate is missing something. Joe runs to the restroom, and we can hear him heaving through the door.

"There's our sign." Mike walks over and fishes his phone out of the bag. Waiting for it to power on, he turns to us. "Kids should be in bed. Guess it's time to go home and get griped at." I can't tell if he's being sarcastic.

Lewis knocks on the bathroom door and helps Joe clean up and get to the passenger side of his car. I'm not sure Lewis is any more fit to drive than Joe.

That leaves me and West. Because he's silent, it's easy to forget he's there, but he's been working.

"Are you writing another book?" I ask loudly, as if he can't hear. He nods.

"Are Mike and Joe and Lewis characters in your story?" He nods again and scribbles on his notebook.

I'm collecting characters.

"Any inspiration tonight?"

West nods. *What's the difference between humans and animals?*

It's a good question. He writes a little more.

What would happen if everyone's secret internet history was made public?

Whoa. If *everything* was brought into the light? "All hell would break loose."

Would it? West jots.

Wouldn't it? Of course it would. Everyone would be exposed. Marriages would have to face it. Teachers, preachers, and politicians would have to own up to their secrets. Wouldn't they?

I think in a silence that has become awkward. Finally, I ask, "What's the name of the book you published?"

He shows me the title: *The Last Great American Novel.* Then he closes his notebook and gets up. He bows to me as a good night and walks toward the dimly lit street.

Just like that, I'm alone. It's cold. Really cold. I close myself in the garage and pick up the bottles. West didn't even drink half of one. *Smart.* Pay attention. Practice what you preach.

I guess I'm staying here tonight. I find a blanket and spread it out on the blue couch. The embers in my chest are still glowing through the gray ash. I need a breath of fresh air or a cold dose of water. I take a deep breath and keep it. The blanket is thin, aged white, dingy with time. Those paper Japanese hand fans that fold up are embroidered open near the top. I pull them over my nose, and the blanket exposes my feet.

My mind is racing and empty at the same time. Ghostly bumper-car thoughts. Electricity snaps and synapses. Electricity and God. Fear. Respect. Sex and society. Whorehouses and churches. Addiction, claws. How we were made. How were we made? Native. How is that different than animals? Truth and grace.

I eye the fridge, think about drinking a beer to see if it would help me fall asleep, but I resist and the thought goes away. *Home.* I curl into the fetal position and slip into sleep. I dream a house is burning. My home is burning. My mom is screaming. There are firetruck lights outside. I'm not there.

CHAPTER 6

TUESDAY: JACKSON HOLE— A DAY OF CLARITY

I **wake up on fire and check** my forehead, but it doesn't feel like fever. I need to be home. I sit up on the couch and notice how cold the air is. I walk to the garage door and look out the windows to see if it's snowing or something. It's not. Piles of chopped firewood line the right side of the driveway. That's a lot of wood. It's May. Winter is over. At least it is in Texas. Has been for a few months.

Back at the couch, I pick up the blanket and wrap myself in it. What do I do now? Are we meeting up with Holy Ghost today? Will I be home today? Tomorrow? I should call my mom.

The heavy wooden door from the garage to the house pulls open from the inside, and the thin, metal-framed screen door pushes out. Grace's silky nightgown robe is tied around her waist, and her hair is in rollers as she walks sleepily toward the clothes hanging by the dryer. She isn't young anymore, but her goodness makes her beautiful still.

"Good morning," I say, the way I would to my mother or distant future wife. She jumps in surprise and makes sure she's covered up.

"Oh, goodness!" she gasps. "I didn't realize you were in here. I'm so sorry. You must have been freezing!"

"I'm okay," I say, not wanting to be a bother.

"You must be hungry. Let me get you some breakfast."

I really do want breakfast, but I really don't want to be a burden. "I'm okay," I say again.

"No, you've already had to sleep out in the garage," she says. "I'm not going to be a total disgrace of a host." She grabs a few things from the drying rack and apologizes before going back inside. "I'm sorry you had to see me like this."

But she doesn't look like a monster, just like a real person who woke up after a hard sleep. I've never understood makeup. When you cover up who you are every day, aren't you afraid that, after a while, you'll be ashamed of what you really look like? Sure, maybe it makes some people a little prettier, but I've seen plenty that it makes them uglier. Like they think they're so ugly they need a pound of it to cover up, but all it does is scream, "I'm self-conscious and ashamed of how I look!" I guess guys do the same thing. Big trucks and tough attitudes. Or a muscular avatar with lots of guns. The grass is not the mountain.

I walk back to the garage door window to see if I can see the mountains. I can't. Trees are in the way. I lean into the garage door for a better angle, and it moves a little; the springs and hinges squeak above me.

The door from the house opens again, and Grace is dressed and carrying a silver tray with a plate of food and a clear glass of orange juice. "It's not much," she says in a way that suggests she would say the same thing if it was a steak with eggs and bacon.

It's steak with fried eggs and bacon.

"Thank you!" I say with my mouth and eyes at the same time. Both open and ready to eat it. I carefully take the tray, trying not to act starving or greedy—and trying not to drop it in my excitement.

"Longstory is still sleeping. He didn't sleep much last night." She blushes with what looks like a tinge of shame. "Anyway, he might be out for a while. I wouldn't disturb him."

My eyebrows knit as an anger rises at the thought of Longstoryshort and Grace. It's not my business. *Chill your eyebrows,* I tell myself as Grace continues talking.

"I've got to get to work. I won't be home until five or so. Longstory said you'll be here another night, so I'll see you then."

Another night? I want to go home. "Have a good day," I say lamely. "And thank you for the breakfast!" I'm already halfway through with it and haven't focused on enjoying it. I take a big gulp of orange juice and wave as she walks back into the house. Medium pulp, so good. Not the knock-off stuff.

The front door opens and shuts, and Grace is off to work. I guess she works close; I didn't see a car in the street, and there wasn't one in the driveway. Joe was the only one with a car. This must be a smaller town than it seems.

I mop up the egg yolk and steak juice with the bacon and lean back on the blue cushion. I'm happy. For a few minutes. After a long sleep and a good meal, I have energy to spend. I have thoughts to think, questions to ask, truth to seek, a world to see. Mountains.

I scoop up my backpack and, with a quick leap and a skip, lift the light metal garage door above me. A blast of frigid air greets me as I step through. A cold front must have blown in. Or maybe it's just that cold in May in Jackson. A shiver of life runs through me. I pull the garage door closed and turn to face the world as an explorer. Maybe I can find Lewis's church and ask him some God questions. What makes Christianity right instead of the other religions? Or are they all pretty much the same thing? Maybe he has an extra Bible I could use. Or keep.

Walking up the road, I see to the west (I think) a greenish-brown hill of a mountain reaching above civilization. Below the gray blanket of clouds, I see scattered patches of white snow. Two houses down, a man runs out to his car like he's late for work. Then he runs back to his house, fumbling with the keys to get back in. Only a few cars drive by on this neighborhood street. Locals going to work, selling memories of a town to tourists. A blond woman in a fleece jacket and workout pants walks her dog. She notices me noticing her and clasps the top of her jacket with her free hand, then faces forward and quickens her pace.

That's weird. Did she think I was checking her out? I noticed what she was wearing, but not in some creepy way like that guy downtown yesterday. Or was it? Did Grace think I was checking her out in a creepy way when she clasped her robe this morning? Is it a common reaction, or is it something that happens only when they feel like someone is undressing them? How can they tell the difference between someone looking at them and someone violating them with their mind?

I wonder what it feels like to be a woman in a world where men are so sexual. Or are a lot of women actually after that sexual attention? The makeup, the tight pants, the low-cut shirts? Is it like the birds, chirping and dancing and flirting in the spring air because it's mating season? *What is the difference between humans and animals?*

Down a few blocks now, a school field is full of kids chirping and dancing and chasing each other. But there's innocence. They aren't trying to mate. I remember the school playground as a kid. For a moment, you're free. You can be who you want, even what you want. One time I was a statue of George Washington during the whole twenty minutes of recess. It was so much fun. School hadn't turned into prison yet. Popularity hadn't turned into a cruel game. No one had committed suicide in our class yet. No one was on drugs. No one had seen porn. No one had been raped or molested. Or at least we didn't know about it.

We didn't know about it.

Like the garden of Eden before Adam and Eve ate the not-an-apple. I had a Sunday school teacher who emphasized, "then Adam and Eve ate *the not-an-apple.*" Then what was it? A pomegranate?

Adam and Eve must've been in middle school. But is knowledge bad? Ignorance good? Innocence is good, but we can't go back to that. A bell rings, and the children turn and run toward the building. It must be eight o'clock.

Across the street, a church steeple without a cross points to heaven. The sign says "Pastor Lewis Clarkson." I read it, then do a double take. I can't help but laugh. That has to be Lewis. I bet people visit the church just to see if he's Lewis or Clark's grandson or maybe if he's here on an expedition. He didn't seem like an explorer to me. I guess I'm not the only one struggling to live up to my name. The church logo is a cross inside a mountain. Why would it be inside the mountain and not on top, or on the side? Is it hiding? I go to the doors, but they're locked. Maybe Lewis is hiding from people needing a counselor but no counseling.

I walk on. There's a glass-walled indoor bus-stop waiting area with benches, a restroom, and water fountains. It must get really cold here. It's heated inside, comfortable for waiting. Three people are spread out and glued to their phones. I sit for a minute to wait comfortably for nothing and get nowhere.

After jotting some notes in my journal, I fill up my water bottle, empty my bladder, and reenter the cold world in search of truth.

I walk up a few streets and over one, guided by my own footsteps. A juicery with a line of people to the sidewalk marks the beginning of downtown. It's not locals anymore. Part of me is tempted to stand in line just because there is one. But I walk on.

An art gallery that isn't open yet displays vibrant, colorful suggestions of buffalo, bucking horses, and mountains. A clothing store employee is putting out a sale rack of twenty-dollar sweatshirts with "Jackson Hole" printed across the chest. A dentist's office is right next to a candy shop. I wonder if they have a secret agreement. I think of the discussion of churches and whorehouses being different parts of the same thing. Is it the same?

A cigar shop is closed, but the open sign is on. Maybe it shares the building with a mouth cancer specialist and they trade hours. A high-end restaurant has a menu framed on the door with descriptions of the food served but no prices. I guess for some people, prices don't matter. Did we walk out on the tab at the Mexican food place yesterday?

I stop at the corner across from the square park, diagonally opposite from where I was standing yesterday outside Pandora's Box. Another arch of antlers invites me to the green grass and budding trees in the middle of town. Last week in Texas it was summer, I just rode through freshly plowed snow, and now it's spring in Jackson. New life? I'll take it.

It's too early for the traffic to be as hectic as it was yesterday, but I still have to dodge cars to cross the street. And a man on a horse, dressed like it's a hundred years ago. People. Time. People don't change; technology does. The machine? Is it technology or people? Or something bigger?

Starting from the antler arches at each corner, the sidewalks in the park meet in an X in the middle. There's a statue of a man on a bucking bronco at the center. X marks the spot? Is the man taming a wild beast in the middle of it all, or is he riding it for the excitement and novelty? Or is he trying to impress a girl?

I walk past an elderly man sitting on a bench; he's smoking a cigar and squinting through reading glasses at his phone. I find a clump of roots that makes a perfect seat under one of the larger budding trees and lean my back against the trunk. I pull out my journal and pen, take a deep, relaxing breath, and am ready to pay attention.

What do you see? I see an Old West saloon with a neon Open sign. Pandora's Box. Gifts and collectibles. Animal hides. A coffee shop with a goddess logo looking out as carefully as I am. Art galleries. A couple, maybe in their twenties, walks by, hand in hand. He's about my height with a clean haircut and expensive clothes. He's cooler than the cool kids. Good posture and a coffee. He's holding his coffee with the care and delicacy that she holds his hand and arm. She's prettier than the pretty girls, and I try not to look at her clothes, but she's in a thick brown coat that looks like it's just off the racks of one of these high-end Western stores. Her body language clings, and her eyes admire him. He doesn't seem to care or notice her affection. If I were him, I hope I wouldn't ignore her doting like he is. Then again, is that what a girl likes? Does he make her a better person? Does she make him a better man? Or is it a fling of convenience, like all the girls I've ever dated? Someone to keep you from being alone. And then, when you get used to each other, it's time to move on. Maybe I just haven't met someone I can see myself spending forever with, making each other better people.

A couple of Asian tourists take each other's pictures posing in front of the cowboy statue, look at the picture, laugh, and move on. I wonder if there's a kid in China sitting under a tree watching American tourists take pictures in front of a statue of . . . What would there be a statue of in China? I never realized how little I knew about America until this trip. Now I'm feeling ignorant of the world in general. Different countries, different cultures, different religions. Are we all really the same?

A Black woman sits down next to the old man on the phone, talking to someone on speaker phone. Am I supposed to say African American? I don't know. I know I'm not supposed to offend anyone, but how am I supposed to know what they prefer? My friend Curtis likes being called colored, "because we're all colored," he says. But with other "colored people," he prefers to use the word that, if I say it, I get suspended for. Our teachers always tell us we're supposed to be "color blind," but that never made sense to me. Why can't people be what they are and be proud of it? Like Native Americans. They have a history vastly different than mine, and it's part of their identity. Isn't trying to make them just like everybody else part of what they're suffering from? If they're proud of their heritage, shouldn't I be too? That way when we cross paths, I don't expect them to think and act like me. Then we'd have the mind to learn from each other and the heart to appreciate each other instead of always trying to fight or fix each other. We can't put white bread, tortillas, and pitas in a blender and say it's all the same. Each one is delicious in its own way. I don't get it, and I don't think society does, either.

The old man gets up and moves to another bench.

"Because I'm Black?" the woman shouts, then continues on the phone. "Yeah, so I just sat down next to an old White man, and he gets up and moves 'cause I'm Black. . . I *know*! And people say racism ain't a thing no more."

What if he moved because she was talking loudly on speakerphone? Isn't it prejudiced that she called him an old White man? I guess that's what he is, but the way she said it. What if what we do and why we do it are two different things? We see what people do, but we don't know why they do it. Like the woman thinking I was checking her out. How was she to know?

A slick man in a rich suit walks by yelling at someone through his phone. "I don't care, just get the job done!" He doesn't care, walking straight through a group of chattering tourists and into the honking traffic. I'd hate to be his kid. I wonder if the suit was worth it. Everyone walking by is dressed in stylish, expensive clothes. It makes me conscious of my generic black sweatshirt that's a size too small. I can smell myself. The unshowered road-trip grime has already taken over the newness of the clothes. Everyone who walks by glances at me. Because I'm a person or because I'm a person who doesn't belong? They can't smell me, but can they tell? I don't see any homeless people or beggars around. I have more in common with them than everyone else here. Wait. Are they looking at me like I'm a beggar?

A police officer is coming my direction. I pretend like I don't see him. He sees me pretend like I don't see him. I open my journal again to show that I'm just sitting here writing. I look up, and he's right in front of me.

"Good morning," he says.

I don't know why I'm nervous. I'm not doing anything wrong. "Hu." Wrong vowel. "Hi."

I'm sure he would have walked on if I weren't so awkward, but the conversation begins.

"From around here?" he asks.

"Texas. Just passing through."

"You by yourself?"

"No, my dad's with me. We're visiting my mom." I just lied. Why did I lie? And why that lie?

"Mind if I see your ID?"

"Oh, um. Sure." It's in my backpack with my wallet, so I shift to reach in.

"Anything else in that bag I should be worried about?" Do I really look like a traveling drug dealer or gangster? How is he to know?

"No sir," I say and open the bag to show him it's just my granddad's journal, a few notebooks, and who knows what else but definitely not anything illegal. I fish out my billfold and hand him my license.

"Redemption Gray," he says and hands it back. "Quite a name. Shouldn't you be in school?"

"I'm homeschooled." I lie again. I hadn't committed a crime before the officer came over, but I've lied to him twice now! Luckily, he didn't run my card through the system or anything. I hope my mom didn't report the car stolen or me as a runaway. I really need to call her.

"Thanks for being honest with me," the policeman says. "We get a lot of tramps hopping off the trains here. This town doesn't look too highly on that type."

He *is* saying I look homeless! Like a tramp! And this town doesn't look highly on me.

"You're welcome," I say, but I'm the one *not* welcome in this rich town.

"Have a nice day," he says. Yeah—a nice day out of the view of the public.

"You too." I'm shaking. Why am I shaking? I'm not scared . . . I don't think. Why would I be scared? His power? Not knowing if I was in trouble just for existing? Not knowing? I'm cold, but not shivering cold. I'm hot. I'm angry.

A woman in high heels and skintight leather walks by. I don't look up past her knees. I'm angry that I can't look at a woman without her thinking I'm a creep.

A fat man walks by, and I'm disgusted. How can someone let themselves go like that? I'm angry that I'm thinking thoughts like this, but I'm on a roll.

I'm angry at the racist woman talking loudly on the phone, calling the old man a racist. I'm angry that everyone has to walk on eggshells about *everything* they say and think, for fear of being shamed for being human. I'm angry that even the old man is addicted to his phone. I'm angry that the businessman doesn't care.

A happy couple sit on a bench nearby, sipping each other's steaming drinks. I'm angry because I've never been happy with a girl. I'm angry that Grace is so gullible and Longstoryshort isn't Jesus.

I'm angry that I'll never be able to afford to fit in here. I don't even *want* to fit in here. Phonies. They're all a bunch of phonies. Phonies on their phones. The guy on the horse is a phony. The woman with the makeup is a phony. Even the buildings are phony.

Phony. I hate that word.

Holden Caulfield was a phony. That's *his* word. I guess I am too. And my friends. My whole life. I should have never left. Should've stayed ignorant of how meaningless my life was. I could've gone to college, got a job that made my parents proud, got married, and had kids to replace me in the machine. But now I know.

I've got to get out of here.

Up from the roots and the moist black dirt, I don't even brush myself off. I feel filthy from the inside. A bath wouldn't clean me.

I walk by the statue. Dude looks like he's having a great moment on the back of that horse. But he's stuck in time. Frozen.

Arms folded and head down, I'm cold.

I walk under the bleached antler arch and cross the street near Pandora's Box. Hope didn't make it out. I don't understand how I can be so positive one moment and so miserable the next. Every time I get it together and think I'm doing what God wants me to do, I get punched in the stomach. Here I am, after I feel like I've found truth, but . . . maybe I can't handle it. Who am I? *Nothing.* I thought truth would be like the sunset on the mountainside, a cool breeze, or a bald eagle. But people are awful. *I'm* awful. If God cares so much about this world, why doesn't He send someone to make it better?

I sent you.

[Bad Habits]

I'm nobody. Nothing.

[Authentic Native American Jewelry]

There's nothing authentic here. Hawking a memory of another time. A simpler time. Society's innocent childhood? Middle school comes in like a cowboy. High school scrambles to buy up all the property and runs the younger and weaker ones out. Is adulthood just building a city on that foundation, going on vacations to buy things that remind you of who you were before the skyscrapers and traffic jams?

[Buckskins & Bookworms]

That's an odd name for a bookstore. I don't know if the nerd tribe would peacefully coexist with the hunting tribe. The bookworms wouldn't stand a chance. Would a book be able to save their lives? The hunters can survive on their own. The bookworms depend on the hunters for food. What would the bookworms have of value to offer the hunters? Wisdom?

I would read a book to save my life.

The door jingles, and I'm greeted by a woman with short hair and glasses who doesn't look up from her phone as she mutters, "Welcome to Buckskins. All local authors are 50 percent off." I wonder if West's book is here.

The store is a maze of shoulder-height bookshelves and displays. Animal hides line the walls with big numbers on big price tags. By habit, I go to the sale shelf first. Local authors share their life stories, their family recipes, the Native history. I pick up one giving an account of the "old" Jackson Hole, read the back, and flip through. The pattern is true. Natives, explorers, trappers, and hunters. Trading posts, early settlers coming with nothing and scraping by. Trains and highways. Rich investors buy what they couldn't have tamed, and now tourists come to visit "the last of the Old West." What will happen when there's nothing left to tame? No horses left to break? Have we already gotten there? I know there's a connection with the soul, but I can't put it together. Innocence, exploration, and adventure, scraping by for survival, selling out. Remembering in an expensive way with no value? Where am I in this? Does it have to be this way?

I explore the maze of shelves and displays for categories of books that could save my life.

[Fantasy] [Historical Fiction] [Manga] [Biography] [Cookbooks] [Spiritual]

Maybe "Spiritual." I step closer to see.

[Yoga and Meditation] [Buddhism] [Hinduism] [New Age] [Atheism]

That's a religion?

[Native American] [Sikhism] [Islam]

All these subsections but no Christian? All these other religions

I've never been aware of or know much about. They think they're right too. So how do I know Christianity is the right one? I look again and find a couple under "Other." But they're those self-help, make-yourself-rich-with-ten-days-of-prayer type books.

"Can I help you find anything?" the woman asks from the counter.

"Do you have any Bibles?"

"No." She looks up from the screen. "No demand for them, really."

Really? My stomach travels back to Sunday morning in Livingston. The preacher read from the Bible and explained it in a way that made me hungry. It was different than what I assumed it would be. I haven't prayed or thought about the Bible or even God that much since then. It's just been a little over a day, but the hunger comes back, and I could eat it like the steak and eggs this morning. *I* have a demand for it.

"Are you looking for anything in particular?" Her eyes are on me like I'm trying to stuff a copy of *Jainism Whole in Jackson Hole* in my hoodie.

I can't believe it. I really don't fit in here. They think I'm a tramp. *This town doesn't look too highly on your type.* Well, I don't have any money anyway. I should steal a book just for spite. I don't, but I don't let the door hit me on my way out.

Walking fast with no direction, I turn toward the hill past the buildings to the west. I don't have any thoughts, just feelings. Anger. Worthlessness. Emptiness. Hunger. The base of the small mountain is right there, but every road is a fenced dead end. They don't want you to escape. Anxiety.

[Dead End]

They don't want you to leave the party. My legs slow down, and I start to see that it's all meaningless. And it's cold. *Where are you, God?* I think about walking back to Grace's, and my feet reluctantly follow.

Kicking a piece of trash, pretending it's my great idea of driving to Montana to prove Mr. Adams wrong, I just want to be home. Safe. Ignorant. Welcome. The wad of paper rolls between two posts.

[St. John's Episcopal Church]

Blue lines sketch the tops of mountains above the words. The defined mountain in the foreground is black and has a red cross near the top, like the one at Living Hope back in Montana. But you can see the base of the cross going through the mountain line, secure in the rock foundation.

Beyond the church sign is a big new building with suggestions of a log-cabin memory. It fits in this town. To the left, though, there is an actual log cabin. Clean, but maybe that was the original church. I'm drawn to it. It's long, a real log cabin. Maybe it's not the original—the logs are varnished and lack the wear of the weather—but it's authentic. Wooden shingles climb the roof to a short bell tower, topped with a proud humble cross.

I walk around to find the front entrance, and the extra-wide wooden door is unlocked.

The floors are smooth hardwood, like in Grandpa's hundred-year-old house. There's a well-worn path between the door and the pews. The lights are on, hanging from the ceiling on both sides of the aisle over the pews. The bulbs are only bright enough to make their red glass vessels glow. Light pours in from the textured stained-glass windows lining the side walls. The red lighting above and the infinite dancing amber-colored refractions from the windows give the impression of being in a fire. But it's cold. Not like the outside cold. Like . . . I breathe deep.

Like new air.

All the emotions and thoughts and walking are still outside. No one is here but me. I walk up the aisle toward the altar, and on the right is a stained-glass window of Jesus with the children. It's not a fancy, overly detailed stained-glass window like the complex red one behind the altar, waiting for the afternoon sun. It's Jesus, one arm open and welcoming, one arm pointing to heaven. And He's smiling. And the children are running like they're on the playground before the school bell. They're smiling. They don't seem to notice how important Jesus is, but He doesn't mind. None of them are bored, yawning, or doing Sunday school worksheets. They're just playing. They don't have cell phones yet.

Across the altar to the other wall is another simple stained-glass window depicting a single fiery-white ray of light coming through thick gray clouds, going *through* the mountains—not between them but actually *through* them—through the trees where a deer is hiding, to a deep blue stream flowing into the person looking at it.

I move toward the altar, and another window of the same inelaborate style gets a smile out of me. It's of an otter standing on the riverbank, basking in a diffusing sunshower. Random. I'd like to be that otter.

The altar is the least lit area of the log chapel. The three-paneled window there is thick with solder and deep with red. On the left, I can make out the doctor's symbol, the snakes wrapped around a pole. In the middle pane, a serious and archaic version of Jesus stands with an orange flickering halo above His head and a yellow sash draping around His neck and down both sides of His chest to His knees. On the right, I can make out what seems to be a feather pen and an inkwell over an open book with blank pages. The rest is so powerfully detailed in metal and crimson, I can't make out much of what it's supposed to be without getting closer. I don't feel ready to get closer. What if a minister walked in and saw this tramp bringing all his dirt and sin to the altar?

I back away with respect for what's holy and find the back pew. The edge of the pew is well oiled by human hands, and the wooden seat creaks and gives as I take off my backpack and sit down. For a while, I just sit.

It's quiet in here.

There are no tourists, no police officers thinking I'm a tramp, no bosses yelling at their employees, no women in workout pants thinking I'm checking them out, no one calling anyone a racist. But thinking about them brings them all in, and my fast walking, anxiety, and sour attitude come in with them. I think about stealing a Bible and getting out of here. I grab one of the Bibles from the line of them on the back of the pew in front of me. But it's not a Bible. It's the *Book of Common Prayer*.

I stand up to see if there is a Bible in any of the other pews. They're all red, hardbound prayer books like the one in my hand. Prayer. I sit back down and notice a padded rail below the pew. I pull the pad down and kneel on it. It's not a very comfortable position. But is prayer supposed to be comfortable?

I bow my head and start. "Lord . . ." But I don't know where to go from there. How do I talk to God? I don't want Him to be my magic genie and woosh me home with a snap of the fingers. I got myself into this, and I've got a way home. I can deal with the consequences.

"Lord, be with everyone," I say, but it sounds lame. He's either already with everyone or already not. He's not waiting for me to pray it.

"Lord, forgive me," I try again. *For what?* For existing. But He made me. But I don't feel like I am how He made me. "How do I become who You want me to be?" I pose the question but don't wait for an answer. My knees already hurt, even though the prayer bar is cushioned.

Back in the seat with a creak, I open the *Book of Common Prayer*. Prayers for Memorial Days, for Children, for Prisoners. Prayers of Thanksgiving, Holy Communion, the Second Sunday before Lent. The Twenty-Second Sunday after Trinity. How am I supposed to know what day it is? The Psalter. The subheadings are numbered Psalms.

I flip to Psalm 23 and find a pressed ten-dollar bill tucked between the pages. *Is that from You, God?* Someone put it in there.

Should I keep it? I don't want to steal it or take what's not mine. Or take it if I didn't earn it. I use it to read the Psalm line by line.

> The Lord is my shepherd; I shall not want.
> He makes me lie down in green pastures.
> He leads me beside still waters.
> He restores my soul.
> He leads me in paths of righteousness for his name's sake.
> Even though I walk through the valley of the shadow of death,
> I will fear no evil, for you are with me;
> Your rod and your staff, they comfort me.
> You prepare a table before me in the presence of my enemies;
> You anoint my head with oil; my cup overflows.
> Surely goodness and mercy shall follow me all the days of my life,
> And I will dwell in the house of the Lord forever.

I read it again. I read it out loud. I read it on the prayer bar out loud. I say it like I want it to be true. I say it like it *is* true. I know they're not magic words that make things happen, but something happens inside me, something turns. It's like I can't have both the beautiful and holy imagery in my brain and heart at the same time as the ugly thoughts about ugly beautiful people. I copy it into my journal, making it as plain English as I can handle.

"Can I help you?" a voice behind me asks with a curious authority.

My heart leaps into my throat. Am I not supposed to be in here? I'm paralyzed. Am I going to get run off from a church?

"I needed some time alone with God," I say, pleading.

"You're in a good place for it," he says. He's a man of about sixty, clean-shaven, short white hair and wrinkles by his eyes. His black outfit with a round, white, backward collar suggests he's the priest.

A wave of reassurance washes through me. He's not going to run me out.

"Are you in trouble?" The concern on his face makes me feel safe.

"No," I answer, and I'm not, or at least I don't think I am, but I want to make sure I give him no reason to second-guess his hospitality. "Just have a lot to sort out."

"Can I be of help?" he asks again, and I hear the compassion in his voice.

"Well," I don't know where to begin. I have so many questions that swim through my brain, but they're smaller than the holes in the net that comes up empty. I have so many half-formed thoughts about God, life, truth, religion—but I don't have the words to complete them.

"I feel like I've lived in a fake world all my life," I start. "But I had to drive away from it to realize it was fake." I expect him to chime in with an answer, some wisdom or criticism, but he's listening with his whole face. "I'm on my way home, and it's like I'm removed from life, watching from the outside. I'm looking for truth, but it all seems to be fake."

"What does?" he inquires, putting his foot on the end of the pew, leaning into a standing thinking position.

"The people. The towns. I don't know." I *don't* know. No, maybe I do, but putting thoughts into words and communicating them is hard, and since I can't communicate it, I don't know.

"What about them?" He's helping me.

"It's like they're living in a fake world. They're sucked into a shopping world, a drinking world . . . an *internet* world when the *real* world is right around them. They're spending lots of money on things that don't matter. As if a new elk-skin hat, a leather purse, or venti-double-mocha-nitro-tetrazino is going to make them happy." *They want to* feel *good but don't want to* be *good?* "They call people racist who aren't racist, call people tramps because they look a certain way, cover their faces in makeup and bodies in fancy clothes." *Play minister during the day but get drunk at night, say they love their kids but avoid them, want to be loved but settle for sex.* "I don't know," I say again, done putting words together to damn the world.

I look up and expect him to be shaking his head in agreement with me with a congratulatory, "You got it!" But no.

"I think you're in the wrong seat," he says instead.

I wasn't expecting that. I start to get up, and he straightens up and laughs. *What?*

"Not the pew! That book in your hand. Turn to Psalm 1."

I fumble through to Psalm 1.

"Blessed is the man who walks not in the counsel of the wicked, nor stands in the way of sinners, nor sits in the seat of the scoffers." He recites it word for word without a book. "You're in the seat of the scoffer!"

I cock my head in confusion.

"If you're living in truth, then of course everything false is going to stand out to you." He says it as if it's obvious. Really? "But as soon as you walk in the counsel of the wicked or stand in the idleness of sinners or sit with the scoffers, you're not living in truth anymore."

"But—" I say it out of habit; I don't have anything else to say.

"*But*"—he points me back to the book in my hands—"his delight is in the law of the Lord, and on his law he meditates night and day."

It sounds nice, but—"What does it mean?"

"Meditate on it. Don't walk, stand, or sit. Delight and meditate."

"Thank you," I react. He didn't tell me the answer, but he pointed me in the right direction.

He turns his body toward the door, but his eyes are still on mine. "I have to get to a meeting, but can I help with anything else?"

I kind of like him being here, listening to me, sharing with me. I really want to know more about the Bible. I don't know what to say, though, so I shake my head with my mouth open, trying to speak words I don't have words for.

He didn't ask my name. I don't think he needed to.

I copy Psalm 1 in my journal, too, and make notes on the things the priest said that I want to remember. Thoughts. Words. I feel like my time here is done and step out of the cool, holy kiln back into the world.

The sun has come out, and I drop my shoulders and smile up at it like the otter in the stained-glass window. *The Lord is my shepherd; I shall not want.* Does that mean *I shall not want* like a commandment, or *I shall not want* like I won't be lacking? It could mean either and still be meaningful. Or both. Delight and meditate.

My mind takes me toward Grace's garage, but I pause. The traffic from the square in that direction is already becoming a chorus of droning engines, like gas-powered crickets. My feet walk the opposite way toward the snow-patched hill mountain. I've already been this way. It's all fenced off. But what better do I have to do? Sit in a garage? I'm not ready to go back downtown. I feel good.

"Lord, guide my feet."

I've only walked a couple blocks, but I'm already halfway to the fenced-off base of the mound. It's interesting how you can be so close to something but not be able to get to it. *The Lord is my shepherd.* I follow my feet to a modern, boxy, two-story apartment complex with bicycles on most of the porches. To live so close to the rock but face the other way. If they could only turn the building, they'd have a slope in their front view.

I turn into the parking lot and see the same dead-end sign on the same fence that I saw an hour ago. A gas station across a privacy fence on my left, apartments on my right, and a couple cars before the dead end, straight ahead. Why am I still walking toward it? But my body is acting almost on its own, and I have to tell my brain not to stop it, even though I feel crazy walking toward a dead end. The sign is right there.

What will I do when I get to it? Touch it and turn around? Climb it? I'm not the trespassing type. I'm not the lying-to-the-cops type either. Would God guide me to break a law? *Blessed is the man who walks not in the counsel of the wicked.* If God is good, which He has to be, He would not counsel me in the ways of the wicked. Maybe I'll sit down at the fence and stare at it.

Just a van parked in front of the apartments a few spots before the fence. I feel foolish walking toward a fence. Is anyone watching from their balcony? I'm thinking about it too much. I need to follow my feet to the fence, touch it, and turn around.

I glide past the van about ten feet from the dead-end sign. A fence. A mountain on the other side. Why? I shake my head. What am I doing? Then I look to the right, and there's a green grassy meadow on the backside of the apartments with a bench under a tree by a three-foot wall of cattails—but *no fence*! I couldn't see it from anywhere else but the dead end! I run to the grass and delight in the hidden Eden. There's no fence! Lush, soft ground, flowers, a stream on the other side of the cattails, and a perfectly placed bench in the shade of a wide pine to look up the spring mountain! I want to sit down on the bench because it's a bench, but I lie down in the grass instead and delight in the clear blue sky and distinct warmth of the sun's rays. Happiness. Thankfulness.

The Lord is my shepherd, I shall not want. He guided me here. Not every dead end is what it seems. Right now, I lack nothing, and I want nothing. *He makes me lie down in green pastures, he leads me to calm waters.* I hop up and find a break in the cattails to watch the stream smooth the rocks it flows over. *He restores my soul.*

I leap over the creek to the other side and run up the mountain. High enough for an overhead view of Jackson, I sit down and see it's just a town. A town with a history, with people living, working, visiting, and relaxing. So what if they're rich. So what if they're racist or mean. From up here, it's a bunch of buildings with people living the life they know. God is with them, whether they know it or not, whether they fence Him out or look other directions.

I pull my notebook out of my backpack and read over Psalm 23 again. *Though I walk through the valley of the shadow of death, I will fear no evil, for you are with me.* I don't want to walk through the valley of the shadow of death. I like it up here where I can see and I don't have to be in the middle of it all.

I think of Grandpa. He would be happy to sit up here with me. He wouldn't say anything; he'd just ask good questions and get me to talk. About whatever. I never really asked him anything. He wanted to know me, search me. I didn't care to know me or search me, so it was always awkward trying to figure out what to say to him. I want to know him now. But it's too late.

I dig in my backpack again for his worn journal and flip through it. A lot of the entries start with the title of a book, the date, and the thoughts that lingered after he read those books.

Under *Robinson Crusoe*, he wrote, "Lower middle class is the smart place to be. No one after your riches, enough for your needs to be met. But the need for adventure is more powerful than good logic." And scrawled at the bottom in a different color ink, "Prepare Red for survival." I feel honored and loved that he was thinking of me, but I don't remember him preparing me for survival. Did he try and I wasn't paying attention? I didn't see him as a teacher, I saw him like a grandpa, and I usually wanted to be somewhere else or on the phone when I was with him.

For *Crime and Punishment*, he wrote, "Everyone is capable of great evil, but there's no getting away with it—even if you get away with it. We commit the worst crimes when we are sick, starved, tired, worn out. Temptation came for Jesus at the *end* of His forty days of fasting. What we do when we're starved and tired still matters. In fact, it might matter more. Stay fed, stay healthy—mind and body. . . A clear conscience in a prison cell is more liberating than being guilty but free. . . Truth and courage go hand in hand."

I flip a few more pages to *East of Eden*. "A great writer supplants truth into a fictional story so it's easier to digest. The first two hundred pages were unbearable, but I couldn't argue that's not the way things are east of Eden." The words *Timshel—thou mayest* are underlined and circled in the middle of the page. "Cain and Abel, *thou mayest*—it's central to the whole book, and perhaps all of life. . . Lee was right. We are not our heritage; we are our choices. We are *only* in control of *our* choices. . . Be careful, the things we hate in others might be something unchecked in ourselves." I should read more.

He's also written a few short prayers throughout. "Lord, I believe. Help my unbelief." "God, help my needs to be little and my wants to be less." "Jesus, protect my children and their children from this evil world. Let them find You and know You in their seeking."

I found Him, Grandpa.

I look back to the stream, the little field behind the apartment with the single tree, the highway of cars coming into town from the north to add to the traffic downtown. I'm hungry. I put Grandpa's journal back in my bag and open mine to the page I was writing on. Psalm 1.

He is like a tree planted by streams of water that yields its fruit in its season, and its leaf does not wither. In all that he does, he prospers. The wicked are not so, but are like chaff that the wind drives away.

The tree by the stream is green and healthy, but I remember one that's by the gas station that still has no leaves. Is it dead? What concern is that of mine? I sit and think, sit and don't think. It's so different up here than in the garage. I'm hungry.

I gnaw on the rest of my jerky as I walk toward the lunch hour race that is happening in town. God is there too. Try to find Him.

I said *Lord guide my feet*, and I ended up at a dead end that turned out to be exactly what I was looking for. And it happened to be just like both Psalms I just read. How crazy is that? Is it crazy?

How does that work? Coincidence? Or can God knit together random Scriptures you read and show it to you in real life wherever you are? What if I was in Dallas? There are no mountains, and the water isn't exactly known for its purity. Would it have been different Scriptures? If I were in downtown Dallas, I'd be afraid to walk by myself in a dead-end alley. I might get shot. It does feel safe here. Maybe it's because they check on people that look like they just hopped off a train. Wouldn't I want the same thing if I lived here?

[Labyrinth]

I'm walking by St. John's when I see that sign, with an arrow pointing past the big building to a path that leads to a courtyard. Interesting. Inside the courtyard, the edges of the path are etched black into the concrete. It looks like a round maze. The outer edge of the circle looks like gear teeth, and the inside paths wind back and forth in four sections with a six-petaled flower in the middle. Is the gear the world and the inner flower life? Like, you have to find your way through the maze to find life? Are there dead ends and false dead ends?

A man in a black suit is looking down and walking his way through the back-and-forth lines. I walk the perimeter of the courtyard, trying not to disturb him. I find a bench facing west to sit and write. I can see the spot on the hill where I was a few minutes ago.

[All are welcome to walk the Labyrinth. Please respect this sacred space. NO skateboarding, smoking, or alcoholic beverages.]

Hey, I know the man in the maze! Well, I don't know him, but he's the guy who was on the phone yelling at someone this morning. He's not so proud and mighty now, squatting with his head between his knees in the middle of the labyrinth. It looks like he's in pain. He clasps his hands and rests his elbows on his knees, forehead on his knuckles, like maybe he's praying. I don't know what he's going through, but I didn't imagine this side of him this morning. A few hours ago he was laying into someone: "I don't care. Just get the job done!" He gets up and takes a deep breath, wiping tears away. He's just a poor man in a rich suit. Just as broken and lost as me.

I expect him to walk straight out of the labyrinth to his briefcase and go, but he follows the winding maze in reverse steps, slow and calculated. The end wasn't the end. I try to write but end up drawing the labyrinth. There are no dead ends, but the way you walk doesn't always take you where you think it will. When it seems like you're getting close to the middle, it takes you back out to the gear teeth, then back and forth, back and forth.

As I finish the detailed drawing and write "No skateboarding!" with a smiley face, I look up and notice the man looking over my shoulder.

"I think you got it," he says.

"Thanks," I reply.

"Have you ever walked one of these before?"

"No."

"I come here every day at lunch. You ought to give it a try."

You ought to come before your morning calls, I think, but out loud, I say, "I feel like I'm already living it."

"Seriously," he says. "It's open for everyone, and there's something sacred about it. It's a three-step meditation. First, you walk in from the east, leaving the world, shedding your thoughts, wants, needs, problems, and sins until your mind is quiet. When you get to the center, it's just you and God in a place of prayer and meditation." This word *meditation* keeps coming up. Is it the same as the books next to New Age in the bookstore? "The last part is the slow walk back out into the world. I like seeing how far out I can take the peace without getting pulled back into the chaos of the world."

He's excited to share this with me, but I can't help but remember that this is the same yelling boss I saw earlier, being so mean over the phone.

"I saw you in the park this morning," I say. "You were yelling at someone that you didn't care; they just needed to get the job done."

His lips purse to one side as he quietly nods his head. He understands I'm calling out his hypocrisy. "I see. Well, you're right. I shouldn't have been yelling. But do you want to know what I was so upset about?"

"Sure."

"Well . . . I don't know where to start. I guess I can say that I'm what the world would call successful. I grew up more than comfortable and always had a gift of finding creative ways to make money. I graduated, got married, had kids. Then one of my companies turned into a multimillion-dollar business. I know every loophole, every trick to the market, and can turn a dime into a dollar with the blink of an eye." Is he bragging? "I even started a nonprofit to funnel the money through and make it feel like I am doing some good in the world. I guess to offset the fact that my business does more harm than good." He pauses and his gaze sinks to the ground. I wait. He looks back up at me. "My wife and kids have seen the world, experienced the best of everything . . . we have multiple houses and everything you could dream of that money can buy. But it turns out, money can't buy a husband and father, and sometimes it costs one. It got its claws into me, and now one of my kids is in trouble, my marriage is on the rocks, and I'm not sure how much of it I've already lost. So a few months ago, I told my CFO to find a way to get everyone a good severance. We're closing shop."

I don't know how to react. I watch his searching for words play out on his face.

"So my CFO, who I hired to make me money, is telling me I'm stupid, crazy, and that if I give all thousand-something employees a fair sum to walk away with, I'll end up with nothing for myself. And that's what you heard. That's the job that needs to be done."

There is a power in his weakness. His back is straight, but his head is hung.

"What are you going to do now?" I ask.

"I don't know. Walk into the maze, get centered, and bring God as far back out as I can."

"Are your wife and kids excited?"

"It might be too late. I've said I was going to change a dozen times, and I don't think they believe me anymore."

I slide into his kids' shoes. "If I was your kid, I'd give you hell for payback." He nods his head. "I'd push you away, maybe even run away. I'd act like I hate you to see where your limit is. I'd test every weak spot in your faith and truthfulness, to see if you're for real. But if you are for real, I'd hang on tight because I need you. That doesn't go away."

He's in tears. I feel bad for judging him earlier. You don't know people's stories.

"Thanks," he says, gathering himself. "What's your name?"

"Redemption," I say with pride.

"I needed you too," he says. "My name's Richard. I've got to make some calls, but it's been good running into you. I'm glad I made the choice to engage. Try out the labyrinth."

He takes a deep breath and pulls his phone from his pocket.

"Get the job done!" I say as he walks away. He turns and waves with a smile.

I study the labyrinth from the bench, writing the three stages in my journal.

Leave the world, enter, shed the world and everything that doesn't matter—thoughts, desires, distractions, anxieties, fears.

Fears. I don't know what to be afraid of. Losing this peace again? Getting all flustered again? Get to the middle. Take a lot of steps to move ten yards.

Be in the center. Be centered. Still. Quiet. Meditate and delight in God's law.

What is His law? It sounds so rigorous. Delight in not speeding? Not killing? Not lusting? Not eating bacon? What do they have in common?

Bring it back out into the world.

That's why I can't stay on the mountaintop. Back to the valley. Back to the show. With new eyes, a different perspective. It led me here, and to Richard. Maybe I helped him. Maybe you have to come through the valley of the shadow of death to bring life to it, to bring hope to it, to encourage people like Richard. And it says *through*. I walk *through* the valley, I'm not here to stay.

When am I leaving? I'd better make it back toward Grace's in case we're leaving today. Plus, a woman and her kids have already claimed the holy space. She sits in exhaustion on another bench while they run, race, and hop through the lines on the labyrinth. I think about a straight shot back but decide to maze back and forth on the wooden sidewalks.

A beautiful girl a little older than me is walking toward me, well dressed, but I don't spend time looking. Her hair looks like it was just done, and her makeup is just enough to draw out her features. She meets my eyes and looks away. I don't blame her. But she's time-slowingly beautiful. Not showy but not sloppy, good posture, and she obviously takes care of herself.

"Excuse me," I blurt as she's about to pass.

"Yes?" she answers reluctantly, still walking the opposite direction, but a little slower. I turn and walk beside her.

"Can I ask you a completely random question? I promise I'm not a creep or trying to pick you up or anything." She looks mildly offended but mainly confused and a little concerned. "I was thinking you could help me." Now she holds her purse tight. "I'm not after money. I—" I'm totally tongue-tied and making a fool of myself, but I'll never see her again, and it doesn't really matter.

"Get to it," she says kindly but cautiously.

"Well—" I spit it out. "I want to be a good person. I want to be a good man, and I eventually want to get married." She stops at the corner, turns to me, and inspects me through my eyes. "Not to you." Oh gosh, that sounded bad. "Umm, but you're a beautiful woman, graceful, and you seem to have it together." Whew, I hope that saved me. "What do women like you look for in a good man?"

She relaxes and smiles a little bit. "Well, it's promising that you're asking."

As beautiful as she is, talking with her makes her not just a pretty part of the scenery but in the scene with me as another soul. I wonder if she thinks she's beautiful or if it matters.

"Number one," she says, "continue not being a creep and working on that good person thing. Most guys want to win a pretty girl for an evening. Be a guy who wants to win a girl for life." She shifts her weight to her left leg and puts her hand to her chest. "It might sound kinda silly, but I always pictured it like we were all made with one wing and we've got to find someone we enjoy working with and being near so that when we're together, we can fly." She is probably in her midtwenties, but in saying this, her face returns to that of a child.

"It's not silly," I say. "You don't want someone with a weak wing that you have to carry. You don't want someone who will drop you when you're flying or make you fly where you don't want to go."

"Yeah," she agrees. "But mainly, don't be a perv."

"If you were younger . . ." Oh no, I'm being stupid again. "I mean, hypothetically, would a guy like me have a chance with a girl like you? I mean, I'm just an average guy and you're, well, you have a wing growing out of your back."

She laughs. "Love should be sacred. Treat it like it is, and she'll know."

No skateboarding, smoking, or alcoholic beverages.

"Plus," she says over her shoulder as she steps off the wooden curb to the street, "I think you're kinda cute."

I stand melted and frozen at the same time. Her eyebrow raised as she said it. I look to the blue sky so that, if she turns back, she won't see a creep watching her walk away. I feel like an otter again. This morning she would have walked by me in the park, and I would have scoffed at her for being rich, shallow, and beautiful. I would have said she was trying to impress some banker or someone that could take care of her. *The seat of the scoffer.* She's a soul, and her kindness to me, her childlike look when she was talking about wings, her desire to be won for life all showed a goodness that is more appealing than her looks. And she said I'm cute!

I skip back the other direction, squeaking a board every few steps. In a giddy mindlessness, I almost run into a couple with their phones in one hand and giant, fancy coffee drinks in the other. An awkward and excited need to engage comes over me. It's like I'm seeing people for the first time, awake and alive amid people going through the motions.

"Are y'all a couple?" I ask, surprising myself. Talking to strangers is so not like me.

Both are stunned for a second, looking at me like I'm crazy. Maybe I am. The man says, "Yeah?"

"It's a pity." What's coming out of my mouth? I'm not brave enough to talk to people I don't know, especially not like this. But I feel a rush of adrenaline, and she said I'm cute!

"Huh?" he says. They're both annoyed by me.

"Your hands are full. If they weren't, you could hold each other's." Why am I doing this? Surely I've overstepped a boundary. What are they going to do? Punch me? They both look at me, puzzled.

Then the girl looks at her boyfriend and laughs. "The kid's right!" She puts her phone in her back pocket, then grabs his and puts it in his jacket pocket. "Now hold my hand, lover!"

He's still confused but goes along with it. They walk off, swinging their joined hands between them.

I'm glad he didn't punch me. This is stupid. This is fun! Leaping across the busy street back to the square, I offer to take a picture for a group of three Asians. They return my kindness with "Sank you, sank you!" How am I not to appreciate their different accent? They are souls from a different culture across the world. They're all smiles. Who's next?

I sit next to a balding old man pestered by his wispy gray hair that keeps getting in his eyes while he's trying to look at his phone. I would have scoffed at him this morning for being rich and overweight and on his phone.

"Hello," I say.

"Good day," he says, then returns to the phone.

"It is. What makes it good for you?" I engage. I'll never see these people again.

He looks up with something important to say. "Today's my fiftieth anniversary!" His posture straightens in pride.

"Happy anniversary!" I say. How do I keep a conversation going? I ask, "What's the secret?"

"Let her shop," he advises. "I used to get on her for spending, but then I realized she never spends on herself. She's in some store thinking about those grandkids, finding the perfect gift to let them know they're loved. And she'll probably come back with a new hat for me. I don't even know my size!"

"Sounds like a good woman," I say.

"We got married in May, and by December I was drafted into the war. She was faithful to me when a lot of women couldn't do it, and she was proud of me when I came back and everyone else was scoffing. I came back a broken mess, and she worked while my legs healed. She read me Scripture every morning and every night to get my brain reset."

He transports back to another time for a moment.

"And now she buys me hats and tells me I'm handsome, even though I'm overweight and can hardly walk on these crippled knees."

"I'd be lucky to find a woman like her," I say, admiring his admiration.

"A good woman is worth more than rubies. Lift her up and a man lacks nothing of value. Charm is deceptive and beauty is fleeting, but a woman who fears the Lord is worthy of praise. That's from the Bible. Proverbs 31."

I wish I knew the Bible like that. To be able to pull out a verse and live by it. I don't know what to say now, but it doesn't feel like the end of a conversation. I ask, "What does it mean to fear the Lord?"

"Knowing there's something bigger, stronger, wiser, and better than me keeps me humble. Same way I fear my wife! I'm not afraid, just in awe." He takes a deep breath and looks around for her. Maybe it is time to end the conversation, not be a bother.

"Thanks," I say with a smile. "It's been a pleasure."

The fire in my chest has been fueled, but it's not hot and burning this time. It's white and dancing.

I see a well-dressed Black man across the statue talking on the phone. Maybe he'll let me borrow his phone so I can call my mom. It's time to. I'm in a good place, and I've mustered some courage to withstand the wrath. Maybe I can ask him about racism too. Walking closer, I can hear him say, "I love you, babe, I'll see you tonight." I sit next to him, and he gets up and walks away. Is it because I'm White? Knowing it's not, I laugh and stretch my arm across the back of the bench, taking in the nice scenery of the same place I was this morning. What's the difference? The people are the same. And they're not too different from me. I don't know them, and I don't know what they're thinking, what they've been through, or what they're going through now. What made it so easy to be critical and hateful earlier? My mind puts the events of the morning back together, retracing my steps, my thoughts, the chapel, the labyrinth. I feel like I'm onto something when I see a familiar face.

I wave my arm with a kiddish smile at Longstoryshort as he's walking my way, looking to the left and right. My stomach and smile drop. I think I can tell what he's thinking by the scowl on his face. He's been looking for me. I've been gone all morning, and now it's midafternoon.

A memory of being ten and getting yelled at on the beach in Port Aransas flashes inside me, and the fire turns yellow and deepens to my gut. I was playing in the water and didn't realize I had drifted a few hundred yards from where my family was. I came ashore and started building a sand elephant head. I was so proud of it, but when I looked up to show it off, my parents weren't there. When I finally saw my dad, he was marching toward me across the sand, red-faced, angry, and letting me have it. I don't remember any words, just the rage. He probably said I was inconsiderate and in my own world, had no regard for others, and was selfish. I heard those words a lot. Because I was. And now I am.

Longstoryshort walks past me with enough pause to push through his gritted teeth, "C'mon."

I leap up with a silent "Yes sir." I hope I didn't make us miss leaving. I was selfish, inconsiderate, and had no regard for Longstoryshort. I was in my own world.

There goes the peace. There goes the blue sky.

CHAPTER 7

TUESDAY EVENING: A BLURRY NIGHT

I **have to almost run** to keep up with him, weaving in and out of people walking, standing, stopping, and taking selfies. We make it to the motorcycle and can't back out because there is a horse in our way, complete with a costumed frontier soldier, posing for pictures with tourists.

Longstoryshort revs the engine, and a gunshot sound comes out below me. The horse jumps and knocks over a portly woman. I'm not assuming Longstoryshort saw it this time. In fact, I don't think he could have. The rider regains control of his horse, and I'm about to get off and help the lady up, but the cycle jerks back and jets between cars stopped to watch.

I glance back as we're turning east, and a couple of men are helping the woman up. A car almost runs over them, pouncing on our open parking spot.

The adrenaline hardly has time to circulate before we're back at Grace's. We get off the motorcycle, and I'm jumpy and flustered. At the same time, I'm feeling guilty and sorry. I feel like a phone in a cold puddle.

I expect Longstoryshort to scream at me: "What were you thinking?!" But he's cool and collected. He just looks at me, walks into the open garage, and sits on his throne.

I don't know what's worse, being yelled at for being thoughtless, selfish, and irresponsible, or facing a silence where you don't know what the other person is thinking. "I'm sorry," I sputter finally. "You were asleep, and Grace told me not to wake you." Great, am I blaming Grace? "I had some energy and thought exploring a little would be harmless." I'm talking to a statue. "I didn't mean to lose track of time." I hang my head and plop on the worn blue couch.

After a few more seconds of eternity, Longstoryshort finally speaks. "You're not in trouble. I'm responsible for you right now. I need to know where you are in case we need to go." That's logical. I could have messed up my own way home. He adds, "You're not getting hurt on my watch."

I wasn't hurt. In fact, I felt kind of healed. And now I don't again. Who would hurt me? Why can't being saved feel safe? Why do I feel like I keep going back and forth, being close to God, then far away? Happy, then anxious. Forgiven, then guilty. Safe, then afraid. Afraid of what? What am I supposed to be afraid of?

"Who did you talk to?"

"Umm . . . a minister, an old vet, and the most beautiful woman I've ever seen." My heart races a little. "I actually talked to her, and she was nice to me and even said I'm cute!" Longstoryshort nods his head and smirks a little. "Oh, and a police officer and a rich businessman."

"What did he want?"

"He wants to sell his business so he can reconnect with his—"

"No, the police officer."

"Oh, he just wanted to make sure I wasn't a tramp hopping off the trains and causing trouble."

"Did he do a background check?"

"No." I feel uneasy. "He just looked at my license and asked me a few questions. And looked in my bag."

"What'd you tell him?"

"Well, I told him I was with my dad, visiting my mom. I didn't know what to say and . . . I kind of lied."

"Don't worry about it." Longstoryshort eases up.

"Why?" I didn't mean to ask, but something seems off.

"Can't trust 'em. All that power, it goes to their heads. If they don't like you or the way you look, they can make something up and haul you away. Their words against yours. Who are they going to believe?"

Is that why I felt so nervous? The power? Power in the hands of a person I don't know in a town I don't know? I was always taught that police are the ones to trust. They're there to help. But he's got a point. That officer could have made something up and hauled me away if he wanted to. You hear about that kind of stuff happening in the news, but it's always with minorities. Is that what it feels like? Guilty of being you, and the police not knowing if you're a threat or not, not liking that you don't blend in?

"Look, Nothing, you've got to be careful who you trust when you're on the road. I've got a few errands to run," Longstoryshort says. "Stay here."

He gets back up and on the bike. It's just me. I'm safe here. I fit in because there's no one here. I guess that's why loners are loners. There's a penalty for not fitting in. And it's not right. I guess that's why it's always the loners that shoot up schools. It's not any particular person they're aiming at; it's the whole machine. I'm not wanting to shoot up the town, but I certainly felt a hate-filled rage come over me this morning. Can the machine be changed without the violence? Because violence obviously hasn't changed anything, and it won't change anything, either.

What made me feel better? The chapel. The kindness of the minister and the guidance of the mysterious invisible shepherd that led me to the better perspective. I picture the gear-toothed outer rim of the labyrinth and the long process into peace and back out. I was able to talk to strangers and see that they were just people too.

Could a chapel with a minister next to the school prevent shootings? Could Scripture and invisible guidance lead an angry loner to a better perspective? They'd have to believe it could first. And a lot of times, the kids who say they're Christians at school are the meanest ones. Could a labyrinth in the courtyard at school make a bigger difference than the metal detectors? I picture the two gangsters that got in a fight last Friday walking in the maze instead of throwing punches.

If the chapel had been crowded this morning, I wouldn't have stayed, and the minister wouldn't have talked to me. All the church youth groups that meet after school are packed with kids. I've been to those. I don't consider myself a loner, but I'm not even comfortable there. It's like they already have their set groups, and the youth minister gives all his attention and energy to the ones that are already popular.

If I hadn't gone out on a limb and believed the Lord was my shepherd, I wouldn't have kept walking toward the dead-end sign. I don't think I would have read Psalm 23 with the same open mind back in Dallas a week ago. Right now I'm searching, I'm open. How do you get someone to search? Without making them drive to Montana? And if you made them do it, would it even be the same?

I didn't walk the labyrinth because someone else was already on it. If there was one at school, no one would use it because it was put there for them by the adults. Plus, everyone's eyes would be on them. I had a tree I'd sit in. No one could see me, but I could see everyone. How do you get a loner alone? Alone with God?

My thoughts fizzle with lack of a solution for something much bigger than my brain can handle. How do you change the machine? I walk to the fridge to see if there's any food in it. There's not. I think about trying the door to Grace's house, but that would be intruding, and I've gotten in enough trouble today. So it's back to the couch. Back to the journal to write. But I can't write. At least not much. I keep going back to the drawing of the labyrinth.

I don't know how much time has passed, but Grace's voice snaps me out of a daze.

"I'm glad you're still here! How was your day?"

"Fine," I say as a reflex to that question. "How was yours?"

"Another day, another dollar. People are crazy, and God is good. I've got to get into something comfortable. Need anything?"

Some more steak and orange juice. "No, ma'am. Thank you."

I don't know what is going on, whether we're leaving tonight or tomorrow, and I don't know what to do with myself. Just go with the flow. I'm in good hands, and I have to trust Longstoryshort, God, and Ghost. The sheep doesn't know where the shepherd is leading. It wouldn't be faith if I knew.

Lord, I'm going home. Help me trust You. I walk outside and look at the billowing clouds above. My aching heart wants to go back to the chapel and talk with not-Saint John, walk the maze, and sit on the side of the mountain. I'm tempted to let my feet guide me again, but Longstoryshort told me to stay here. My head would probably get lost in the clouds again. I don't want to make him upset. He's my only way home, and he's been good to me.

Back on the couch, I can't get over not wanting to be here. But I can't leave. What choice do I have? "Sit there and be quiet," I hear my dad say. Sometimes that's all you can do. Like school. Like church.

"Hey, Redemption!" Lewis says from the open garage door. He's in a coat with the symbol of his church on it, the cross inside the mountain. "You the only one here?"

"Grace is inside, and Longstoryshort is running some errands."

He puts his phone in the bag, goes to the fridge, and grabs a beer. It bothers me, and I think he sees it because he puts it back. That bothers me more. He sits next to me.

"I tried to go by your church this morning," I say, "but the doors were locked. It was still early."

"Yeah," he says. "We try to keep the doors locked outside of service hours. There are a lot of tramps who pass through town looking for handouts."

"Any counseling today?" I ask.

"Not on Tuesdays. I've got to have a day where I'm safe from the crazies."

I don't think Lewis realizes that I'm looking to him for hope. He's got a chance to minister to me right now. I'm open. I'm hungry for truth. But I don't know what to ask. Something about church.

"Why are there so many denominations?" I ask randomly.

"Well, Christians have never been able to agree on what matters," he answers quickly. "Take baptism. The Catholics sprinkle the kid at birth in case something happens to them. The Methodists sprinkle you later on. The Church of Christ says it doesn't count unless you're fully submerged. The Baptists say it doesn't count unless you've been baptized by a certified Baptist preacher, and you can't be a member or take communion with them until you have. And communion is another biggie . . . and I've seen churches split over pads on the pews . . ."

He goes on for a while, until I interrupt.

"Then what does matter?"

"Well," Lewis answers in a thoughtless rehearsed tone, "that they believe Jesus is the Son of God, He died for our sins, and was raised for His glory." He blinks at me.

"What does that mean?" I ask sincerely. I think back to the cross with my name scrawled across it that I left on the hill in Montana. I think I know what it means to die and be born again—to let go of the past and be open to new life. Right now I feel like an infant. Like I'm a remnant of myself. But the religious language seems so easy for the person saying it and so hard for the person who's trying to understand it.

He blinks at me again, not realizing how much I want to understand.

"Well," he says, "it means that Jesus is the Son of God. He hung on the cross for our sins. And on the third day, He was resurrected."

I'm a little frustrated now. He said the same thing with different words. Maybe if he said it louder and with hand motions, I would understand. He talks to me like adults talk to a kid. But I am a kid. That's what he sees. He doesn't see that I'm a thirsty soul. How can he? I'm just another kid needing counseling but wanting a pat on the back instead. He pats me on the back.

Grace comes in wearing jeans and a Grateful Dead T-shirt. Her face is still professional, but her body is relaxed.

"How are you, Lewis?" she asks with a hospitable but tired smile.

"Better than I deserve," Lewis responds. "How long are you going to be able to keep hold of Longstoryshort this time?"

"Now, you know no one can keep hold of that man," Grace admits, like she's brushing a boulder off her shoulder. "He says he'll be here another day or two." Another day or two?! I don't want to be here *another day* or *two*! "He's waiting on a friend who's going to take Redemption back home to Dallas." She says it like it's a victory. Getting home will be the victory. Another day or two feels like defeat. "Speak of the devil!" she says as an engine rumble comes to rest in the driveway.

Longstoryshort carries his helmet under one arm and a heavy paper grocery bag under the other. He sets both on the couch and heads to Grace for a kiss.

"Hey," Lewis says, getting halfway up to shake Longstoryshort's hand as he makes his way to his throne. "What's in the bag?"

"The best surprises are the ones you've got to wait for," Longstoryshort says. "Where's everyone else?"

"They'll be here soon. I think Mike's wife is mad at him again. They've signed up for counseling. And Joe is Joe."

"What about that writer—what's his name?"

"West," Lewis says. "Sometimes he's here, sometimes he's not. He just shows up."

"Makes me uncomfortable," Longstoryshort responds. "Just watching and writing. When a man doesn't speak, it's hard to know what he's thinking. Can't get a read on him."

"He's a good guy, Longstory," Grace says. "Everyone's welcome in my garage, tongue or no tongue. Everyone needs a place to be accepted for who they are, poor guy."

"The more the merrier," Mike chimes in. Joe's right behind him.

"How ya feeling, Joe?" Lewis asks.

"Like a million dollars." Joe holds up his arms to the sky and grins just as wide.

"No beer?"

"No money." Joe drops his arms and his grin.

"There's plenty in the fridge," Grace says accommodatingly as they walk their phones to the purple bag.

"Even better—" Longstoryshort gets up and pulls five bottles of whiskey from the brown paper bag on the sofa and hands one each to everyone.

Mike admires the bottle, impressed. Joe jumps up and down. Lewis holds it up and says, "Thanks."

Grace sets hers between Lewis and the arm of the blue couch. "You know I can't hold my liquor, Longstory. I'll take a sip or two from yours."

"What's the celebration?" Mike asks.

"Tonight, we celebrate tonight," Longstoryshort explains. "To-morrow will bring its own troubles."

Grace goes inside for glasses, and Lewis gets up to sit with Mike and Joe on the long couch across from me and Longstoryshort on his recliner. Joe takes a drink straight from the bottle while the others make small talk waiting for Grace to return. I don't fit in here. I don't belong.

I glance at the bottle Grace left at the end of my couch. I don't want to be here. I don't want to drink either. She comes back with a tray of short, clear glasses half full of ice.

The ice melts quickly with the refills as the guys try on conversations. Mike gets on a rant about modern cars not being able to be fixed by an everyday mechanic. He's upset that you need a computer whiz just to tell what the problem is. Longstoryshort is upset about GPS being in everything and how we have computer chips in everything, even our clothes. Longstoryshort seems less and less like Jesus or an angel. Lewis doesn't have a car—if it's not in walking distance, it's not part of his world. Joe is pretending to drive a lowrider. Grace's car is in the shop still, and she thinks the mechanics are ripping her off.

I just sit on the couch as time goes by, hungry. I don't belong here.

They talk about the Elk Fest and share memories of being kids searching the melting snow for antlers. They discuss the upcoming Old West Days, who's going to be playing, and what new beer is going to be served.

The conversations warm up, a buzz fills the air, and the dark liquid almost becomes another character in the room. And it wants to talk to me. It wants me to loosen up. It wants to make me feel warm and comfortable.

When no one else has anything to say, Joe brings up football. Everyone stares at him.

"What?" Joe asks.

"You're the only one here who likes football," Mike says.

"So?"

"So if you're in a group that you know doesn't watch football, don't bring it up."

"Why not?"

"Because everyone will stare at you." Lewis grunts.

I see a chance to jump in with something. "It's kind of like being a bum in downtown Jackson. It can get you run out of town real quick."

Now they stare at me.

Longstoryshort jumps in to defend me. "Kid's got a point. Tourism depends on the nice scenery, and questionable characters don't make you want to hold your money loosely. Just like our conversation depends on football not being brought up!" He laughs, and everyone else laughs. He refills his glass, and the conversation turns to complaining about tourists. I'm nothing more than a blip in the conversation, an uncomfortable reminder that I am there.

It's dark outside, and the false lighting illuminates the false friends and deteriorating conversation. Watching grown people drinking is like watching humans devolve into animals. Joe is a hyena, sitting on the outskirts of the discussions, waiting for the right moment to attack the dying conversation and laugh at the moon about it. Mike becomes a groggy bear, tossing his hairy limbs about as he talks in his low and slowing voice. Lewis is a chameleon, finding something to agree with on everything, bending his argument to not actually disagree—holding on to his branch of thought with eyes scanning for danger. Grace devolves to a hen, clucking at the guests and pecking at the dropped thoughts and seeds of ideas.

Longstoryshort, though—he hasn't changed. He's more stoic, more red, thicker skinned, and looser lipped, but he's still in complete control. Not only of himself, but also the mood and tone of the conversations. It's like he's playing. He makes Mike mad, then calms him down. Makes Lewis retract a belief, then assures him he's right. Builds Joe up, then blows him down. But he treats Grace the same as he did before. He holds her close, like he knows she's the only one with the power to get rid of him. He keeps her off balance and plays on her loving nature. I can't stand it. I want to get out of here, but I'm stuck.

I reach for the bottle, unscrew the cap, and take a big swig. My throat-singeing cough gets everyone's attention and stops the conversation dead. My eyes almost pop out of my head.

"I see you've joined us," Longstoryshort says with a smirk, and the others raise their half-empty bottles and celebrate.

I've been here all along. The cold fire that was already in my chest from the wreck was dying down, but I just doused it in napalm. Warmth flows through my veins to my fingertips like a hot tsunami. I am Yellowstone, smoking from my pores.

There is an immediate change in me. Beyond the fuzzy warmness, I sit at the edge of the couch seat and feel like I could fight a tiger. I feel like I *should* fight a tiger.

"I've been here the whole time," I say, but the words coming out sound more like the voice in my head than usual speech. Like the filter between the two has been reversed. I want to arm-wrestle someone. Mike.

"Sorry, man," Mike says. "It's easy to forget you're here if you're not in the conversation. Is West here?"

"W-e-e-e-s-s-t," Joe calls, looking under the cushions.

"I know, but how does a person who doesn't fit in, fit in?" I ask, still clear minded. I felt so apart from them, further and further as they imbibed. Taking that long swig with that heart-jolting cough seemed to crash me through a thin, crystal barrier into their bubble. I take another gulp and gasp to prevent a cough. This isn't so bad. I feel good.

"Who says you don't fit in?" Mike growls contentedly and leans back into the couch.

"Well, I'm a kid, I'm not from here, I don't know you, and I don't think we have much in common."

"Everyone's got something in common," Longstoryshort says. "It's up to you to find out what it is." He looks me in the eyes and slowly raises his bottle to his lips. I slowly raise the bottle to mine and take a long slow sip that tickles my tongue before numbing my esophagus and coating my ribs.

"Does you like football?" Joe asks, throwing his wadded-up whiskey label at me like a quarterback in slow motion.

"Not really," I answer. Everyone cheers as I drop the pass. The room is starting to sway a little, or maybe I am. Pop Rocks spark in my brain instead of thoughts. "Y'all don't seem to have anything in common. How'd y'all all meet?"

They all look at each other as if for the first time.

"I guess we are an odd bunch," the bear bellows with a hearty laugh. "How did we all meet up?"

They all are swooned in the brain, thinking back.

"I was kicked out of my house one day," Joe pipes up, "cussing the sssunset walking down the street. Longstoryssshort pulled up on his motorcycle ashkin' if I needed a drink. I says yeah! And that's how I met these guys." He gives Mike a bear hug.

"I guess I was the first," Mike adds. "My wife and I was havin' troubles, and I was stepped out of the saloon downtown, looking for a fight. Only the first person I saw was a cop, and he warn't pleased with me. I drop my keys, and Longstoryshort picks 'em up and says, 'You're not driving tonight, Bill,' then turned to the officer and apologized for me. Showed up at the right time and saved me. Brought me over here and met Grace. The others showed up, and we been like family e'er since. We all even go to Lewis's church."

"I found Lewis not long after, alone in a bar." Longstoryshort emphasizes *bar* and glances at Lewis. "He was drinking up some courage to talk to a lady."

"I just moved here," Lewis says. "Didn't know anyone and was questioning everything."

"Din't you witness a murder or something?" Mike asks.

"Not exactly," Lewis answers.

"No, but he was in the wrong place at the wrong time," Longstoryshort explains with a chuckle. "And now he's in the wrong place at the right time!" Everyone laughs.

"So how'd'you become a minshter?" I slur.

"It's an easy place to hide." Longstoryshort answers for him.

Lewis looks ashamed, but used to it. "No, I got Longstort to thank for that."

"I had a foot in the door in a church that was desperate for a leader," Longstoryshort tells me. It sounds like he's being cruel, but Lewis is resigned to it.

"You do a good job," Grace encourages.

"Yeah!" Joe agrees.

Isn't a preacher supposed to be ordinated—orderved—whatever. I'm even slurring my thoughts now. I'm losing control of my brain. I take another drink to control it.

Longstoryshort says something, and Mike says something.

I can't tell if Lewis is thinking or just doing his best to sit up. He's more like a sad ape at a zoo now. I'm doing *my* best to sit up. No tigers now. I become my arm, wrestling myself to stay up. The bubble of talking I entered becomes a distant, puddled world of sound and flickering artificial light. Longstoryshort says something to me after Grace gets up from the arm of his chair and heads inside. He follows her. It's a blur. I think I'm lying down. I think Joe is headed to the bathroom.

Black spinning. The height of temporary pleasure crashes into a canyon of dark hell. The wrong waters wash over me. *Lord, I'm sorry. Get me through tonight. Please. I don't ever want to feel this way again. I'm Yours.* The last thing I remember is the lights going out. Or maybe not. I don't know.

CHAPTER 8

WEDNESDAY: A HAZE OF A DAY

I wake up with the dank blanket over my face. I don't remember where I am and half imagine I'm home at a friend's house. Then the pounding starts in my brain, and I'm thirsty for water like a frog in the sun, crusty and slimy at the same time. I push back the blanket and squint at the daylight coming through the garage door windows.

I remember where I am, and the spinning night seems like a different lifetime ago. I run to the bathroom and drink as much water from the faucet as I can get. Too much; I'm going to puke. But there's already remnants of what looks like salsa all over the toilet. I turn back to the sink and drool into the basin for a thousand years.

When it passes, I wash my face again and again, as if water could cleanse me. It doesn't. I just need to lie down. Eyes closed to stop the spinning, I can't tell if I'm hot or cold. Whiskey seeps through my pores, and I use the blanket to get it off. It doesn't work.

The square glass bottle is wedged between my head, the cushions, and the arm of the couch. It's mostly empty. Did I drink that much? I don't remember drinking that much. But no one else was over here. What else did I do or say that I'm not aware of? I replay the conversations the way I remember them, and I have a vision of Longstoryshort laughing, Grace crying, Mike yelling, Joe shocked, and Lewis falling. But none of that happened. Did it? It doesn't fit.

I don't remember it. It must be the whiskey playing tricks on me. Right? I nod off.

Waking up again, I'm thirsty and go back to the sink, drinking slower this time. My stomach gurgles with liquid and begs for something solid. I walk to the door going into the house and put my hands and face to the window. All the lights are out. Who knows what time it is. Grace must've already gone to work. I go back to the couch and lie down. The pulse in my temples punches out the passage of time. My eyes hurt. I never want to drink again. I've thought this before.

The bottle taps my head as I turn to get comfortable. I can't. The blanket is too short. I curl fetal to fit, tucking the sides underneath me. I want it all to go away. I want to go home.

I take deep breaths under the blanket, starved for oxygen, and the lingering whiskey calls for itself. The smell in those deep inhales is like a wicked aromatherapy, temporarily suggesting relief. I become acutely aware of my neighbor the bottle, and my body tells me it will make the headache go away. No, it won't. Just a swallow to stave off the craving. I'm sitting up with my head between my knees, the bottle in my hand. It's logical. *God, help me.*

I pour it down the drain, and three other bottles say they still have drops of liquid Tylenol in them. I pour them down the drain and throw them all in the trash. The refrigerator becomes the only thing in focus. Is this what alcohol does? I don't need it. It needs me.

I need You, God. Where are You?

I need a Bible. I need the chapel. No, I need to lie down.

Time passes, and I just take up space. I try to write, but my brain is all fog. I read Psalms 1 and 23, but after I'm done I realize the words merely passed through my eyes and brain but found nowhere to call home. I flip through Grandpa's journal, and it's just ink on paper, squiggling squiggles. I don't want to write, don't want to think, don't want to exist. Not like this.

I bathe in shame for being so weak so soon in my new life. I'm not changed at all, am I? *You are.* I'm not. I'm deadened. The burning in my chest from the wreck isn't even there anymore. It's not even pain, just empty suffering. A sunken ship. *Nothing.*

Lying at the bottom of my sea, I feel worse than my body. Like the new life is only a memory. I wanted to battle the hard questions, but now I don't have enough will to fight gravity. I can't pay attention. I'm sluggish. And salty. Sleep.

Each time I wake up, I don't know how much time has passed. Waiting in this garage with nothing to do and no motivation to do anything bothers me. Just waiting for something to happen. A meteor would be best.

The day has slipped away, meaningless. I don't want this to be my life. Fresh air would do me good. I walk to the window to gauge what time it is. Sometime in the afternoon? Longstoryshort's motorcycle is not here. Grace is at work. I think of Mom and Dad thinking about me. Are they mad at me? Worried? I still haven't technically broken up with my girlfriend, but she's just as distant as my friends, and they're no more friends than Mike and Joe and Lewis are. Just people to try on conversations with and maybe have some fun with. I don't know what we'll have in common when I get home.

Loneliness.

A leaf falls.

It's not as cold as it seemed this morning, and my sweats have tapered. Fresh air. I push the bottom of the garage door with my foot, but it pushes back. I try harder, but it resists. Is it stuck? I bend down, pushing on different parts. I stand tall, pulling from the top. It's locked. I try the door to the house. Locked. I've been trapped all this time and didn't even know it. Great.

Why would he lock me in? So I can't get out. And he's probably right. With a breath of fresh air, I'd need a walk. With a walk, I'd end up at the chapel, on the hill, roaming around, losing track of the train of time. Derailed, that's what I am. Back to the couch.

I feel trapped, but it has nothing to do with the garage door. Trapped in time. Trapped in consequence. Trapped in someone else's world. And I'm not so sure I trust it anymore.

Longstoryshort isn't Jesus. Who is he, then? Surely not the devil. I know as little about the devil as I know about Jesus. I wish I had a Bible. And someone I could ask questions to, someone to guide me. *The Lord is my shepherd . . . God, how can You guide me when I've got nowhere to go? I'm stuck. Where are You?* A car pulls into the driveway. I jump up and look out the garage door window. It's not Joe's. It's Grace. *Thank you, God.* She must've gotten her car from the mechanic. I think about tapping the glass as she walks by, but I don't want her to think I'm in trouble or upset. I know why Longstoryshort locked me in. I deserved it.

I wait in the garage for her to come through the door to check on me, but she doesn't. A sigh and a step back to the couch. Grace is so close. *Where are You, God?*

Silence.

I'm in no condition to listen.

Another hour or so passes, and I hear Longstoryshort's motorcycle pull up. I don't get up. The garage door rattles and opens.

"You look like hell," he says with a welcoming smile.

"I feel like it too."

"Sorry about locking you in."

"That's okay, I understand. And I probably would have gone

back downtown smelling like day-old whiskey and gotten arrested for bringing up football. Any word from your friend?"

"I got ahold of him this morning. We'll be on our way soon."

I perk up at "soon" and start putting things in my backpack.

"Not quite, son." He laughs. I'm uncomfortable with his calling me son. A couple days ago, I would have relished it. "I'm taking Grace on a date tonight. I've got to go get cleaned up." We both look at his dirty hands and greasy shirt. "The machine is ready for another go."

I'd like a shower too. And some food. "Great!" I'm not a machine, but I need fuel and a tune-up too. How are they supposed to know no one else has taken care of me? Grace doesn't even know I'm here.

Don't be a bother. You'll survive. You're almost home.

Something's not right. A gut feeling. An empty gut feeling.

About the same time Longstoryshort walks to the front door, Grace comes out to the garage to put some laundry in the wash, still dressed in work clothes. Her necklace sparkles.

Something's not right.

"Does he treat you right?" I ask. She jumps and holds the top of her blouse at the chest.

"I'm so sorry," she says. "I didn't know you were here. I thought you might be out with Longstory. You were both conked out this morning. You feel okay?"

I feel like hell. Do you have food I could eat? "Does he treat you right?"

"Yes," she says, turning her head side to side. "He loves me for who I am. I've got an awful past that most people wouldn't be able to look past. He's been so good to me."

"God does." Where did that come from?

"God does what?"

"Look past your past." I don't know why I'm saying this. It's the same unfiltered speaking I was letting loose in the park with all those

137

people, but it's different. It's not coming from giddiness or happiness. It's coming from sorrow.

"I know, hon. But I can't."

What do I say to that? I'm not a preacher or a minister. I barely understand the cross. You die to who you were, and God lets you start over. It's that simple. Isn't it? Dread comes over me in a flash. I thought I was figuring things out. I thought I was understanding something true. Are there some things God won't look past? What do I know? Nothing. Who am I to try to help a grown woman who knows a lot more about life than me? *Nothing.*

She looks at me with a tilted head and tired but kind eyes. "It's not that simple," she says, I guess not knowing what else to say. "But thank you."

Can I have some food, please? I can't ask.

"Well, I've got to finish getting ready. Longstory's taking me on a date tonight." She puts a little skip in her step and heads back inside. "Lewis and the others should be here after church. You might go join them for the service. I think it starts at six thirty. I'll see you later."

I don't even know what time it is. I stink. I'm tired. I don't belong here. I don't belong at the church. I'm not sure Lewis does either. Shouldn't a minister be more . . . holy? Is that too much to put on a person? Probably. The jacket with the cross on it. It's something he wears on the outside, hides under. I don't know, is that scoffing? Or just being leery? I don't know his mind. I don't know his heart. Or do I? Aren't actions a reflection of belief? Still, I've only seen him when he's tired and worn out; it can't be an easy job. Then again, who said ministering was an easy job?

I pull out my notebook and Grandpa's journal, flipping back to his thoughts on *Crime and Punishment.* There it is. "Temptation came for Jesus at the end of His forty days of fasting. What we do when we're starved and tired still matters. In fact, it might matter more . . . Truth and courage go hand in hand."

138

Lewis is supposed to represent truth, but he wasn't able to communicate it to me. And it doesn't seem like he has that much courage, either.

I know I'm not supposed to judge and I'm not supposed to sit in the seat of the scoffer, but when something bugs you about someone, isn't it important to be able to put into words what it is? I search back over to Grandpa's notes on *East of Eden*. "We are only in control of our choices. Be careful, the things we hate in others might be something unchecked within ourselves."

Lewis lacks truth. He lacks courage. Grandpa's right. That's me too.

I finally have the brain juice and inspiration to write in my journal.

Notes to my future self:
1. Know your beliefs enough to explain them. You never know who's going to ask.
2. Have courage. Don't be timid like Lewis (or yourself right now). Believe in yourself enough to stand up for yourself. Believe in others enough to stand up for them. Believe in your beliefs enough to stand up for them.
3. Don't drink. You need a clear mind, and you never know when someone will need you. And you'll feel awful the next day.
4. Pay attention to people. Take notes on who you want to be like and who you don't what to be like. Imitate what is admirable.
5. Read more.

I stop writing and stare into space. I don't know. It's easy to write, easy to say. What will it take to live it?

Grace waves at me as she walks to the motorcycle. Longstoryshort points at me. I know, stay here. Follow the rules, don't be a bother.

I lay my head back on the couch and try to breathe myself into a world where I'm not hungry, tired, hurting, lost, or lonely. My mind is as empty as my stomach, and each breath empties my lungs of air. I try to exhale as much air as I can and hold it, but I'm not dead.

New life keeps pushing itself into the depths of my lungs. My heart thumps without my will, and I have to accept it. I become just my lungs and my heart.

I am *not* nothing. I am at least two organs working. They are not parts in a machine, they are living. Where does that life come from? Biology can explain *how* they work, but can it explain *why*? To what end? What will I do with my breath? What will I do with my pulse? We are our choices. No, much simpler than that. We are living, we have life in us. What we choose to do with it doesn't make us who we are, it reflects what we think about the life already inside us. I want to cherish it. To use it for good.

I think back on all the time I've spent not even aware that there is life inside me. I've always felt like life was on the outside. Somewhere else. I think about the life in Grace, Mike, Lewis, and Joe. What are they doing with their heartbeats and breaths? Are they aware it's in them? They don't seem to cherish it. Why not? Longstoryshort seems to be aware of it. He does things on purpose. But he doesn't seem to enjoy it. No, that's not it. It's like he wants to be bigger than it.

My brain is tired.

As the light dims outside, I turn on the garage lights. One bulb is flickering, so I drag over a chair, climb up, and wiggle it till it stops. Joe pulls up in his boxy brown car. Mike and Lewis get out of the back seat. Joe unbuckles and grabs two boxes of beer from the passenger seat. They seem to be in a good mood.

"That was quite a message, Lewis!" Mike's voice carries.

They come in and plop themselves on the couch across from me, not even bothering to put the beer in the fridge. It's a late start.

"I never thought about Jesus being tempted *after* His baptism," Mike continues. "I always thought my life would get easier after getting dunked, but it didn't. It's like my problems got even worse. Like God was testing me."

"Were you paying attention, Mike?" Lewis is more full of life than I've seen him. "God didn't test Jesus. The devil did."

"Right, but God allowed it," Mike answers.

"Yeah, why does God allow things like that to happen?" Joe asks. "Why can't He put Satan in jail or something? I thought He was all powerful and stuff."

"Resist the devil and he will flee," Lewis says and pops open a beer. "God gives us free will. He won't take that away. There's something about us choosing to resist, choosing God instead." He takes a deep swig.

"Why's it have to be so hard?" Joe whines, popping open his beer. "If God wants us to follow Him, why can't He make it easier to?"

"Jesus said, 'My yoke is easy, my burden is light.'" Lewis quotes.

"But isn't Jesus's yoke suffering and His burden the cross?" Mike says.

After a moment of thinking, Lewis takes a deep draw and answers. "You've got a point, Mike. And He says, 'Pick up your cross and follow Me.' That's something worth thinking about."

West walks in, waves hello to everyone, and puts his phone in the bag. The others remember their phones, turn them off, and put them in the bag too. West sits next to me and opens his notebook. For a second, I wonder why West needs a phone if he can't talk. Another quick and dumb assumption. Phones are for more than talking. My brain races through all the things I use my phone for, and I briefly miss the distraction.

Before the beer gets in their blood and while they're talking about it, I ask, "Does the devil exist?"

"Of course he does," Mike says, "but not like the red pitchfork guy Joe sees in cartoons."

But Joe disagrees. "No. He's just made up like the bogeyman to make us scared. And so we have someone to blame. The devil made me do it!" He thinks for a second, then adds, "It don't work."

Lewis is still contemplating his answer, sipping instead of gulping. Finally, he turns to me. "Is there such thing as light?"

"Yes," I say.

"Is there such thing as darkness?"

"Yes."

"No. Darkness isn't a thing at all. It's just the absence of light. Is there such thing as warmth?"

"Yes."

"Is there such thing as cold?"

Catching on, I think back to science class. "No. It's just the absence of heat."

"Right. Is there such thing as God?"

"Yes. So Satan is the absence of God?"

"I'm satisfied with that answer," Lewis says, looking at the others for admiration. They give it. An engine revs down before we see the motorcycle pull up and park between Grace's car and the pile of logs. They both dismount and head our way with smiles.

"There's the guy to ask," Mike says. Lewis slouches back and finishes his first can.

Joe stands up to welcome them and throws the conversation at them for a conclusive answer. "Is Satan the real deal?"

"Of course he is," Longstoryshort answers as he catches the beer Mike's tossed to him. "The more important question is, why would God make a being as powerful as He is, knowing what Satan was going to do—being all knowing and everything—and then punish him for doing it?"

I look to Lewis for an answer, but he's cleaning his fingernails.

"I think," Grace says, "there's a whole spiritual world where there's a lot going on that we don't know about."

"Meh, enough of this drivel," Longstoryshort says with a jump to his throne. "Who's up for some Texas Hold'em?"

"Yeah!" Joe shouts with his whole body as he jumps up and sets up a card table in front of Longstoryshort.

Grace gets the cards and chips off a shelf while Mike and Lewis move the couch closer to Longstoryshort's recliner and the table.

West taps me on the shoulder. I look at him, and his eyes move mine to his notebook.

Are lies real?

I think about it a second. Is a lie just the absence of truth? No, it's a real thing. I nod yes, forgetting that just because he can't talk doesn't mean he can't hear. He writes out a few more words.

Satan's name in Hebrew, ha-satan, means "the liar" and "the accuser."

He shows me, then keeps writing.

Are accusations real?

I think about my accusing attitude in the park yesterday morning. It wasn't the lack of something; it was real. I nod.

He writes some more and shows me.

When we lie, believe, or spread lies—when we have an accusing spirit, we are participating in the works of the devil. He is real. And he is here.

And he is here?! My eyes widen and look around. The hand has already been dealt, and the chips are on the table. Everyone is leaning in, hiding their hands, and controlling their faces. Grace sits on the right arm of Longstoryshort's chair, watching.

"Why are you even here?" I whisper.

Research.

"Are you writing another book?"

He nods.

"What's it about?"

I wait for his quick pen.

The story of Abraham and Lot in Sodom and Gomorrah, set in modern times. I seem to remember something about that story from Vacation Bible School, something about a pillar of salt. He shows me more.

They've got to find ten righteous people to save the city from destruc-

tion.

"What's it called?"

9 Righteous.

"Do they find the tenth?"

The story is still unfolding.

Mike laughs as the others groan, and he takes the pile of chips in the center.

I wish . . . "I wish I could write a story, but I don't know what I'd write about."

West is responding.

You can only write what you know. You already have a story.

That makes a little sense, but I don't know much, and I definitely don't know where it goes from here or what's going to happen. "How do I know how it ends?"

The story is still unfolding.

I consider this for a moment and look back down.

How would you like to be a character in my book?

"Am I one of the righteous?"

It depends.

"On what?"

On how your story ends.

He writes down his email and tears it off for me.

Let me know.

He closes his notebook and walks past the table, unnoticed, steps outside, and disappears.

I put the slip of paper in my journal, and while I have it out, I write a few notes. How does my story end? How do I get out of here? I lie down, tired and empty but awake and breathing.

God, where are You?

An occasional burst of excitement comes from the table, always matched with a set of grumbles. Longstoryshort's stack of chips grows, and Joe stacks his empty cans. Lewis is quiet; his eyes dart around as he conceals his hand. Grace seems out of place, and Mike is having a great time. I think about his kids.

I'm lying down, pretending to be asleep. I don't want to join in. I don't want to be a part of this. Outside, a rustle of people chatting bursts into an a capella chorus.

"On a hill far away stood an old rugged cross, the emblem of suffering and shame."

I sit up, and a warmth stronger than whiskey courses through my veins. That's my story. That's how it starts.

"What's that all about?" Longstoryshort hides his hand and asks.

"Miss Greenhill isn't doing too well," Grace explains. "I guess that's her church coming to sing to her."

"They must sure love her to do something like that," Mike says. "It's beautiful."

"Do we do anything like that, Lewis?" Joe asks. "It sure is pretty."

Lewis looks like there's a battle inside fighting for his voice. "We should, shouldn't we," he ends up saying.

"I will cling to the old rugged cross, and exchange it some day for a crown."

Longstoryshort picks up his hand to continue the game, and the others follow suit.

"Amazing grace! How sweet the sound, that saved a wretch like me . . ."

"Hey, Grace, it's your song!" Mike exclaims.

Longstoryshort seems anxious. "What's your play, Mike?"

"I once was lost, but now I'm found; was blind, but now I see."

Their voices are crisp as the evening air, harmonizing highs and lows and everything in between. It's angelic. Old-fashioned but timeless. It's not just the singing, it's the love they're showing by singing, through singing. It's holy. And real.

"Through many dangers, toils, and snares, I have already come. 'Tis grace hath brought me safe thus far, and grace will lead me home."

Home. That's how the story ends. It has to. The angelic choir ends one and starts another.

"There is coming a day when no heartaches shall come, no more clouds in the sky . . ." I close my eyes and soak it in. "What a day that will be, when my Jesus I shall see . . . What a day, glorious day that will be."

Yeah. That's how I want my story to end.

"It's getting a little chilly in here," Longstoryshort says as he gets up and closes the garage door.

I can still hear the music of their voices, and it fills me. It's going to be okay. I'm lulled into the hard sleep I need.

CHAPTER 9

THURSDAY EARLY, VERY EARLY—JACKSON HOLE TO LITTLE AMERICA

"**G**et up. It's time to go." Something hard lands on my stomach. My helmet. Is it finally time to go? Right now?

By the time I sit up, the garage door is opening, and by the time my eyes adjust, Longstoryshort is already on the motorcycle, fastening his own helmet.

I put on my shoes quickly, double check to make sure my journal and Grandpa's are in my backpack, then sling it over my shoulders. I'm still mostly asleep when I hop on behind Longstoryshort.

"Wait!" I say, still pulling on my helmet. "Can I say goodbye to Grace?"

"Sirens," he says, muffled. "We're late."

It's black outside, and I don't hear any sirens. The neighborhood is still too deep in sleep to notice the loud engine and bright headlight as we whiz through stop signs and turn south at the square.

My groggy brain only half registers the empty parking lots and streets lit up under darkness as we speed out of town. The frigid, almost wet air stings my bare skin. Trying to get comfortable without falling off, I lean into Longstoryshort's leather back.

The dark road winds enough to rock me back and forth, and

I have to fight hard not to slip back into sleep and onto the road. The waking part of me is glad to be out of the garage. At least we're moving.

I close my eyes and will myself to wake up. The dampness in the air becomes a drizzle, and I fight the shivers. I'm less comfortable now, but more awake because of it.

Clouds rise slowly out of the ground over the miles, and a thick fog settles on and around us. I don't know what lies ahead, not even twenty feet. Again.

We're going faster than my spirit. It doesn't feel safe going this fast on a snaking wet road with no visibility. *Just hold on.* Survive.

The fog lifts and returns to the ground as rain. I'm chilled to the bone, sopping wet, and still groggy. How long ago was it that I thought riding a motorcycle would be a thrill? My hips, back, and muscles disagree.

I've never had pneumonia and I'm not really sure what it is, but I feel like that's what I'm headed toward. At least in the garage, I was dry and had a warm blanket to curl under. But it wasn't home. I'm going home. The discomfort is worth it. It *has* to be worth it. I'll be in a van soon.

No thoughts. Just the glossy blur of passing trees.

There was only one other time I felt like this. When I was six, my dad dropped me off at a soccer game. It was February, and it happened to be one of the cold days Texas sometimes has. I had socks on my arms with holes cut out for fingers because we couldn't wear sweatshirts under our jerseys. A storm blew in, and the game was called because of sleet and rain. Everyone else ran to their cars and trucks and drove away. Somehow, I ended up overlooked, and I waited in the rain on the side of a hill by the soccer field. And waited. After a while, Mom drove up in the far parking lot, but I don't think she saw me waving because then she drove off. The storm wouldn't pass, but I didn't think too much of it because when you're a kid, things just are the way they are. Sometimes you get left in the rain. A few kid eternities later, I started walking home. It was probably five miles, and it felt like forever. It was warm inside when I finally got there. Mom and Dad were fighting.

"You were supposed to stay there!" Mom yelled. "Where were you? What were you doing?" Mom yelled a lot. But she ran to me when she saw me. She gave me a big hug, looked me in the eyes, and asked, "Are you okay?"

I nodded. She got back up and yelled at Dad some more. I went back outside and sat on the curb in the cold downpour.

Not the best memory, but neither is this. If God wants the best for me, why am I so wet and miserable? No. I won't feel sorry for myself. I got myself into this, and I can get myself out of it. Well, no. I'm depending on Longstoryshort to get me out of it. I shake my head. That's not right either. I need *God* to get me out of this, and I have to believe He is, but I'm holding on to a man who has become more of a stranger the longer I've known him. What if—no.

Think positive. At least I'm getting a shower.

It's not until we start a gentle decline that I can tell we've been getting higher in elevation this whole time. We must be a long hour in, and the rain has finally stopped.

After winding east for a while, we take a southward curve, and the scenery opens around us. We're not in the mountains anymore. The black sky traces a jagged outline of even blacker mountains. A faint hum in my ears separates itself from the pain.

The road straightens south, and my head stays turned to the east.

The black sky turns deep purple above the peak lines. The sun is going to rise. *Hope.* I peek over Longstoryshort's shoulder. It looks like a mad black hole that we're heading toward. I put hope back in the box for safekeeping.

Brilliant orange becomes the line between the heavens and earth, and feathered wisps of distant rains scatter along the widening horizon. But those rains are someone else's worry.

I don't know if we're going slower or if it feels that way because we're on a long, straight road. The sun rises on the scattered storms, and there's nothing new.

Mountains on the horizon turn into mesas. I close my eyes and pretend to be warm.

The light is changing on the other side of my lids. Pastels paint the sky like no work of art I've seen in a frame, not even hanging in a museum. It's living, changing. Am I?

There are still patches of rain streaking down in the distance, and behind us the clouds are dark, almost evil. I think about what West said about the devil. *He is real. And he is here.*

Was he talking about a real person or just the people living lies? Which one would be the devil? Not Joe or Mike. Surely not Grace. Lewis was squirmy but powerless. Longstoryshort was the only one with power. He's the one who brought them all together for their every-night drinking ritual. But it's their choice, and he's hardly ever around. Would he have to be?

I shudder at the thought of Longstoryshort being Satan. And I'm clinging to him. But he saved me. I think back through the days—all he's done and all he's said. A shiver of terror shakes me. He *is* the devil. The liar. The accuser.

Wait. Am I accusing Longstoryshort of being the embodiment of evil? Doesn't that make *me* the accuser?

I look at it all another way. He's just a loner on the road with a dead-dad complex. It could go either way. If I'm looking for the devil, I see him. If I'm looking for a man covering his brokenness with machismo, I see that too. I think the cold is messing with my mind. I'll be happy when I'm in a van. No, I'll be happy when I'm home.

[Big Piney]

No pines are in sight. Not even small ones. We're not in the mountains and forests anymore.

The mesas are closer on both sides, a scrubby desert landscape beneath the watercolor sky. The storm ahead seems to be growing and growling. *It's going to be okay.* I whisper it to myself. Longstoryshort is not the devil. Why would the devil be afraid of fire? I close my eyes to let time pass.

Time passes. The vision returns, the dream of my mom screaming in the fire, the school burning, the world in flames. I open my eyes to get rid of it, and the sun is breaking through dark clouds in a shower of majestic light, landing on a nearby stream. A deer turns its head to us. Another band of white light spreads toward the looming black we drive toward. It's going to be okay.

We veer around and speed past a yellow school bus.

Farther along, a group of kids are waiting for the bus by a cluster of mailboxes at the base of a cliff. A scene unfolds in my imagination. One kid has the fruit of the knowledge of good and evil in his lunchbox. He wasn't supposed to pick it, but it'll be the talk of the lunch table. He's already showing it off on the bus, other kids huddling around with curious fascination. Through class, it's all he can think about. A little bit of guilt, a little bit of shame, and a body full of adrenaline. By lunchtime, he's decided to keep it hidden away and throw it away after school, but the other kids are anxious to see what happens when someone eats it. The crowd has already formed, and they're tossing around the words "dare" and "chicken."

It's in his hand. His eyes are watering with the external pressure and internal resistance. Decision time. What does he do?

Longstoryshort slaps my forearm to get me to loosen my grip, and I snap out of it and lull back into a daze.

The road cuts closer and closer to mesas and cliffs, near enough to make out the layers of the history of earth. There's nothing new; it will all be exposed in time by the wind and water, making its way to new ground for tumbleweeds to grow in. What thoughts I have clear with the sky, and the sun becomes too bright for my eyes.

I squeeze my lids tight and hum hymns I don't know the words to. I'm thankful for the people in my childhood who took me to church, even though I hated it at the time. Neighbors, friends, the old lady who holds the stop sign for the crosswalk. My mom and dad on Sundays, especially the ones after big arguments. Grandpa. I miss him. *Amazing grace, how sweet the sound, hmm hmm, hmm hm hmm, hmm hmm!*

Note to self: learn the words to a bunch of hymns . . . and sing them.

Longstoryshort taps my arms and points to the southeast. We're now in a rolling desert with occasional landforms of beauty. A giant mountain range makes its presence known far, far in the distance. Is that Denver? Little America? It's sunny over the mountains like a good omen, but the roiling black clouds still swallow all light to the west. Maybe not everything is an omen.

We take a long curve around a wide mirror of a long lake, away from the storm. Then the road hooks back to the west, and it looks like we're headed straight for the entrance to hell. The road straightens out to the south, and we travel the line between.

Heat from the midmorning sun battles with the wind for attention from the nerve endings in my skin. Both win, but I'm starting to feel warmer inside. It can't be from the wreck. It's like the sun is inside me too. It's been uncomfortable at times, even painful, but right now it feels like a little flicker of life.

A long train carrying coal progresses east, crossing underneath us as we drive over a low bridge. I picture timing a perfect jump and landing in a coal car. I've watched too many action movies.

We turn onto a major east-west highway and zoom by a giant billboard showing a line of penguins waddling below a white silhouette of snow peaks.

[Little America—Almost Home]

Almost home.

CHAPTER 10

THURSDAY MORNING— LITTLE AMERICA, WY

I **expect to see a town,** but all that sits between two stretches of tan desert to the east on one side and the west on the other is a long, busy parking lot north of the highway and several matching buildings. We exit and park close to nothing, away from the other cars.

"Stay here," Longstoryshort says as he takes off his helmet, scans the surroundings, and walks west toward a cluster of white-trimmed brick buildings with numbers on the doors. It looks like a hotel of duplexes set in thick green grass that is either freshly mowed or artificial. A father is taking a picture of his young wife holding their baby on the neck of a green brontosaurus.

The wind has mostly dried my clothes, but my skin still feels wet and uncomfortable. I lean against the bike, relieved to be off that hard, straight seat—hopefully for the last time. I get to be in a van now.

I'm alone in the vacant back row of spaces, watching cars, trucks, motorcycles, and vans compete for the spots twenty feet closer. RVs and motor homes are parked in the lot west of us, and semis in the lot to the east. It's a convergence of everything you would see on the road. Little America.

Longstoryshort walks from the hotel lobby up the sidewalk and waves me toward him as he passes a playground next to the busiest building in the strip. I walk between a refurbished pink Cadillac and a sleek new black Tesla toward an unmarked red-brick building wrapped with large mirrored windows. The front doors don't have time to shut between people going in and coming out.

Inside, the room looks bigger than the building from the outside. It's part convenience store, part gift shop, and part restaurant.

"Order you some breakfast." Longstoryshort seems nervous. I suppose it's all the people vying for spots in lines all around us.

"Thanks," I say hungrily. But my bladder is speaking louder than my stomach right now, and I head through the crowded entryway toward the restroom signs in the back.

I follow a white-haired man who's about my size and build, whose gentle authority is parting the sea of people in front of us. He's wearing a brown shirt that says "Older than dirt" on the back. It seems like a shirt we would've gotten Grandpa. He would have worn that shirt with pride.

Relieved, I find my way back through the chattering crowd to a window seat in the restaurant area. My stomach growls at the sound of bacon sizzling. I'm surprised to find Longstoryshort leaning against the other side of the window. I don't mean to spy on him. I think about tapping against the glass to let him know I'm here, but he seems to be focused on looking for his friend, letting him know where we are.

"Can I take your order?" a frazzled girl about my age asks, holding a pen and pad. I haven't had a chance to look at a menu but see it on the wall above the kitchen area. An oversized digital clock says 9:00.45.

"Number one, please."

"Bacon, sausage, or ham?"

"Bacon."

"How would you like your eggs?"

"Scrambled."

"Toast, biscuit, or English muffin?"

"English muffin, please."

"Anything to drink?"

Coffee. "Orange juice." I guess my mouth knows what it needs; orange juice sounds refreshing.

Looking around, I see this really is a "little America." There are young people, families, retirees. Men and women in military clothes, bikers in leather, a businessman talking on his phone. A man in a turban, a kid dressed like a rock star, nodding his head to the music in his earbuds, a professional-looking woman handing out fliers or something. Black, White, Hispanic, Asian, Native American. Tattoos, tank tops, well dressed, blue jeans, short, tall, fat, and thin.

All of America has converged on this one spot for food, refreshment, gifts, refueling, and rest. Fried food, grilled, kosher, keto, dessert. People are sitting, standing, spending, talking, and quietly reflecting. A group of three laughs at a table next to me, absorbed in their conversation. On the other side of the room, a toddler is crying, and the parents are snapping at each other. It's all going on right now, at this moment, under this wooden beam-lofted roof. There is nothing new under the sun. All the differences, all the variety, all in one place and one time. And they all have backgrounds and stories that are unfolding, intersecting here.

I pull my journal out of my backpack to try to capture some of the fleeting thoughts in the constantly changing but somehow unchanging scenery. I flip to the next blank page, and a ten-dollar bill falls out. It's the ten-dollar bill from the church. I didn't mean to take it, but maybe I can find a Bible here, or a small gift for my mom and dad.

I leave my backpack on my chair with my notebook on top in case Longstoryshort comes in. Right now he's pacing.

Candy, health food, trail mix, chips, energy bars. Soda, beer, water, juice, energy drinks. They have something for everyone. Blankets, shirts, paintings, mugs, toys, canes, and socks. Crass, crude, rude, funny, sweet, sentimental. Knives, key chains, postcards, books. Westerns, romance, best sellers, mysteries. No Bibles. My stomach says my food is probably close to ready.

Back to the padded wicker chair at my table. I'm more than excited to see my plate is awaiting me. The large glossy white plate is loaded with steaming eggs, peppered hash browns, bacon, and the biggest buttered English muffin I've ever seen. The cup of orange juice looks fresh and is full to the brim. It takes me back to Baker's Bakery in the Black Hills. That was only a few days ago, but it seems like a different world ago. The food is about the same, but I'm not. I mean, I'm still the same person, but something has been awakened in me that I've been asleep to all my life. Or at least since I was a kid. But it's still not really awake, not all the way. It's like an old world has shattered or maybe a cocoon has broken, and I still have the glass and sticky residue on me. I'm small again, and the world is bigger. There are so many different people and perspectives, and we're all trying to figure it out. On my drive to Montana, I found something true, and since then it's been getting lost in a haystack. For the first time in my life, I'm the right kind of hungry.

Once I dive in, there's no stopping to wipe my mouth until the plate is half-empty and my stomach is pushing tight against itself. I smile. Longstoryshort leans against the window again, looking toward the entrance of the parking lot.

I pick slowly at what's left of the salty, greasy food on my plate as what I've already shoved down my throat is working its way past my stomach. Now that I'm satisfied, I don't feel like writing all my thoughts, but I jot some notes anyway. All these different people living, moving, breathing. We are all in the same reality. But does anyone have it figured out? Or are we all just different recipes? But how can everyone be right? I'm not sure anyone was right in Grace's garage, except maybe West. I guess some people get it more than others. But how do you know who to listen to? These thoughts and questions don't mix with the endorphins pumping from my stomach to my brain. I just need to sit and enjoy.

Longstoryshort pushes off the glass and walks toward a tough-looking guy in a short-sleeved button-up shirt. Tattoos spill from his sleeves to his wrists and up his neck from the collar. He's got spiked, blond-tipped hair and a thin goatee on his chin. They shake hands and turn toward the reflective pane between us. He's taller than Longstoryshort and is built like a bodyguard. What was I imagining the Holy Ghost to look like? Longstoryshort isn't Jesus, so what if this isn't the Holy Ghost? Can I trust him? Do I have a choice?

The two come in laughing and find their way to me.

"Well, this is the kid I was telling you about."

"Good to meet you, bro." The strong man sizes me up. He has three teardrops tattooed by his right eye. "M'name's Ghost. I'm gonna get you where you're needed."

"Good to meet you, too, sir," I shake his hand with as much trembling authority as I can muster.

"Longstoryshort says you're headed to Dallas. That's on my way, but I've been driving all night and need a little shut-eye. Longstory says he got you guys a room; you can hang out, and we can be on our way tonight."

He got us a room? Something doesn't feel right.

"Okay." I just want to be home. I don't want to linger where I don't belong anymore. But what choice do I have?

The waitress brings the ticket and takes my plate.

"Bring a couple of coffees, would you?" Longstoryshort asks before she leaves.

"Anything else?" she asks to their backs as they walk away.

"No thanks," I say for them.

Outside, Longstoryshort and Ghost seem to be in an argument. Considering that the windows are mirrored on the other side, I sit back down and lean closer to hear what's going on. The orange juice is too acidic to drink now. Longstoryshort is near the window, and I can make out some of what he's saying.

"Yeah, he's a little old, but someone will want him." My brain scans itself for all the options of what that could mean.

Ghost is shaking his head. Longstoryshort doesn't have control over him. I don't like this.

"Look, he's off the grid, confused, malleable. The kid thinks I'm Jesus, for Chrissake!"

No I don't. What's going on? I'm paralyzed and listening hard. Ghost is relaxing a little but still listening, his hands on his hips.

". . . and he's got no backbone . . . weak as a child." Why is he saying this?

Arms crossed and thinking with a scowl, Ghost gives in and eases up. "Okay," he says. Then he reaches in his pocket and aggressively hands Longstoryshort a thick wad of cash.

The waitress sets down two cups of coffee on the table, and it scares the daylights out of me. "You okay?" she asks.

"Yeah, fine," I say, feeling for my backbone.

I turn back to the window and flush white as Longstoryshort is on the other side of the window looking right at me. He smooths his hair back and inspects his teeth with only a foot and a mirror between our faces. My eyes bug out, and I'm not sure I'm breathing. He turns back to Ghost.

"I'll get him hooked this afternoon, and then you can break him."

The words are crystal clear. I'm paralyzed. Just like watching the kid get thrown by the buffalo. A lifetime is frozen in a second, and my brain computes a thousand algorithms searching for meanings other than what was said. Nothing. Is this real? I'm trapped in my inaction, and there isn't even a locked garage door. What do I do? Something. What are my options? Go with it and get hooked and broken? Scream and cause a scene? What would happen? I'd be the crazy one. Find a way out? Where would I go? It's desert for miles in all directions. I'm stuck between a dozen bad options. Dead end. Time speeds back up with my racing brain. I need to do something. They're coming. *Dead end.* A fire flares up in the kitchen.

Lord, guide my feet. I snatch my journal and backpack, put the ten-dollar bill from the chapel on the table, and bolt toward the bathroom. Ducking behind the candy aisles, I peek through some displays and see Ghost and Longstoryshort looking around for me. They didn't see me. Their faces change as the seconds on the large digital clock tick away. Ghost's attention glares toward Longstoryshort. Longstoryshort is angry but increasingly panicked, a feature I haven't seen on him before. He's not the devil. He's just an imp in the presence of a superior. The thought satisfies some part of me that loathes him, but the rest of me is terrified. He's coming this way!

Someone drops a tray, and he turns around. I dart stealthily out the east-side doors as someone else is coming in, then sprint toward the back of the building to hide.

I can't sit and hide, though. There is no hiding. I run behind the gas station next door, using it for cover. I try to get as much space between me and the doors as I can.

Leaning my eyes around the corner, I see Ghost outside now, scanning the grounds with clenched fists. I can see his jaw muscles tighten and loosen even from here. Longstoryshort must be tearing the place apart inside.

When Ghost is looking the other direction, I make a dash to the cover of a line of parked semis. Where do I go? What do I do? I run down a path at the edge of the property along a wall of sand dunes, the freight trucks creating a blind between me and the men who want to hurt me. How did I end up here?

[Dead end]

I've been here before. Where is the green pasture and the quiet waters? There's a giant sand dune to my right and people who want to hook and break me back to the left.

At the dead end, just like before, I turn right, and there is another way. It's a maintained path wide enough for a four-wheeler to follow a barbed-wire fence hidden behind a sharp drop in the sand dune. *Thank You, God.* I'm barricaded from sight and all I want is to sit down and cry, but my feet carry me into a run.

The barbed wire fence keeps me behind the dunes and below the access road for about a mile. I'm out of breath—I can't sprint anymore, but I keep moving as fast as I can.

Think. Don't die. I can't. Unbelievable. How can this be real? I always thought kidnappers were junkies in ski masks or pervs in cars with candy. I walked right into it, willingly. Happily. Could I have seen it coming? I should have seen it coming. I'm so stupid. Jumping on the back of a motorcycle with a stranger. Thinking he was Jesus. Something was starting to feel off, but this?! It's too much. I can't believe it. But I have to. I have to keep going.

The sand hills that were my cover level out with the road, and I've got no more place to hide. I could burrow in, cover up, and just die. But my legs keep moving. Walk quick, look back, run, look back, keep going. What does Ghost's van look like? I could jump the fence and aim for the horizon, but it's so flat and bare I'd be easy to see from a mile away in any direction. *Follow your feet.* My heart thumps like a rabbit in the shadow of a hawk as I trip over a clump of weeds and hit my knee on a rock. There's no time to hurt. Keep going.

The air is cool, but the sun radiates on my skin and in my eyes. A ball of fire so far away, but impossible to run away from. It makes life possible. Also death. Death in the desert or whatever they were planning for me. Did Ghost really pay Longstoryshort for me? I saw it. Hooked and broken? Too old for what? *Someone* will *want* me? I heard it. I feel sick. I throw up, and my knees hit the ground. I'm dizzy.

A car zooms by on the two-way access road. I've got to pay attention. The busy highway is just beyond the access road on raised concrete pillars. I wonder if any of those cars have a kidnapped kid in them. Human trafficking. In America? Is that real? Is this real?

I look up to the spinning sky. The hellish storm looms behind me. And a motorcycle is coming out of it. I want to hide. There's no place to hide. I can't move. On my knees I pray, *Lord, make me invisible.* Please be someone else's motorcycle.

He pulls up near me with an aggressive stop, then calmly dismounts, opens his cyclops visor, and walks toward me.

I'm afraid. What's he going to do?

But he's cool and collected. I'm petrified.

"What's going on, Red? You had me worried."

He walks right up and towers over me. Reaching out his hand, he helps me up, and his stormy eyes look deep into mine like the conversation I heard never happened. I'm weak. Powerless. He puts his arm around me and guides me peacefully toward the motorcycle. "Look, son," he says, "you're almost home."

I am not his son. A flame bursts in me and I resist. "I'm not going with you," I say forcefully. "And I'm *not* your son."

"Whoa, Red," he says, tightening his grip on my shoulder. "What's going on?"

"I heard you!" I shout. "I know what you're going to do!"

"What did you hear?" he pauses, his mind filtering through what I might have heard. "Are you sure you caught the whole conversation?"

"Enough of it," I react, breaking free from his vulture arm.

"Did you?" he asks, gently putting his arm back around me, trying to coax me to the bike. *Did I?* "I think you're confused." *I am confused.* "C'mon, I'll take care of you."

My feet don't move, but my mind is fuzzy. Surely it wasn't real. He's not an evil guy, right? It's far-fetched, all of it. Maybe I didn't hear what I thought. I'm confused. This isn't a book or a movie.

"Sorry," I say, but my feet still won't move.

"What's your problem, kid?" What *is* my problem? His hand grips my shoulder a little too tight, just enough to trigger a reflex. I try to jerk away but his claws dig deeper.

"*Jesus*," I whisper. He yanks me forward, but my feet are glued to the ground and I twist free. He lashes around and boxes me in the ear with the full force of a sideways catapulting fist. My head rings like a bell, but I stay upright in shock.

"I took care of you!" he roars and grabs my arm as I'm about to fall. No, he didn't take care of me. I fight to get my arm free, and he tries to pick me up.

"Quit fighting!" he spits through his teeth. Everything in me is fighting, but he's so much stronger.

I twist my arm up and against his grip to his open visor and push against his face. He squeezes harder, and so do I. I feel my strength weaken and try to adjust, but he holds me tight like a python with a mouse. He feels the fight flicker in me, but I can't give in. With my hand still on his face, I muster a surge of anger against him and scream with one last push against his clutch. All of my muscles flex in an explosion of resistance and one of my fingers digs deep into his eye socket. It pops to a sudden, unnatural, wet depth.

He howls in pain and lets go, hands going to his gouged eye.

I back up, and he walks toward me. Taking his hand away from his bloody face, he looks through me with the one eye while the other pulses crimson down his cheek.

My ears are ringing like after a big bang, and his voice muddles around in it, trying to find a way to echo.

"I was wrong about you," he growls with little wincing. "I fed you, I clothed you, I protected you from yourself, and this is what you do to me? You ungrateful little child." Blood puddles in his left eye, and he stops his advance to shake off the pain. I stop retreating. It's affecting him.

"You're nothing, kid!" He shouts at me. "You never were, and you never will be. They were right. They were all right. You're not even worth it. You're a coward! You don't know anything!"

The ringing in my ear rises, pulses. The sun spins in a circle right above me. I'm between Longstoryshort and the motorcycle. He's disoriented. I stumble out of the way, my fists ready to fight and feet ready to kick. I won't let him get hold of me again, and I won't hold on to him again.

"Your family isn't even going to want you back," he sneers as he walks by, staring at me with his bloody socket. "I'm coming back for you. You can't hide. You're going to die out here. You need me."

I don't need him. And I've already died. He could kill me right now. Why doesn't he? I've got to figure out how to get away.

"You think you're good? You're weak!" he shouts, not finished taking it out on me. "You'll *never* be good enough for God!"

I try not to listen, but his words sink deep. Like he knows my fears and shame, and he's attacking me there on purpose. I turn my back on him and try not to waver in my steps on the side of the two-way access road. The motorcycle starts behind me with an angry roar. He turns around and faces me with his black helmet, revs the engine, and speeds toward me. I shuffle out of his path and stumble into the thorns of the barbed wire fence. Then he's gone, headed back to Little America.

God, don't let him come back. He's going to come back. Or Ghost is. *Protect me. Help me get home.*

I continue walking east along the access road. Crazy as it is, I feel a strange and unfamiliar freedom of sorts. I'm free from Longstoryshort. And I want to stay that way. I think I'm in shock. I look back to make sure no one is coming.

I don't know how long I've been walking or how far I've gone, but my feet keep moving.

I don't think he's coming back for me. Wouldn't he be here by now? No, he said he'd be back. *Stay alert.* I keep an eye out for hiding places, but there are none. No more dunes and not even a sufficient bush. Maybe I can catch a ride with someone. How could I think that after this? Who can I trust? My eyes study cars coming from Little America fearfully. If it's Ghost, what will I do? *Lord, protect me. Guide me.*

A red Corvette heading toward Little America speeds by and passes again a few seconds later in reverse. It swerves backward onto the shoulder and waits for me.

"You okay?" a beautiful blond woman asks, leaning over from the driver's seat. I keep walking. There's no room in my scenery for her. It doesn't make sense. I was being kidnapped. I was going to be drugged and "broken." Someone was paying money for me. No, I'm not okay.

She backs up to keep up with me.

"Hey, kid, you're bleeding."

My ear is ringing, but I think there's a cut on my cheek. Yep. I wipe my right cheek with my sweatshirt and feel it.

"It's just a little cut," I say, walking in pace with her backward moving sports car. "Looks worse than it is."

"You sure? There's a great stop up ahead," she says. "Besides, it looks like a storm's coming."

It's already hit.

"I'll treat you to lunch and get you cleaned up." She seems kind, but why would a woman in a nice car stop for a beat-up tramp like me? And why now? I can't go back.

"Thanks," I say. "I'm almost home." I'm so far from home.

The shoulder is narrowing, and another car is coming.

"Okay," she says. "Take care." She puts it in drive, and I won't look back.

My ear is still ringing and throbbing, head is swimming, and knees are wobbly. I need a break. There's a turnout up ahead.

The turnout is for a historical marker that must be about the small mesa that juts out of the flat desert to the north. There's nothing else here.

I take a break at the turnout and try not to black out. *Breathe.* Focus on something other than anything.

[Follow the Trona Trail]

What on earth is trona? I look at the map of the Trona Trail below the sign and try to estimate where I am and how long it will take me to get somewhere. Green River is the next town, it looks like, and I'm probably a few hours, walking distance. I've got to sit down.

I try to rest, but I'm restless in pain and get back up. I try reading the informational plaques to distract my mind.

Trona is something mined in the area . . . been used since ancient Egyptian times . . . in every American home—most of it comes from here. Soda ash. So much I don't know . . . I didn't know. Why didn't I know? It's not supposed to be like this. What am I going to do?

I shake my head and try to focus on something else. Soda ash is used in glass, baking soda, glue, paper, fire extinguishers, detergents, soap. I need a bath. And a change of clothes. And something to hold on to.

I lean against the sign, close my eyes, and breathe to keep from passing out.

A large engine purrs into the turnout behind me, and my heart stops.

It's an RV. Act normal. Be invisible.

Two doors open and shut. A man, not Ghost, stretches and yawns.

"Max, you act like you've been on the road for ages. You've been driving five minutes. And do we *have* to stop at *every* historical marker?"

"Only the ones we stop at," he replies. They haven't noticed me yet. Act casual.

I saunter out of the way of the signs. The old man sees me. "Hello," he calls.

I wave to him politely to interact but not engage. But he's looking at me funny. His mouth is gaped and his eyes are in panic.

"M–Maxine, get the first-aid kit!" he hollers and runs toward me.

"It's just a little cut," I say, touching the small gash on my right cheek. It's already starting to scab. "It looks worse than it is."

"No! your ear! It's bleeding!"

I lift my other hand to my left ear, feel the wet, sticky fluid on it, around it, down my neck, and look at my soaked shoulder and bloody hand. It's not just a cut. I look back at him and feel myself sway. Knowing my ear is leaking makes me aware of it. Weak-kneed and woozy, I do my best to stand up.

"What happened?" he asks, holding my shoulders enough to keep me from falling.

I can't answer. I lean into his arms and sob.

CHAPTER 11

THURSDAY AFTERNOON: FLAMING GORGE

I sob chest-heaving sobs until I can't anymore. The old man holds me in his arms and waits. The flood of emotions ebbs back into a stream, and I'm finally able to breathe again.

"I'm sorry," I say, backing away a little. The old woman has the first-aid kit open on one of the informational signs about trona, digging for the right bandage. "I'm okay, really."

"No, you're not," she argues matter-of-factly, "and you've nothin' to apologize for. We're going to fix you up good as new."

Good as new? How can I go back to good as new? I wasn't hooked and broken, but now I know that world exists. I was that close to being forced into it. That didn't exist before, and going back to "before" would just be ignoring it. I look at the old man.

My hand shakes as I point at him. "I got blood all over your shirt. I'm sorry."

"I guess you did," he says looking down at it. "I've been washed in the blood, honey," he says to his wife, winking at me. "It's just a shirt. I have more than a few in the motor home. What size do you wear?"

"Large," I say, "but I don't want to be a bother."

"Quit your bother," he says in a light voice. "I'll be right back." He turns and walks to the long motor home. The back of the shirt says "Older than dirt."

"What's your name, hon?" the short, soft, white-haired lady asks. *Nothing.* "Redemption Gray, ma'am."

"What a beautiful name," she says, dabbing my neck and bloody ear with wet gauze. "God must have big plans for you."

Part of me wants to argue; part of me wants to be hugged by her. I simply hang my head and let her wash me. New blood runs on my clean skin.

"Hold this," she says, gently pressing fresh gauze against my pounding ear. "We should get you to a hospital. Where do you live? Do you have parents? Can we take you home?"

I hold the cloth and feel woozy again. "Can I sit down?"

"Of course, of course," she says, like she's upset at herself for not thinking of it first. Toward the western horizon, a truck or van is speeding our way, and I urge toward being led to safety. She takes me by the hand and guides me into the motor home just as the old man is coming out. "Max, will you get this young man some water?"

"Of course, of course," he says, like he's upset at himself for not thinking of it first. He hands me a fresh shirt and points me to the restroom before turning to get me water.

I put down my backpack, go into the restroom, and sit on the closed toilet seat, holding my head and resting my elbows on my knees. With my arms this way, my sweatshirt sleeves are almost at my elbows. The clothes are too small for my body, but my body feels too big for my soul. *What do I do, Lord?* Can I trust these people? A vehicle outside comes to a quick stop, and I hold my breath. The engine purrs, then it peels out as quickly as it came in. I lift my head, exhale slowly, and feel a little relief. I need to get as far away as possible. There's a small shower cramped in the tight space of the restroom. I need to be clean.

I go back out, unchanged, and Max and his wife look at me eagerly to find out what they can do to help.

170

Trying to find a way to explain the situation and my need to get far away, I end up asking awkwardly, "Is it possible I could take a shower?"

"Of course, of course," Max responds with goodness. "We're about the same size," he adds before arising. "I'll get you some new clothes too."

A tear runs from my eye as I blink, partly from shame of being in the situation I'm in, partly from the unfamiliarity of their generosity.

"Bless your heart, Redemption. What has happened to you?" Maxine asks.

It all runs through my head: the long drive up the Great Plains, the warm liveliness inside Baker's Bakery, the happiness of finding happiness in Montana, the dedication of my life to God, the wreck, thinking Longstoryshort was Jesus on a motorcycle, the chapel and labyrinth in Jackson, the blur of alcohol, being trapped in the garage, West's unfolding story, the dark drive to Little America, the kids waiting for the school bus, Ghost walking up and shaking hands with Longstoryshort, the conversation, "he's a little old, but someone will want him . . . he's off the grid, confused, malleable . . . he's got no backbone . . . weak as a child . . . I'll get him hooked this afternoon, and you can break him."

"Here you go," Max interrupts my stupor and hands me a stack of clothes. The old lady is still sitting, with her hands in a prayer position over her mouth, her teary eyes studying me as if she feels my hurt. Am I in that bad of shape?

The shower head is low and the pressure is weak, but it's almost a religious experience. I was so dirty, so chafed in every hidden crevice of my body, so rotten smelling and raw. Now I'm naked and clean. If only it could get to the depths of my soul.

In clothes that are not my own, I feel like I could be a younger version of Max. The soft gray lady takes my old clothes and puts them in the trash.

"Thank you," I say, sitting on the three-cushioned couch that only fits two people. Max sits next to me.

"I'm Max, and this is the bride of my youth, Maxine. It's good to meet you, Redemption."

I don't know what to say. I just look at him.

"You don't have to say anything," Max says as Maxine hands me a blueberry muffin and sits across from me. He holds out a cell phone. "Would you like to call someone?"

I don't know. I need my mom right now. Maybe they wouldn't mind coming and picking me up. Or maybe not. A few months ago when I was in an argument with them, I said I'd rather live on the streets than with them. "Go ahead," Dad told me. "Do what you need to do." I didn't want to live on the streets; I just didn't want to live in a house of constant fighting. My mom yelled at him for telling me to go and yelled at me for wanting to. I went to my room, turned out the lights, and put in my earbuds.

I can't put in my earbuds now. I have to face it. I ran away, but I'm coming home. They need to know I'm coming home, that I want to.

I take the phone and dial. It goes to voicemail. "Hey, Mom," I stammer. "I got in a wreck, but I'm okay. Kind of. It's a long story—" My throat closes, and I squeeze my eyes shut to get that name out of my head. When it unlocks, I try again. "I'm trying to get home. You can call me back at this number." Oh. She doesn't answer calls from numbers she doesn't know. I hope she listens to the voicemail.

"She probably didn't recognize the number," I tell Max and Maxine. I hold the phone and wait for it to ring back. Max holds Maxine's hand, and we all look at the screen in front of me. It doesn't light up.

Max clears his throat. "Well, we have a few options. We could let you keep walking, but there's not another town for fifteen miles. We're passing through there anyway. Would you like to ride with us?"

"I don't want to be a bother."

"Quit your bother," Max says again.

"You always say that, Max. I don't think it means what you think it means," Maxine tells him with a smile.

"As you wish," he says, winking at her.

"Or we could take you home. Where is home?"

I feel like a deer in the headlights. They don't know where my home is, how far it is.

"Denver?" It's close, right? I don't want to be in their way. As much as they don't seem to mind helping, I don't want to be a burden.

"Great," Max says. "We can try your parents again on the way. It's quite a drive, but we have reservations outside of Denver tomorrow night. It's on our way home, and we wouldn't mind taking you if you're comfortable with us."

I'm caught off guard again. Tomorrow night? I thought it was close. I tap the phone to wake it up again. I try to call, but it goes to voicemail and I hang up. I feel like I shouldn't get on the road with strangers again, but I don't want to keep walking with Longstory-short and Ghost still out there looking for me.

My gut says stay with them.

But my gut has been wrong.

There is something safe about them.

I don't know who to trust. But I have to trust in something. *God, I need You. I don't know if I trust You, but I need You now.*

"Do you like dinosaurs?" Maxine asks. It's a weird question.

"Yes ma'am," I say politely, curious.

"Wonderful!" She claps her hands with delight and stands up. "Tonight we have reservations in Jensen, and in the morning we can go see the dinosaur bones if you want to. And tomorrow night, we can have you home."

Home? No. I don't know what I'll do from Denver. Maybe Mom and Dad will come get me.

Max hops up, kisses Maxine gently on the lips, and they head to the front seats. They let me keep the phone.

Leaning back from the front seat, Max says, "Make yourself at home. There's food in the fridge and water in the cooler below."

Make myself at home. When I was home last, I was a different person. I'd stand at the full fridge with the door open, complaining there was nothing to eat. I'd eat snacks and leave the trash on the floor or shove it in the couch crevices. I'd yell across the house and ignore anything Mom and Dad asked of me. How do I make myself at home now?

Max takes a handful of almonds from a bag on the console and puts the engine in gear. We pull onto the access road and drive away from Little America. Max and Maxine make small talk with each other. I lean back on the soft leather couch and close my eyes.

Quiet. The adrenaline is gone from my body. The sobbing has left me drained.

The access road crosses under the busy highway, and I turn to look out at the traffic. Trafficking. A white van with tinted windows. My gut twists. I've always heard about trafficking in the background of the news, always got the alerts on my phone of some kid missing. But it was always some other city, some other kid. Things aren't real until it's close to home.

But it was real; I just wasn't aware of it. How was I not aware of it? I thought he was Jesus, wanted him to be my dad. I thought he was looking out for me, helping me. But it was all a lie. How was I to know? Surely God knew. But how could He be aware of it and not do anything to keep me from it?

A black motorcycle speeds by on the elevated highway, going the same direction as us. I swear he looked at me. My ear throbs, and my skin turns clammy. I close the window shade and slump sideways on the couch, below the level of the window. My heart is racing, and I feel the motor home speed up as it gets on the highway. Cars zoom past us. *Breathe.*

I try my mom and dad a few more times. Voicemail. "It's me again. Please call me back." Why aren't they calling back? I close my eyes against the pain and confusion.

I awake to a rhythmic thump-a-thump of the wheels on the road. Max and Maxine are done with their small talk and are listening to the radio. I don't recognize the song, but its clean progression of piano chords and notes catches my attention. I perk up, remembering the last time a song stood out and spoke to me in the car. I dig in my backpack for my journal. I'm a little surprised I still have it. A man's slightly raspy voice enters the music.

"Waking up to a new sunrise, looking back from the other side, I can see now with open eyes. Darkest water and deepest pain, I wouldn't trade it for anything 'cause my brokenness brought me to You, and these wounds are a story You'll use."

I feel like the words want to say something to me, but I can't relate to them. I'm *not* on the other side, the sun is still up, and the storm is still stirring. I *would* trade it. I don't see how God can use this. The reality of Longstoryshort's world is too big. It's too much a part of the machine. And how can God use *me* for any good? *Why would He use me?*

A rippling crescendo on a cymbal raises the intensity of the music as his strengthening voice leads into a chorus. "So I'm thankful for the scars, 'cause without them I wouldn't know Your heart, and I know they'll always tell of who You are. So forever I am thankful for the scars."

I don't get it. I'm thankful for the distance between me and Little America, but the cuts are still fresh and deep. I don't understand how this tells who God is or what His heart is like. Drums kick the next lines into a tempo with a purpose.

"Now I'm standing in confidence with the strength of Your faithfulness and I'm not who I was before. No, I don't have to fear anymore."

Confidence, strength, faithfulness—not how I feel right now. I'm not who I was before, but I've got a lot of fear and good reason for it. It goes back to the chorus, and I want to run up and turn it off. How can I be thankful for the scars? The words change and repeat.

"I can see, I can see how You delivered me. In Your hands, in Your feet, I found my victory."

Okay, I guess I can see how He delivered me. The escape from the diner, the strength to fight Longstoryshort, Max and Maxine showing up at the right place and the right time. But it doesn't feel like victory. It feels like a close scrape with an evil that will still be there, no matter how far away I go. And I hurt.

"I'm thankful for Your scars . . ." *Your* scars? I thought the song was about *my* scars. Hands. Feet. Oh. It's talking about the cross. I thought I understood the cross. Maybe Grace was right. Maybe it's not that simple. One last line stands out above my thoughts.

"And with my life, I'll tell of who You are."

Whose life will tell of who is? Me or Jesus? Right now I don't know enough about either one of us to tell. But at least, if nothing else, the song is sparking thoughts and questions I haven't felt like thinking or asking.

It's hard to write thoughts about things you don't understand, and I scratch out every sentence I start.

Maxine looks back and sees me awake and writing.

"Ooh, Max, we've got another writer!" she says.

"I'm not really a writer," I say, looking down at my page of scratched-out sentences.

"Are you writing?"

My half laugh is more defeat than humor. "Well, more like trying to take notes."

She unbuckles and walks back through the moving vehicle to sit across from me, leaning in.

"How did God create the universe, the earth, and everything?" she quizzes me.

I don't know. I know the big bang theory from middle-school science. I remember a girl in class who got her feathers ruffled, and she argued with our teacher that God made it. The teacher said there was no room in science for religion, that you can't prove God. But couldn't the big bang be *how* God started it all?

"I don't know."

"Words," Maxine says. She seems excited, so I listen closely. "God *speaks* things into existence. 'In the beginning was the Word. The Word was with God; the Word *was* God. Through the Word all things were made, *in* the Word was life, and that life was the light of all mankind. The light shines in the darkness, and the darkness cannot overcome it.'"

She waits for it to sink in. It doesn't. But it seems important.

"That's from John chapter one, in the Bible." She smiles. "God also made us to speak, to use words to define our reality, and to use them to bring a life that outshines the darkness. Max is a writer. He's touched a lot of lives with words. People without words are lost, so it's important that you're taking notes and writing down your thoughts. Not everyone is so wise." She offers an open ziplock bag of dried fruit. "Would you like some dates?"

But people with too many words are lost too. I've always felt bombarded by words and ideas. It's like everyone is arguing and fighting to make you agree with them and if you don't, then you're stupid, hateful, or closed-minded.

Maxine places the bag of fruit on the table between us, the open end facing me. "You know, in the book of Revelation, all the evil in the world is defeated by two things." She pauses for me to think about it.

Atomic bombs and otter flu? Meteors and fire? Sticks and stones? Christians with guns? Meditation and—

"The sword of truth and the songs of angels."

Okay. I write it down. I don't understand it, but it sounds good. Truth was what the preacher in Montana was talking about. I remember wanting more when I left. And those people singing hymns to the dying lady next to Grace's. That was pretty angelic.

And Longstoryshort couldn't stand it.

"Keep taking notes, but don't stop there," Maxine says. She's so excited to be my temporary whatever-day-it-is Sunday school teacher. "Put your words together, and you have a testimony!"

Testimony. That's another church word I've always heard but don't know what it means.

"What's a testimony?"

"Sweet thing!" She says it with a laugh—more at herself than at me. "You've seen a court trial on TV, right?"

I nod.

"So, a person who saw what really happened is a witness." She waits for a nod of understanding.

I nod.

"The witness comes to the stand to give their testimony, their *story.* They tell their story to help the judge and jury find out what really happened." She looks into my eyes with concern, and I try to suppress my awareness that I was just almost more than a witness to a crime.

Reading something in me, Maxine tries to make it more specific. "There are a lot of lies in the world that we grow up believing. Your testimony helps you sort through them. And it can help others along the way too."

I catch myself shaking my head. I don't want to deal with sorting anything out right now. For me or for anyone else.

Maxine switches seats to sit next to me on the small couch. "You've been through something, and you don't have to tell us if you don't want to. You can, and we'll listen without judgment, but that's all up to you and only when you're ready. You're probably still figuring it out, and you should. In fact, I should let you write instead of giving you a Sunday school lesson." She gets up to go back to the front with Max.

You don't have to go. "I'd love some dates," I say.

I've made her day by taking her up on the offer. She hands me the bag with a smile. They're soft and sweet and keep me here on the couch as I flip back through my journal. I add some details I remember but that didn't seem important at the time. I read back over the days since hitting the elk. I can make notes for my future self, but I can't talk to the guy I was a few days ago. The truth changes everything.

Was I just an opportunity for Longstoryshort to make some money? I wanted him to care about me, but did he at any point? Did he feel any guilt or shame? How could a person be so evil? Or is he just a part of the machine? If so, I say let the machine break.

I lift the window shade. We're far from civilization, cutting between striated cliffs. Sputtering through layers of history.

You're nothing, kid. You never were, and you never will be.

Get out of my head!

I shut the blinds again, along with my eyes.

You're nothing.

I focus on the songs playing on the radio, willing them to replace the words in my head, and let myself slip back into darkness.

But it's not darkness, and it's not quite a dream. It's like the brightest part of a flame, but brighter. So bright it . . . registers as darkness? And I'm there, like time or the world doesn't exist.

I come to as we slow around a long, declining curve. I sit up and look out the window. We're crawling across a high bridge over a deep gorge with a river flowing through it.

Leaving the bridge, we turn right into a parking lot, and we're at a lake that comes right up to us.

"Lunchtime!" Max hollers back. Maxine makes her way to the small kitchen area. I like them. I liked Longstoryshort too. I feel like I can trust them. I felt like I could trust Longstoryshort too. But something is different about them. Is it because they're older? A couple? A few days ago, I looked down on people in mansnails. No, they're motor homes.

"Can I help?" I ask.

"No, no, no," she insists in a grandmotherly voice. "You go on out and walk around with Max. As much time as he spends with me, he could probably use a little guy time."

Max is outside stretching to the sky, to the ground, and side to side like his back hurts.

"Ah, I can't make these drives like I used to. Did you get some rest?"

"Yes sir."

He walks by and pats me softly on the back, inspecting the cuts on my ear and cheek.

"Still hurting?"

"A little."

"Follow me," he says, guiding me away from the parking lot, through a picnic area, and down to the edge of a short, rocky beach flanked by a long aluminum floating pier. The water ripples to rocky red hills covered with tall green pines finding crevices to thrive in. Clear blue above, but a black sky still threatens to the west. There's an island in the lake beyond the pier, and it has a little metal boat resting on its shore. *No man is an island.* But it must be nice to get away alone to one sometimes.

Max is quiet, but not unto himself. I think he's waiting for me to talk. I don't want to. I pick up a flat rock and skip it. This water is a lot calmer than the last time I tried to skip a rock. Max picks up a rock and tries to skip it, but it just plops.

"It's all in the wrist," I tell him and skip another. After a few tries he gets it, does a little jig, and picks up another.

We do this for a few minutes, and it's like he's telling me it's okay even though we're not saying anything.

"I want to make a difference in the world," I say, disheartened.

"That's a great way to be!" Max says. "Why do you sound down about it?"

I skip another rock. "See those ripples?"

"Yes."

"They just go away. It's just like anything we do, don't you think? There's no real effect."

He rubs the rock with his thumb, in thought.

"Follow me," he says finally.

We walk along the rough beach and around a short drop-off below the picnic area. Another metal pier, shorter than the first, juts out toward a concrete wall where the water ends. Max guides me to a historical marker plaque.

[Flaming Gorge Dam]

I look up and understand we're on the lake side of a dam. The water is about fifteen feet from the top, and cars are driving across it.

"What you can't see is how giant that dam looks from the other side," Max explains.

That must be the bridge we drove over before turning in to the parking lot. The deep gorge.

"It's massive," he says. "That's what happens when humans want to make a difference in the world. When you have a grand vision, knowledge of how the world works, and the teamwork and resources of people who share that vision—anything is possible. That dam makes a big difference for a lot of people. It has for a long time, and it will for a long time to come. Without it, a lot of the towns around would dry up, a lot of farms would turn into desert, and people like me couldn't come fish in one of the most breathtaking lakes in the United States."

He pauses for it sink in, and I let it. Water laps on the pebbled shore. We stand quietly for a comfortable moment and let nature speak in our silence.

I really want to sit down and go to sleep, but not wanting to be awkward or rude, I ask, "Why's it called Flaming Gorge?"

Max smiles. "Up the lake from here, the Green River cut a canyon out of the red rock. Take a boat between those red cliffs on a yellow, sunny day, and the rippling water makes the light dance. The moving colors and lights are a sight to see—makes the whole canyon look like a giant flame, like you're right in the middle of a fire."

"Like hell?"

Max looks at me sideways, considering. "No," he says after a minute. "There's no sense that this fire can hurt you, and instead of wailing, screaming, and gnashing of teeth, you hear the gentle breeze between the high cliffs, fish jumps echo, and osprey call. It's a refreshing fire, if that makes sense." He gazes toward the horizon, probably reliving the last time he saw it. "It's otherworldly beautiful."

A refreshing fire.

Maxine's voice carries over the whispering breeze. "Max? Redemption? Lunch is ready!"

"Coming, dear!" Max smiles at me and has a happy, hungry step in his walk.

"Max," I say without moving, "why would the devil be afraid of fire?"

He stops and turns to the question with a pondering expression. "That's a good question, Redemption. I'll have to think about that."

Maxine made me two sandwiches with chips, hummus, carrots, and a couple of clementine oranges. I don't hesitate, and then I'm embarrassed when I look up to see Max and Maxine holding hands, praying. I stop, wait, and apologize.

"I'm sorry."

"No need. We blessed your food too," Max says lightly. "You're a guest with us, Redemption. We don't know you or your story, and we're probably some pretty strange strangers to you as well. How about some rules."

Don't be a bother; don't cause a scene. "Okay."

"First, you're never a bother. You're a guest, and for the time being, we are your hosts. It's our pleasure to take care of you, and it's hard to take care of someone who sees themselves as a problem.

"Second, you have nothing to be sorry for. Every time a person says 'I'm sorry,' they've missed a chance to say 'thank you.' Isn't it better to have a thankful heart than a sorry one?

"Third, ask anything you want; tell us only what you want. You don't owe us anything, and we're not requiring anything of you. Freedom is the highest form of love. That way, it's all your choice.

"And that leads us to the last rule I can think of. You're our guest, and we're happy to get you to Denver and take care of you along the way, but you can leave our care at any time. You won't have to explain or anything. The magic words can be 'Thank you for your hospitality,' and we'll drop you off wherever you want. No questions asked. Can we agree to these terms?"

Okay. "Thank you."

"And be our photographer!" Maxine adds. "We have all these pictures of one of us, and hardly any good ones of us together!"

"I can take one now if you like," I offer, retrieving their phone from my pocket. No missed calls.

"Perfect!" Max says with his mouth full. Maxine gets up and looks for the best spot.

"Well, come on!" she tells Max.

They pose with the red rocks in the background, the dark sky contrasting with the bright reflections on the shimmering lake. The sun illuminates them perfectly as they position, negotiate arms around each other, laugh at each other, and finally smile at the camera. I can't imagine what they looked like when they were young, but they made a life together and their young love survives.

"Okay," I say after taking a few.

Maxine looks through them and compliments my photography. "Do you want a picture?"

Do I? A few days ago, I was bemoaning the picture-taking obsession people have. But I really do want to remember the right things, not just show off to friends that I was someone trying to be somebody. I want to remember feeling safe with Max and Maxine. I want to figure out what makes them trustworthy. I want to think more about the flame of Flaming Gorge and how fire can be refreshing. I want to remember that a person can make a difference. But does taking a picture mean I will? I want to.

"Sure?"

Posing, I don't know how to stand. Awkward feels natural. I try to smile, but a deep breath is all I can really muster.

Maxine shows me the picture, and I compliment her photography.

"What's your phone number? I'll text it to you," she says.

"I don't have a phone."

"Good for you, Redemption. Email? Or I could print it and send it to your house?"

I give her my email, and lightning cracks the sky beyond the lake. A long, low roll of thunder eventually makes its way through us.

"Time to go!" Maxine says and scurries to the motor home. I didn't notice the small metal boat hitched to the end before. It has to have been there the whole time.

Note to self: just because you don't see something doesn't mean it's not there.

"She's deathly afraid of lightning. Always has been," Max explains. "Did you get enough to eat?"

"Yes sir."

"Let's clean up and beat this storm out of here."

Maxine is looking out the driver-side window at us, waving us on. A drop of rain hits me on the forehead. A vulture circles above. *But God, I've already died.*

"That's all I need, another storm," I mumble without meaning to.

"Not everything is an omen, you know," Max says.

"It has been for me lately."

"Can a little rain ruin you?"

"I'm sorry."

Max stops packing up and puts his hands on his hips to look at me.

"I–I mean, thank you?"

He smiles. "Don't apologize for the rain making you wet. Storms are normal in life. You're either coming out of one, about to go through one, or smack dab in the middle of it. If you understand that, it's easier to weather the weather. Look at that osprey up there riding the current! That's not a sight you see every day!"

The vulture is an osprey? I don't even know what an osprey is, but I'm starting to notice I'm wrong a lot.

We carry the lunch setup back to the motor home in a sprinkle. Maxine has already started the engine and is strapped in the passenger seat. Max says she's cute and buckles himself in. The rain pitter-patters softly on the roof as we get back on the road. I can't help but notice Max takes the curves slow and careful, not going faster than his spirit. Or mine.

I'm not tired, but I'm exhausted.

Slipping in and out of sleep, I find we've outpaced the rain. I open the window shade to let the warm light and green trees give me a sense of the scene.

We leave the high forest to find working bulldozers, excavators, and dump trucks deconstructing the mountain. It's a huge operation that spreads for miles to the south. Who knows how much mountain they've already moved and shipped off. There's so much—they could work for generations and still not make a dent in the range we are leaving. It doesn't seem like coal; it's all just barren, tan-colored dirt.

I wonder if it's trona. A few weeks ago, I would have seen a picture of this and gotten mad at them for violently destroying the earth. Now it looks more like people going to work, using the abundance of earth to make stained glass and laundry detergent possible. Making the world a better place?

A motorcycle speeds past us on a long straightaway. I duck from the window, and my gut churns.

You're nothing.

Get out of my head. I want to be home.

Your family isn't even going to want you back.

Yes, they will.

Why haven't they called back?

CHAPTER 12

THURSDAY EVENING: JENSEN, UTAH

"**A**lmost there," **Maxine shouts, and** it's not long before we slow down into a town.

Maxine is trying to give directions from her phone, and Max is getting frustrated. Finally, he pulls into a parking lot and looks for himself. Maxine seems embarrassed.

"All our arguments any more have to do with directions," she says back to me. "Even with technology, there's no app that solves the communication barrier between women and men!"

I laugh to ease her mind.

We're back on the road. I've never really tried to communicate with girls. Other guys try to convince girls that they're studs; I just tried to convince them I wasn't a loser. I've never really thought about it, but in high school, talking seems more like a dating-and-mating game than anything deep and meaningful. I can't picture Max and Maxine making out. I guess there has to be something more in a relationship for it to last when teenage hormones go away.

Mom and Dad don't really talk much, not on a deep level, anyway. Maybe they do, and I don't see it. Or maybe raising me has been a stress on their relationship. I want to be different. I *am* different. How will it be when I get home? Mom will yell at me, and Dad will give me the cold shoulder because I made Mom upset. I'll go to my room and get lost in the phone. No, I won't. I'll start washing the dishes and mowing the lawn without being told. I'll do my homework on the kitchen table and help with supper. I'll make it better for them. I won't be the problem anymore.

We pull into an RV park after another ten or fifteen minutes of driving. Maxine checks us in, and Max teaches me how to unhook the fishing boat before he backs the motor home into a narrow gravel space between two house-sized RVs. Max pretends like he needs my help to get the electric and water hooked up.

"Thank you so much, Redemption," he says. "These things are supposed to be convenient for us retired folk, but even still, our bodies can't do what they used to. It's a lot of effort to carry a house on your back!"

"Are they worth it?" I ask.

"Well, there's nothing like tent camping. Maxine and I used to love roughing it—just a tent, a shovel, and a campfire. But you get to an age where sleeping on the ground, tying your trash up in a tree, and digging your own holes becomes more torture than relaxation. We got this one used from a fellow church member, and we've gotten great use out of it. It has three extra beds for our grandchildren. I don't know if they'd know nature if we didn't take them along with us sometimes."

Max pulls out his wallet and shows me pictures of his grandkids, tucked in protective plastic sleeves.

"Their parents don't take them?"

"We raised them to, and they always talk about it, but something about life nowadays makes the years pass quicker."

We sit at our spot's picnic table, and Maxine announces a much-needed nap. Max seems to be comfortable in our long silences, not anxious about anything or expectant of my talking. I study him, and there seems to be no mystery. He's just a man who's lived a full life, loves his wife and family, and is content. More than happy. I want to be there, even if it takes a lifetime.

"What did you do before you retired?" I break the silence.

Max smiles his way out of his thoughts. "I'm not so sure anyone ever *really* retires, but I used to be a science teacher and a minister of a small church."

"I thought science and religion weren't supposed to mix," I respond as a half question, half statement that I'd never questioned.

"A lot of people think that, and it does both an injustice." Max pauses like he has to be careful about how he proceeds. I didn't mean it as a prompt, but I can tell he enjoys teaching, so I let him talk, doing my best to pay attention. He mentions creation, archaeology, mystery, and discovery, but none of it sticks until he says something that prods a real question.

"But if you look at creation assuming God created it," he says, "we can learn more about His . . . personality, for lack of a better word."

I've looked at the world now. I've seen more in the last week than I did my whole life before. A lot of it was beautiful, but I also saw Ghost give Longstoryshort a wad of cash for me. I saw Longstoryshort's fist slam into the side of my head. I saw blood spattered with lies and threats. And I am someone who got away. Not everyone does. My heart starts to boil, thinking about it. If what I've seen tells me about God's personality, what kind of god am I trying to find?

"So God is part evil?" I can't help it.

"Not at all!" He's surprised at my seemingly random interjection. He pauses and regroups to my question. "Evil is a difficult but real problem. I've spent years grappling with that one, and many people have. Maybe you have too."

"If there is a God," I try to put words to it, "He'd have to be God of everything and everyone, right?"

"Right."

"I don't know if I want to believe in a god who would create evil to do harm to the people He supposedly loves."

"So you're assuming God created evil?"

"Where else would it come from?"

He rubs his chin. "If your mother or father twisted your ear and told you to say 'I love you,' even if you said it, would it mean you really do?"

I don't see where he's going with this, but . . . "No."

"So what would allow you to love them?"

I say the only thing I can think of. "Their love."

"God first loved us, but He doesn't twist our ear and make us say 'I love you.' He gives us the choice."

"So evil is just when we don't choose to love God?" Longstory-short chose not to love God, so he was going to sell me like a drug? That doesn't make sense.

"Love can only come from the freedom to choose love," Max explains. "God created choice. Choosing ourselves over God doesn't necessarily make a person evil, but it causes sin. Some people get so deep in their sin that they fall in love with it. When they get that deep into it, God doesn't represent a savior, He represents the one who will destroy what they love. Evil is outright rebellion against the pure, virtuous, and selfless love of God."

It's a lot to comprehend. Silence stretches between us as I think about what he's said. Max just waits. Interesting—he can tell I don't understand, but he's not squirming like Lewis would be. But maybe I'm not asking the right questions. I still don't understand how, if God is so good, He lets people like Longstoryshort get away with what they're doing.

"But there are people out there, hurting others on purpose. Why does God let that happen?"

"He doesn't."

"Yes, He does! I *know* He does." My voice is hard. I'm angry at such a simple answer. How can he say that?

Max sees my pain, that it's close to home. "Hmmm. We aren't talking hypothetically, are we?"

"No, I'm not!"

"It's still a matter of choice. He doesn't require us to—" He stops and rubs his chin again. "Okay, so does the highway patrol allow you to text and drive?"

I think back to getting pulled over in Kansas. "No."

"Do people still do it?"

"I guess."

"And sometimes the people doing what's not allowed get in a wreck and hurt innocent people."

"Okay." My eyebrows tighten, but I'm listening.

"So the suffering is caused by selfish disobedience, not because the highway patrol didn't have enough rules or control."

"Okay." I wish he would just answer directly.

"It's the same way with sin and evil. God doesn't allow it, but people choose it anyway. It's important that we put the blame on the sin and the—"

"But God is bigger than the highway patrol! He knows everything, right? So He knows when something is about to happen. He knows when an innocent person is about to get hurt. Why doesn't He hurt the one doing what's wrong?! Or stop them, at least." I picture Ghost and Longstoryshort in handcuffs, unable to roam free, picking up kids and selling them for who knows what.

I decide to be direct. "I'm not talking about bad drivers, Max. I'm talking about real evil. Evil on purpose. Like . . . like kidnappers and rapists. Why doesn't God stop them? How can He sit back and just watch?!"

Max's eyes show a sudden rush of understanding and compassion that isn't pity. "Oh, Redemption, God doesn't just sit back and watch." He stops to think for a minute. Then he says, "There is a war going on right now that most people are oblivious to. We need to be aware of it and on guard. And as Christians, we cannot sit back and watch. We *must* not. It's the job of strong Christians to stand in line and protect the weak and vulnerable. God *does* care about the innocent and the victims—it's accounted for over and over in the Bible."

"But He still lets it happen." I'm frustrated. "So how are we supposed to defeat evil? How do we make it stop?"

"Redemption. The devil knows God won't betray His gift of choices, and that's exactly where the battle is. And he attacks us with everything he's got in as many ways as he can." Max stops and leans toward me. "Especially when he recognizes a person is becoming a danger to him."

A silence lets me calm down and think about it. I gave my life to God, and in rode Longstoryshort. It's like he knew. It makes me feel good, almost powerful, that the devil would notice and be scared. But why would he be scared of me? I'm nobody. *Nothing.*

Almost like Max is reading my thoughts, he says, "The devil fights because he knows who he's up against. He'll do anything to make you think God is not with you. But God promises He will never leave or forsake us. He commands armies of angels on behalf of His children and gives us authority over evil in the name of Jesus. He plants His Spirit in us to guide when we are lost, instruct when we lack wisdom, and provide strength when we are weak. He speaks and acts through others along the way. He gives us the sword of truth—that's Jesus's own words—to cut through the devil's lies, and songs and hymns that drive him crazy. It's a war, and it's ugly and it's full of pain—"

"But how do we make it stop?" The words explode from me. "How do we stop evil?"

Max's eyes gleam. "It sounds like you're about ready to put on the armor of God and join the fight."

He says it like it's a fight that he's a part of, like it's a battle that's been going on for a long time. I feel so weak and unequipped for anything like battle. But I fought off Longstoryshort. And now that

I know this side of reality, I can't go back to not knowing. My head is spinning.

Max stops and looks at me. "Do you have a Bible?"

"No."

"I'll be right back."

I am so overwhelmed by information and lost in language. Or maybe I'm just overwhelmed and lost, period. Information and language are just easy to blame.

Max comes back with two books. A Bible and a hymnal.

"These are yours," he offers. "I'm going to let you be alone with them for a while. You're not going to get through the whole thing in an hour or two, or even a lifetime, but they'll be useful on your journey and powerful in your battle."

"Where do I start?"

"I'd start with some silence and a prayer. I'm afraid I've dumped a lot on you. But when you're ready, I always start with Jesus. In fact, everything Jesus said is printed in red in this one."

"Thanks," I say, thumbing through the pages looking for red, cherishing the gift.

"We'll have supper after a while, then start a campfire and roast some s'mores. We always end the day with a devotional, so have some questions ready if you have any and want to share. I'm right inside if you need anything, and if you want to come in and lie down, too, feel free."

Feel free. I'd like to.

Before exploring the contents of my new book, I walk around to get closer to the water I hear in the background. A few hundred feet away and through a tuft of tall grass, I find the river. Part of me wants to get in, but it's shallow and muddy. There's no good place to sit, so I stand at the edge. It's calm, and the mountains beyond the scrubland are simply and quietly there. A storm still lingers ominously behind me. Would I be in it right now? Would I already be hooked, mind numbed and body deadened, with thunder shaking the window-panes? Would I be scared? What was Ghost going to do to me? I'm pretty sure I know, but—would I already be broken? It's warm, but I shiver. How close was I to not getting away?

But I'm not there, I'm here. *Breathe.* My thoughts pause, and the river's constant *shhhh* makes its way through my ears. The gentle breeze moves around me and quiets my stirring soul. My eyes open to the vast, empty scenery around me and within me.

Thank You, God, for guiding my feet away when You did, for giving me strength to fight. Thank you for Max and Maxine stopping when they did. Please stop Ghost and Longstoryshort. Break the machine they're a part of. Why is there such evil? Why can't it stop? Surely You can do something. I don't understand You or how You work, but I want to. Amen.

It feels good to sit in silence for a while. Bits and pieces of Max's talk about choices, rebellion, and armies of angels roll around in my settling mind. The sun goes behind a cloud, drawing my attention back to where I am. How long have I been out here? Suddenly worried, I head back to the picnic table. I don't want Max and Maxine to think I've run away. I open the Bible to the book of Matthew, the first place I find red ink.

I don't know what I'm looking for. Something relevant. Something I can understand. The first red ink is when Jesus is baptized and goes into the wilderness, where He's tempted by the devil. Mike and Lewis were talking about this Wednesday night after church.

The first sentence in red doesn't make sense to me, but I can relate to the second. It's in chapter four. "Man shall not live on bread alone, but on every word that comes from the mouth of God."

But what stands out more isn't what Jesus says, but what the devil says to him: "He will command his angels concerning you, and they will lift you up in their hands, so that you will not strike your foot against a stone."

That's familiar. The past few days are a blur, but I've heard that.

I can't place it at first, but then I read it again. My blood turns to ice when I realize it's what Longstoryshort quoted that first night.

Shake it off.

I keep reading, and a verse or two later, Jesus says, "Away from me, Satan!" I read it again. I repeat it out loud. I feel the power of those words. I close my eyes. The *shhhh* of the nearby river is still audible, and the air breathes new breaths onto my face.

I skip ahead. Chapter five is almost all red letters. "Blessed are the poor in spirit, for theirs is the kingdom of heaven. Blessed are those who mourn, for they will be comforted. Blessed are the meek, for they will inherit the earth."

I sure feel poor in spirit, but where is this kingdom of heaven? I mourn the reality of Ghost and Longstoryshort and their evil world, and I'm sure not comforted. And I had a coach tell me one time I'd never make it on the field because I was too meek. The strong ones always got the playing time.

I don't get it. I keep reading.

"Blessed are those who hunger and thirst for righteousness, for they will be filled."

I think of West's book, *9 Righteous*, and realize I don't even know what *righteousness* means, but it sounds good. How will my story end? Will I end up righteous? I want to. I want to be filled. Right now I'm empty. Empty of tears, empty of energy. Empty of the ability to think.

Part of me wants to be blessed, but it seems kind of meaningless, knowing there are people in an aboveground world being abused. I'd rather them be blessed than me.

Thoughts going nowhere, I try to read on. I don't know what I was expecting. Maybe something that felt like it was talking to me. I am the salt of the earth? I am the light of the world? I feel pretty bland, and my light is dim. It's like Jesus is talking to people who are leaders or something. I'm just a kid.

The next few pages have headings you'd expect to see in a religious book: Murder, Adultery, Divorce. Right, don't do that stuff. But I read it and it surprises me.

"You have heard that it was said to the people long ago, 'You shall not murder, and anyone who murders will be subject to judgment.' But I tell you that anyone who is angry with a brother or sister will be subject to judgment. . . . Anyone who says, 'You fool!' will be in danger of the fire of hell."

What? So being angry is the same as murder? Saying "You fool!" puts you in hell? I knew the virgin birth of Jesus was going to need some explanation, but I wasn't expecting Jesus's teachings to be confusing too! I read the next part on adultery.

"You have heard that it was said, 'You shall not commit adultery.' But I tell you that anyone who looks at a woman lustfully has already committed adultery with her in his heart."

The image of the man on the corner in Jackson undressing the women with his eyes flashes in my brain. The woman who was walking her dog, covering up because she thought I was doing the same. Mike's kid and the question about porn. It clicks. It's not about what's worse, porn or sex—it's about lust. Lust is the root of the problem. But the next lines seem extreme.

"If your right eye causes you to stumble, gouge it out and throw it away." I cringe, replaying my hand against Longstoryshort's face. "It is better for you to lose one part of your body than for your whole body to be thrown into hell. And if your right hand causes you to stumble, cut it off and throw it away. It is better for you to lose one part of your body than for your whole body to go into hell."

No one gave Mike *that* answer. Is Jesus really asking us to sacrifice parts of our body? The world would be full of people with one eye and one hand!

But Longstoryshort's world wouldn't exist. There wouldn't be a demand. *Demand.* Mike's kids. It hits me. Longstoryshort's malevolent world exists because there are people who do anything to satisfy their lust. Even if it means harming innocent people. My gut churns remembering that I wasn't the first kid Longstoryshort took to Grace's garage. The girl who was going to jump from the bridge. I feel sick as I remember him bragging that he got her a "job" and a "purpose." Or the twelve-year-old runaway . . . I try not to think about where they are now, what happened to them. How is this real?

As hard as it is to imagine, at some point Longstoryshort was an innocent kid, right? At some point, Ghost was too. The kids on the playground in Jackson Hole, the kids waiting for the school bus outside Little America. They're innocent. But the fruit of lust will be there. On the school bus. In the lunchroom. In their bedrooms. How many of them will become rapists, abusers, or just addicted to it? How many will become victims?

My stomach tightens again as I think about my friends back in Dallas who are already neck deep in sex and porn, acting like it's not a big deal. I never realized before how much of a big deal it is. "It doesn't hurt anyone" is always what I hear. But it's a part of the machine, and it *does* hurt people.

I wish it could all go away. Gouge out the eye, cut off the arm for a world without lust? It almost sounds worth it. In heaven, there won't be lust. But that doesn't seem very near. I don't want to think about this anymore. I read on.

Anyone who marries a divorced woman commits adultery? That doesn't make sense. Do not resist an evil person? Turn the other cheek? Love your *enemies*?! I feel myself getting angry. I can't love Longstoryshort. I won't! I was right for fighting back and running away. I thought God led me away! I was so sure about God in Montana. I was so sure about the cross. But this doesn't sound right; it can't be right.

The last verse in chapter five. "Be perfect, therefore, as your heavenly Father is perfect." *Perfect?* I can be good, but I don't know if I can be perfect!

Longstoryshort's last words to me ring and echo: *You'll never be good enough for God!*

I feel defeated. I thought I would read the Bible and be encouraged.

Expectations. Ha! It's the same feeling as finally making it to Montana and being welcomed by a billboard advertising mountains but finding nothing more than more rolling plains. I was so desperate for a Bible, but now that I have one open in front of me, I'm *dis*couraged.

"How far did you get?" Max interrupts my self-defeating thoughts from the door of the motor home. How long have I been out here?

"Chapter six."

"Different, isn't it?"

"Yeah." I don't want to let him down. "I don't know what I was expecting." Something to tell me what to do right now. A voice from heaven? *Right.* No, I just wanted something to be clear. Something to tell me everything will be okay.

"Do you have any questions?" He sits down with me.

I flip back through the pages, not knowing what to ask. "Do you have to not ever be angry or have lustful thoughts to be good enough for God?"

Max looks over my shoulder at the sea of red letters on the pages. "Oh," he says. "Sermon on the Mount."

I don't know what that means.

"Good place, but tough place to start."

"But that's where you told me to start—with the red ink!"

"I did, didn't I? I guess it's so familiar to me I forget how much it needs to be unpacked. To answer your question, no, you don't have to be perfect—"

"But Jesus says it plain and clear: *'be perfect'*!" I interrupt, pointing right to it.

Max holds his ground and starts where I cut him off. "You don't

198

have to be perfect, but you do have to allow *Him* to be perfect *in you*. Quite the difference."

I want to understand, but I don't. I'm trying hard to restrain my frustration.

"Redemption, God loves you the way you are—but He loves you too much to let you stay that way. He meets you where you are." Max lets his words have weight as he tries to get a read on me.

I want it to be true. I want to believe in the God I was so convinced of a few days ago. But I have so many questions. Why is there so much evil? How do I know what's true? Why is the Bible so confusing?

That's a good one. "If God wants everyone to know Him, why is the Bible so confusing?"

"There are a lot of ways to know God, and I get the feeling you two have already met. He speaks in many ways—Scripture is one of them, but it's a valuable and reliable way." Max pauses, then asks, "When you meet someone, do you know everything about them all at once?"

"No." He waits for me to say more. I don't.

"The more time you spend together, the more you learn about their history, and the more you get a sense of who they are. Right?"

"Yeah. And if you can trust them." I didn't mean to say that.

"Right! God has a long history and an immense personality. You can meet Him in a day, but even after a lifetime of walking with Him, you'll still find new things that amaze you. And the thing you'll see in the Old Testament, the New Testament, and even today is that He is the same then, now, and tomorrow."

I feel bad for asking, like I'm not believing or something, but Max seems to get me. "It's hard to believe some of it, and I don't know if I agree with what Jesus was saying."

"You're asking questions, and that's good. Never stop at the questions. Problems in the Scriptures are like speed bumps—they're supposed to make you slow down and pay attention to the scenery. You can either speed right past them, or you can stop and turn around. It takes courage to wrestle with God. Scripture is good at raising the questions worth grappling with. Put marks by them, and later, when you read back over them, you'll slow down and see things a little bit different—with new eyes and new knowledge."

"Does it all make sense to you?"

"Well . . ." Max takes some reading glasses out of his pocket and puts them on. "That's better," he says and pulls my Bible a little closer. "Have you ever had your eyes checked?"

What's that supposed to mean? "Yes?"

"Do you have human eyes?"

Of course. "Yes."

He nods. "There's the problem. I do too. But God has divine eyes, and He sees things very differently than we do. We can seek God kind of like an eye doctor—as we learn about Him and ask our questions, He slowly adjusts the lens we look through, and over time we see the world, Scripture, ourselves, and others more the way He does."

"So it will make more sense over time?"

"As long as you keep going back to it and keep getting your eyes checked, yeah. For now, keep doing what you're doing. Read it so you know what it says. So many Christians don't even know what their own book says. They keep looking at the world through their kiddie glasses."

"I wish I could just get it," I say.

"Some things you already do! Your hatred of evil, your desire for good. And more will come. I'm far from a scholar, but a lot of things make sense now that didn't when I was young in the faith."

"Max," Maxine calls from the motor home door. "Are you squeezing a thousand sermons into a single conversation again?"

"Yes, love," Max replies. "Would you like a helping hand with supper?"

"I would love a helping hand," Maxine answers. "Please send Redemption in." I laugh.

"You'd better go help her," Max whispers to me with a wink. "Thanks for trusting me enough to ask your questions."

I help Maxine in the kitchen, and I try to listen as she dotes grandmotherly wisdom on me, but my brain is full. It's already losing most of what Max and I talked about. I think back to Jackson, the day I was sitting in the seat of the scoffer. When I realized that, I learned I really didn't know what people were thinking or what their intentions were. I wanted them to be detestable, and they were.

I thought I knew what Longstoryshort was thinking and what his intentions were. I couldn't have been more wrong. I wanted him to be an admirable, rugged American individual, so that's what I saw. I was blinded by something *behind* my eyes, not in front of them.

I want to see things as they are. *I want Your eyes, God.* Can I handle what I'd see?

The room gets bright, too bright for my eyes, so I close them. But it's still blinding. Am I passing out? I'm not dizzy. Was that God? Nah, I must just be that tired. I smell smoke. Fire?

"Redemption!" Maxine's voice breaks through my thoughts, and I realize there's smoke coming from the pot I was supposed to be stirring. "That's okay," Maxine says. "Max likes his beans a little burnt. Here, let me see it. Will you carry the plates and napkins out?"

Before I know it, we're eating, and I'm vaguely aware that Maxine has taught me how to set the table properly.

"You overloaded him, Max. He's got the same look the other teenagers have after one of your sermons."

"It's okay," I say. "I'm just really tired. A lot has happened this week. I've got a lot to process, and everything he said is helpful. And the chicken is delicious. Thank you, Maxine."

I eat two suppers' worth, then help clean up. Max teaches me how to start a campfire as if I were one of his grandkids. Instructive but not bossy, helpful but not controlling. "Now, get low and give it some fuel. Blow on it. Gently, gently. A little more . . ." He can't help but jump up to celebrate when the flickers turn to flame. I'm a little proud myself.

The s'mores are sweet, sticky, and delicious next to the crackling warmth of the fire. Max and Maxine are full of joy, laughing at each other's messy white faces. They go inside to wash up, and I gaze into the dancing flames of the campfire, watching the embers' sustained glow. I think of my dream and try to picture Mom and Dad not burning, my friends and school uncharred, the Great Plains growing into fields, and me sitting here—on this side of the fire.

By the time the aged lovebirds come back hand in hand, I've licked all the sticky off my fingers twice. Maxine is carrying a lantern, and Max has his Bible. It must be devotional time.

"Are you familiar with devotionals?" Max asks.

"A little," I say, only knowing I've gotten books of them for Christmas, but I've never read them past January first. I don't know if I have room in my brain for any more input.

They talk a while about what "doing devotions" means to them as individuals and as a married couple. Then they help each other remember their favorite devotional books over the years, who they've given devotionals to, and who they've received them from. They read a passage from a book, then some from the Bible. I don't have much attention to devote, and my focus gets blurred. I can't follow the conversation, but the way Max and Maxine talk to each other about God lingers, dances, and spins with the crackling embers that spit out of the fire. Their voices become background noise, blending with an occasional sound from a neighboring RV and a continual chorus of evening insects.

More than any words they could have said to me, who Max and Maxine are is convincing. They have a testimony. I know, eventually, I'll probably need a philosophy on life and God all worked out, but right now all I need is to feel safe. To feel worthy of protection. And

I do.

The hushed and gentle pops of the fire take over as the conversation eventually dissipates like smoke upward into the night sky with prayer and a gentle "good night."

CHAPTER 13

FRIDAY: DINOSAUR NATIONAL MONUMENT, COLORADO

Waking up to the smell and sounds of bacon, I open my eyes and see Maxine dancing in the kitchen. Max is on the couch, reading and writing in a journal. I watch them for a few minutes. I can't picture them without each other.

I wonder what Grandpa was like before Grandma died. I only knew him afterward. He was sharp minded but always seemed to be looking for something lost. He moved slowly, not because he couldn't be quick, but because he was never in a hurry. Was Grandpa spry and active like Max when Grandma was alive?

The purpose of relationships is to make each other better people. That was his advice to me. I want to be old and happy like Max and Maxine. It wasn't too long ago I wanted to be a rugged lone wolf on a motorcycle, scraping by and exploring the world. I don't want to think about it. I don't even want to think his name.

"Good morning, sunshine!" Maxine proclaims to me.

"Good morning, Maxine."

We eat a hearty breakfast, and compared to their early-morning energy, I'm dragging. They chatter like squirrels over nuts and try to include me, but I'm physically, mentally, and spiritually exhausted. I feel like I've been hit by a bus and trampled by a herd of buffalo. Still no word from my mom.

"Are you ready to see some dinosaur bones?" Maxine asks excitedly.

I don't know what I'm ready for. I'm tired. All of me. "Yes."

We're not on the road for more than ten or fifteen minutes before we pull into a parking lot. I step out of the motor home and wait for Max and Maxine. We're surrounded by low, dust-colored, rocky desert mountains. We walk toward a small building with a roof shaped like a backward checkmark, like a valley rather than a peak. Max and Maxine swing their hands between them like a teenage couple, still in love. Maxine has me take their picture in front of a life-size replica of a stegosaurus, but I decline a picture of myself.

[Dinosaur National Monument Visitor Center]

Inside, Max strikes up a conversation with the young ranger. Maxine tells me we have to wait on a shuttle, then sits down on a nearby bench. I walk around, looking at the maps and pictures of the park and its history. Not knowing what I'm looking for, it just seems like information. I'm looking for that piece of God in me. Facts can't help.

I find myself standing in front of a visual demonstration of the twenty-three layers of rocks here, dating back to the Precambrian era—the beginnings of the earth. Millions and millions of years of limestone, sandstone, shale, conglomerate, and here we are on the surface of the present day. It's like looking at the vastness of the universe in reverse, investigating down instead of up. We really are a speck in the overall scheme of creation, a blink in the history of time.

"Shuttle's here!" Max calls and helps Maxine up.

An open-air shuttle awaits us and a few others. Max and Maxine are talking; they open their conversation to me a little but not enough to force a response. Max is excited about a book he bought.

The shuttle lets us out about a minute later at another building that's a larger and more interesting version of the visitor's center.

Three walls are made entirely of glass windows. The fourth wall is set against the side of a large rock formation, making it look like the building grew out of the rock and clung to it.

Inside, I see why it's been built the way it is. The rock has been carved back to reveal a concentrated trove of hundreds of fossilized dinosaur bones. A few dozen people mill around, taking pictures from the lower level and the balcony above. Several people wait in line near a place where you can touch the fossils. Considering the crowd, it is surprisingly silent. The glass walls offer a three-sided view of the brown mountains, breaking the panorama with bones that have turned to stone from another time, another world. We are present in a private scene of the past.

It's not like downtown Jackson Hole or Little America, where travelers are busy and distracted. It's more like a chapel. Why?

"Make yourself at home," Max says. "We'll stay as long as you like, and then we've got something special for you before we take you on to Denver."

I don't know if I can handle another surprise right now. A landslide of fear crumbles over me. "I don't need anything, but thank you."

What do I need? Answers? The right questions? A long hug from my granddad? Home? All of a sudden I feel guilty for making Max and Maxine change their plans so they can take me to Denver.

"I know I'm supposed to say 'thank you' instead of 'sorry,' but I can't help but feel bad that you're changing your plans because of me. If you were going to stay longer, I'm fine." I'm not fine, and I won't even be home in Denver. Another big question mark. I hope Mom or Dad will come get me.

Maxine brushes off the concern. "Don't you worry about us. We've been here a dozen times. Max got another copy of the book he lost, and we just planned on sitting around enjoying the silence for a while, remembering the good times we've spent in these rocks. Our days of camping, hiking, and rafting are behind us."

I take another picture of the gray lovebirds in front of the fossil wall and let them look around a bit. I sit on a bench along the back wall and try not to think. Here I am at an amazing place, and I can hardly enjoy it. Can a person enjoy anything when they realize they're not where they're supposed to be? I belong at home. I'm out of place here with these petrified bones. It's not their time. Their time has passed.

I don't want to miss any more of my time than I already have.

"You look like you're ready for the next step," Max says, touching me on the shoulder.

I lift my head from resting on my hands. "Sure."

We shuttle back to the RV and drive further into the desert rock hills for a few miles before pulling onto the wide shoulder on the other side of the road.

"This is your stop!" Max says, looking over and gesturing toward the door.

It catches me by surprise. My stop? In the desert? My gut drops. Did I do something to upset them? They seem so nonchalant about it. I don't move for a second, then grab my backpack with a hung head.

"Max, you can be so insensitive sometimes," Maxine scolds after looking back at me. "We're not abandoning you, hon. Come here."

She gets up from the passenger seat and meets me with a short, soft hug. I'm embarrassed that she saw me doubt them. Max follows, apologizes, and unfolds a map.

"Here we are," Max says, folding the map back to a simpler view. "Right at the head of the Sounds of Silence Trail. See how it meets up with the Desert Voices Trail? Take that over to Split Mountain, and we'll be at the picnic tables with lunch. Take as much time as you need. This is your surprise, and I think you will like it. Silence isn't silent at all. Take this map; it's hard to get lost if you know where you are."

"Thanks." It's all I can say.

I walk on the path through the desert bushes and tufts of grass toward diagonal rock protrusions cutting sharply out of the ground toward the sky. The sound of the motor home fades away, and around me, everything is immediately still and quiet, like time has paused and I'm walking through it. There isn't much magnificence to the landscape, which makes it easier to slip into thoughtlessness and let my feet do the roaming.

Yesterday doesn't seem to exist. Or the days before. Or the long drive. It feels like looking back at a book I remember reading. Denver and Dallas are dots on a map. I climb an upward-tilted rock formation, a sideways strata, and sit on a distant era. Nothing is moving. Time ceases to exist.

I close my eyes and watch a slow time-lapse come to life from the darkness behind my lids. Grandpa dying. The drive to Montana. Longstoryshort. Grace's garage. A fight by the highway cutting through the desert. Max and Maxine. My mom is crying. My friends are the same, and my girlfriend has moved on. This vision, waking dream, whatever it is, then focuses above me where I am, slowly zooming out to reveal how it is all connected, overlapping, and happening at the same time. A billion choices and a billion consequences in the framework of power lines and highways. Some good, some bad. Zooming out more, the earth and the current state of everything on it spins in space, revolving around the sun. Even further, the light from the burning star seems to swallow it all. Then, even the sun becomes an indecipherable speck in the galaxy.

You are where you are supposed to be.

A familiar high screech above me breaks the silence, and I look up and around. Another big bird like the one at Flaming Gorge soars on the high currents. I'm quickly aware of where I am. Where I'm supposed to be?

I yell at the sky, disagreeing with myself or God or whatever that voice was in my mind. "What do you mean, I'm supposed to be here?"

Silence.

A burning anger rises in me, and I don't know why.

I throw a rock. It plinks meaninglessly to rest a few dozen yards away. I scream. The silence swallows it. I try to unearth a rock to flip it over. It doesn't budge, so I kick it.

I think I broke my toe. It's time to go.

Walking on the side of my right foot, defeated, I limp around the long circular path, look at the map, and find where the Sound of Silence Trail cuts over to the Desert Voices Trail. I could use some voices other than my own right now.

This whole week has seemed like a dream. A lucid one that makes my life before seem like sleepwalking. I was taking up space but not filling it. I can't say I'm even awake now. I'm stuck in some sort of in-between. In this rocky desertscape, I'm hardly even sure I exist. Except I *know* I exist. Why? Because my bones will be in this layer of earth? Because my mind is having thoughts? Because I have feelings? Hurt and confused little-kid feelings.

I hobble, muttering decreasing nothings to the Desert Voices Trail. The path before me splits, and I have two to choose from. One is wide and flat, and the other disappears into some brush between growing rock formations. I don't know if it will make any difference, so I turn left into the hills because it looks like the short-er path. I'm ready to go. I'm not supposed to be here; I'm supposed to be home.

On the map, it looked straight, but in reality it's a winding path, zigzagging through the curves and cuts in a valley. The rocks rise on both sides, and desert plants huddle along a dry wash. I can't see beyond the steep slopes on either side and can't see too far ahead or behind. The sky is narrow and blue with the white sun looking down on me.

I don't hear any voices from the desert, but I'm not really listening. The silence is the same, but the vantage point couldn't be more different. On the rock a few minutes ago, I could see the long horizon in all directions. Now, the entire environment slopes toward me.

I find a rock to sit on and take off my shoe. There's no blood, just throbbing. It's probably not broken, but it sure hurts. My neck itches like someone or something is watching, but there's not a person or sound around. Just the sun, the mountains, and the prickly shrubs. A few days ago, the mountains stood for truth, and I would search my brain for the metaphor of me walking in it, but today I'm tired. I don't feel like writing in my journal, reading Grandpa's, or thumbing through the Bible. I want the truth, but I don't want to listen because I'm hurt and tired and empty. I don't need thoughts and ideas. I need healing and rest and . . .

What *do* I need? I need it all to go away. No. I need to keep moving. No. Getting somewhere quicker when you're lost doesn't solve anything.

I'm not lost. I know right where I am on the map. I don't know where I am in life. I know I'm going home, but that's just a place. It's a simple *where*. I need a map for the *how* and the *why*. Is that what the Bible is? I don't know how to read that map.

I breathe deep and try to quiet my mind again. It's like I'm trying to figure something out but I can't with all the chattering my brain is doing.

Silence.

Who are you?

Redemption Gray. High school senior, middle-class son of parents, Texan, escapee of a trafficking ploy. Average kid. Lost kid trying to get home. Sitter on a rock in a desert valley. It seems like I'm describing a character in a book. Is that all I am? Is God writing a story, and I'm just a character in it? How does it end for me?

"Who am I?" I shout into the valley.

"Who am I!" it shouts back.

211

A bush on the other side of the gulley catches my eye; it seems to be on fire. I'd better put that out before I'm caught in a wildfire. I put my shoe back on and jog to the plant, only to find an aluminum can reflecting the sunlight.

I continue on the path. The back-and-forth reminds me of the labyrinth. Am I going inward to God or outward to the world at this point? Or just walking? Truth could be close, but I'm not really looking. I hear Grandpa saying, "If it were a snake, it would've bit you!" Snakes. I'd better pay more attention.

I'm relaxed now and well aware that my toe has taken the pain from my ear. I decide to listen carefully for the voices of the desert instead of hurrying to the end, but all I hear is silence. And the humming of existence. And my footsteps on the pebbles and hard ground.

I think back to the long drive up the Great Plains, settling into the silence and hearing the humming of my own existence. How I found clarity in the silence. And from paying attention. I thought I found who I was, or at least who I was supposed to be. Maybe there's more of me to find, more of who I'm supposed to be.

It'd be nice to have answers again instead of these unending questions.

The trail ends on a road leading to a boat ramp next to a brown river. Children are laughing in the distance. Shouldn't they be in school? Maybe they're homeschooled. Max and Maxine's motor home is parked to the right, near some covered picnic tables. Maxine sees me and waves, then they both get up to welcome me.

"You're limping!" Maxine says with concern.

"Did you wrestle with God?" Max asks.

"No, I stubbed my toe. It's nothing." I don't want to worry them.

"Are you hungry?" Max asks, inviting me to the table. I am.

We eat, and I feel like they were expecting me to have some grand revelation, but they don't push or interrogate me. I'm glad because I don't have any more answers now than I did before.

We clean up, then get the RV ready for the highway.

"There's one more place here we like to stop at," Max says. "Would you mind? We'll still make it to Denver by evening." Another stop? Is Denver that far away? Is it that close? What will I do when I get there?

"I'm just here for the ride," I say. Do I mind? I do, but I don't. I'm comfortable with Max and Maxine, stalled in time in a safe place. But I can't stay here.

Back up the road and halfway to the visitor's center, we pull over and park.

[Swelter Shelter Petroglyphs and Pictographs]

We join a dozen or so people walking around a group of rocks, quietly observing drawings Natives drew hundreds of years ago. More pieces of history. There's one of a lizard. On the far side of the rock, I find a drawing of a group of square-bodied people, some with horns on their heads. Another shows several clusters of people, some huddling and bowing to a larger person. Another looks like he's teaching with his oversized hands attached to wavy arms. One looks like an alien with large head. There is a long-necked cat, a possible dog, a star, and some random wavy lines. One figure looks like it's fighting one of the horned beings—a buffalo man? The devil? A few with horns lurk on the perimeter, and there's one featureless figure that looks like it's lying there dead.

They were drawing their life. Their world. It wasn't realistic or even idealistic. They simply made an image of their world as it was. Smart characters, powerful ones, ones that lead, and ones who follow. Evil was present among them. One was willing to stand against it and fight. Another one died. Some images, you can't tell if they're human or animal.

I keep walking until another picture draws me in. There's a smaller person beside a larger, detailed one, standing front and center.

Other than a buffalo and a faint figure with a bag or a mask over his devil-horned head in the background, there are a few scattered circles and a random, floating stick-arm. The larger character is dressed in lines of power and wisdom and is holding a detailed round object with spots in it, like maybe it's the solar system or the night sky. I try to figure out what it means, what it symbolizes, why I feel a connection to it, but I'm stumped. Something about it draws me, and I somehow relate to the smaller character next to the one holding the universe. Maybe it's because it looks like he's shrugging his shoulders.

I pull out my notebook and begin copying the drawing.

Max walks up beside me. "That one's my favorite," he says, "but I can't tell you why."

He waits while I finish the drawing. Together, we complete the loop through the area.

"Ready to go home?" he asks.

"Yeah." *More than you know.*

The drive from Dinosaur National Monument toward the mountains and away from the ever-present, unmoving storm behind quickly becomes a blur. It's as if my brain, my body, and my soul can only take so much. Thoughts come and go like the towns, and people become pictographs with square bodies and no faces. Trees turn into formless seas of green, and the highway becomes an eternal ribbon of asphalt under our wheels. I take notice of dark clouds behind the white mountains but apply no metaphor. Everything just is. Nothing isn't. I slip in and out of naps while Max eats almonds and plays on branches of thought with Maxine.

They check on me regularly, making sure I'm not hungry or thirsty, letting me know how many more hours . . . as if I'm looking forward to being somewhere else. Time becomes a long tunnel boring through the mountain as the engine works hard in a long, slow climb.

At some point, the careful incline becomes a delicate decline, the engine gets a break, and the brakes fight gravity in the opposite direction.

We pull off in a town nestled below the highway between two cliffs. I can't see the sun, but if I had to guess, I'd say it's close to sunset. That or we're deep in the shadows.

I get out to help Max check the engine, brakes, and levels of fluid and air. Well, I stand there wanting to listen as he teaches what everything does, but it makes me think of the last person who talked to me about machines and how they work. I don't mean to, but I shut him out and become anxious about leaving them. Our paths split tonight. Where will I go? How will I get home?

Over dinner in a family-run cafe, Max lets me know we're about an hour from Golden, where they're staying the night, and that he can drive me to wherever I'm going in Denver. They think I have a place and a plan. I try to show thankfulness and happiness that I'm almost there, but I can't. I don't know where I'm going or what I'm doing next. Maxine senses my trouble and confronts me.

"You're picking at your food, Redemption. What's on your mind?"

Do I tell them I don't have a plan? What will they do, take me to the police on a Friday night? If I'm reported missing, will they arrange a way for me to get home, or will I have to stay locked up in a cold police room? What if my mom reported the car stolen? Why haven't they called back?

"I—" I hesitate. "I don't think anyone is expecting me." It's not a lie.

They both analyze the not-a-lie.

"Would you like to stay with us another night and figure it out in the morning?" Max suggests.

A rockslide of relief. I don't have to have it all together tonight.

"Would that be okay?"

"We'd be delighted for another night," Maxine says.

"And I've got a great idea for tomorrow morning's devotional," Max adds. "Maxine, do we still have those pans and buckets?"

Maxine smiles like she doesn't quite understand what he's getting at but is familiar with his shenanigans. "We don't pass through here without them."

A quick hour downhill and we emerge from the mountains to the edge of a flattened-out ocean of streetlights and distant skyscrapers. Maxine is giving directions, and Max pulls in at another parking lot to look at the map for himself. In no time, we're checking in and hooking up in an RV park that is basically the same setup as Jensen—a narrow space with a picnic table—except this one is packed with fancy RVs and motor homes, has lights strung, and is alive with festive people walking, talking, and having a good time.

Max tells me I can walk around if I want, for as long as I want, or I can stay and make s'mores in the microwave with them. I could use a little more alone time, so I decide to explore.

A man and a woman are arguing outside the RV next to us. He sounds drunk, and she has a pleading sound in her voice. He slams the door and leaves her crying on the picnic table. She looks up and sees me looking at her, leaves the lantern burning dimly on the table, and goes inside. She just wants to be loved.

The next couple of RVs are quiet, but there's a family laughing and playing a card game beside a healthy, crackling campfire at the next. Part of me wants to join them. In the past or in the future, but not now. My brain is overpacked with thoughts, my soul a knot of emotions. My feet carry me on.

The flame is native in all of us. Is that it? Why did I dream that my house was burning? Layers of earth. History of the world. Nothing new. Evil. The petroglyph of the man fighting the devil. Was the horned man trying to hook and break the other? Am I just living out a story that's been going on for ages? How do I make it stop?

A loud engine revs behind me, and I turn to look and get out of the way. It's a black motorcycle with a man wearing a matte-black helmet. Without thinking, I jump out of my skin and run. Between some RVs, through a playground, and over a fence. Was that Longstory-short? Surely not. Could he have been tracking me this whole time? It can't be him. I'm breathing hard. My heart is in my throat. It could *not* have been him, I reason with myself. This guy was taller, I tell myself.

But if God knows where we are at all times, does the devil?

I take no risk and edge around the fence to a river behind some trees. I don't like hiding. I feel like a shivering coward, but I don't know what else to do. Curled in the darkest shadow in a curved trunk, I wait for my heartbeat to slow down and normal breathing to return. I want to cry. Ashamedly, I do.

It takes a few minutes, but I manage to get myself back under control. Finally, mustering the tiniest bit of courage—all that I have—I follow the water behind the tree line and back into the RV park. I stay hidden and alert with my eyes peeled. There's no sign of him, no engine.

I find Max and Maxine's motor home, look both ways, and listen hard before sprinting across the pavement to their door.

I open the door and try to enter like nothing is wrong, but Maxine jumps up. "Redemption," she cries. "You look like you've seen the devil!" I don't argue as she gives me a grandmotherly hug.

Still trying not to cry, my body trembles, and I'm weak at the knees. Maxine leads me to the couch next to Max and sits across from me. Both lean in, looking at me, waiting on me. I feel like I'm going to throw up.

We wait in silence for a good while. Max and Maxine's attention is still focused and patient. What do I say? That the devil is after me on a motorcycle? That I drove away from school and wrecked my dad's car? That I was walking willingly into my own kidnapping? I'd sound crazy. I'd sound stupid.

Are they going to outwait me? What do they want me to say? I try, but nothing comes out.

"You don't have to say anything." Max finally breaks the silence.

I can breathe. Why can't I speak?

I can tell them, I can. But I've shoved it all in a box. I don't want to open it. I don't know what will come out. Or even what all is in it. Max pats me on the shoulder reassuringly. They know something's up. Of course they do.

"How do you shake the devil?" comes out of my mouth.

Maxine looks concerned and waits for Max to put words to an answer.

"That's a good question." He thinks about it.

"Redemption," Max finally says, "we can't sit here and pretend like you're not in trouble." Oh, no. They think I'm a fugitive. "Now, I don't think you're in trouble with the law, and it would surprise me if you were. But something happened that put you in this situation, and I'm glad you've landed with us. Someone is after you. Either out there or in your mind or in your soul. Maybe all three. It's not as rare as you'd imagine." It isn't? I can't look at him.

"I don't think you have a plan after you leave us, and I don't estimate you have a place to go in Denver. I may be wrong." *You're not.* "Now, we can't keep you forever, but we can help you figure out the next steps. In the next day or two, we can get ahold of your parents or go to the police to help you sort it out. Eventually, you're going to have to face whatever has happened in order to get to where you need to go. Otherwise, you'll be running *from* something all your life instead of *toward* something. Understand?"

"Yes sir," I answer. "Thank you."

Max looks at me thoughtfully for a second. "Do you know who Moses was, Redemption? In the Bible?"

"Uh, kind of. Something about Egypt and the Red Sea?"

"Yeah, that guy. Did you know for a big part of his life, Moses was a man on the run?" *He was?* "He got in big trouble in Egypt and ran away to live in exile. He went from being a prince to tending sheep in the desert. But he couldn't run away from God. God had plans for him. He was going to use Moses to bring the Israelites out of the suffering they were enduring in Egypt. Maxine, honey. Would you read the first part of Exodus three for us?"

Maxine reaches over to pick up her Bible from the counter, flips a few pages, and starts reading. I listen closely as she reads about Moses watching the sheep and seeing a burning bush but it wasn't being burned up. A voice came from it, calling him by name. Moses answered, "Here I am," but he was afraid to look at the fire.

Maxine looks up. I'm still listening and actually following along. She smiles and says, "Verse seven," and continues to read. Phrases keep standing out: "'I have indeed seen the misery of my people' . . . 'I have heard them crying out'. . . . 'I have come down to rescue them' . . . 'So now, go. I am sending you'. . . 'I will be with you' . . ." It's like what Max was talking about earlier. God does care about the victims, the people who are being hurt. God does send help and is involved with what's happening down here.

Maxine stops and looks up again. I realize I got distracted with my own thoughts. She smiles and looks at Max. Max smiles and looks at me.

What did I miss?

"I see a lot of Moses in you, Redemption," Max says. "God can make a difference through you."

"Me? I'm no leader," I say, almost automatically. "No one would listen to me."

Maxine giggles. "Moses said the same thing. Right here, look." She points to the page. "Chapter four, verse one: Moses said, 'What if they don't believe me or listen to me—'"

Max peers over her shoulder and says, "Read verse ten too."

"'Pardon your servant, Lord,'" Maxine continues. "'I am slow of

219

speech and tongue.'"

"I guess it does sound like me."

"But listen to God's promise in verse twelve," Maxine instructs. "'Now go, I will help you speak, and will teach you what to say.'"

"I appreciate the encouragement," I say, "but there are a lot more people out there that could do a lot more for God than me."

Max touches the page and laughs. "Hang on, Redemption. Look at what Moses says in the next verse. 'Please send someone else.'"

Their lightheartedness is refreshing, but the weight of the topic is a little terrifying. My face turns to stone, and my caretakers must notice. Max looks at me wisely.

"Do you know why God chose Moses and not someone else for the job?"

I shake my head.

"Because God knew Moses would have to lean on Him for guidance and instruction to get the job done. And that's why He's choosing you too. He knows you'll rely on Him to do the work, to guide your feet, to give you the words."

"But—but I hardly know God!" I protest.

"Do you know Him enough to seek Him?"

"I believe He's there, but that's about it."

"That's what He's looking for. Other people think they know more than they do, and it gets in their way. Some people see evil and spend the rest of their lives running away from it. A lot of people hide in the walls of the church and hope God will do something, but they sure don't want Him to require anything from them in the process. True Christians aren't afraid to face evil, resist it, and speak truth to it. A disciple of Jesus will run to the fire and through it instead of away from it."

I didn't tell them about my dreams, did I?

"Max, you're getting preachy," Maxine says. "Redemption, awful things happen all the time. You're going to have a choice. You can ignore it, hide it, and run from it for the rest of your life, or you can face it with prayer and petition and move on into the life God wants for you."

She stands up and squeezes my shoulders in another grandmotherly hug. "We never had those s'mores. Would you like one?"

"No, thank you."

"It's always a good time to pray," Max says. And then Max and Maxine each put a hand on my shoulders and pray specifically for me.

"God, our Father, we thank You for this day and this chance to serve You. We thank You for Redemption, the person and the offer of new life. Thank You for sending him into our hands. Let us be an example of Jesus's reality in love and wisdom. Thank You for your Scriptures, for letting us see Your relationship with us through them, even as imperfect and incompetent as we sometimes are. Help us to seek You, to lean on You and not our own understanding. Be with Redemption as he figures things out. Speak to him in every way he will listen. Open his ears and his eyes to Your calling. Protect him from evil, guard his heart and his mind. Make all things that are true, evident and attainable to his open mind. Guide his feet, renew his soul. Tonight, tomorrow, and forever. In Jesus's name"—Maxine joins her voice in unison as they squeeze my shoulders—"amen."

They let go, and I open my eyes, not sure how to respond. Max grins, then lets out a giant yawn.

"Well, it's getting past this old man's bedtime. Do you need anything?"

I don't know what I need, but the devotional and prayer helped. Max hands me a new set of clothes.

"Get some rest," he says with a little dance. "I've got something fun planned for the morning."

Maxine rolls her eyes and says to me, "I swear he's a kid in an old man's body." She kisses me on the forehead, flips the furniture to make my bed, and spreads out the long, heavy comforter. "Good night, Redemption. Sleep well."

I do.

CHAPTER 14

SATURDAY MORNING: GOLDEN, COLORADO

Maxine wakes me up with a heaping plate of breakfast. Max is already outside, rummaging around under the RV. The sky is blue from the window. I don't know if this is my last day with them. I don't know what I'm going to do or how I'm going to get home. I don't know what will happen today. Will I ever?

I think back to the routines of my life before this trip.

7:30 a.m.—Wake up.

7:45 a.m.—Head to school.

7:50 a.m.—Sit in my tree in front of the school.

7:59 a.m.—The minute bell rings, run to class.

8:00 to noon—English, US History, Chemistry, Theater

Lunch

12:30 to 3:30—Pre-Calc, Spanish, Art

After that, make out with my girlfriend, ride home with Dad, do homework, sit in my room on my phone, eat, sit in my room on my phone, go to bed.

Do it all over again.

Life was stable, predictable, and stagnant. Grandpa's dying changed the routine. I think knowing he was there was part of the stability. Even though I knew he was sick, someone dying isn't predictable. Stagnant was comfortable, but it wasn't enough. Classes were always the same—I knew what was coming. But the framework of my routine world wasn't based on anything. When Grandpa died, all of a sudden, none of it was important. None of it was safe. Predictability was my paper castle, and I was a miserable king. I thought I knew what would happen next, but I didn't.

Maybe that's why the drive to Montana was so eye opening. I never knew what would be next. I didn't know what I was looking for, but I was searching. I don't remember ever feeling so alive, even though I was grappling with death. Maybe it's *because* I was grappling with death. Even now, while I'm terrified about the unknowns of today, I'm free from the illusion that I know what's going to happen next.

But the danger is real. I can't trust everything and everyone. I almost ended up drugged in a hotel room and broken. I was lucky to get away.

No, that wasn't luck. I made a choice. I didn't wait to see what would happen—I ran. I put up a fight. But none of it really seemed like me. Except for saying, *Lord, guide my feet,* it's mostly a blur. Bits and pieces flicker through my brain as I relive it. Max and Maxine just happened to pull up, right? What would have happened if they didn't? Of all the possibilities of the ways that day could have played out, how did I end up in good hands? Was it God? It had to be.

Where will I end up today?

Maxine takes my empty plate, and I help her clean up. My time with Max and Maxine is coming to an end; I can feel it. Not like I've overstayed my welcome, but like if I could stay longer, I would. And I need to keep moving. I have this faith that I'm going to make it home.

Faith. What is faith? Knowing even though you don't know? Blind hope?

"Maxine?"

"Yes, dear?"

"What's faith?"

She answers like she's answering a trivia question. "Faith is the substance of things hoped for, the evidence of things not seen."

"What does that mean?"

She's quiet for a moment, putting books in a deep grandma purse. "You're making me think again about what I already know. Let me see . . . You're going home, right?"

"Yes ma'am."

"That makes me happy. Now, how do you know your home is still there?"

It was there when I left. I think of my fire dream, and my stomach drops. What if it's not there?

"I guess I'm counting on it being there."

"Right. You're acting on hope. And I'm sure you're hoping that you'll be welcomed home with open arms."

I disappeared with Dad's car, wrecked and abandoned it, and missed Grandpa's funeral.

"I don't know that they'll be happy, and I'll probably be grounded all summer"—and working to buy Dad a new car—"but it'll be worth it."

"Can you know for sure?"

I guess not. "No ma'am."

She nods. "That's faith. You can't *know* it, but you act on it. Your action is evidence of something existing that can't be seen. Your hope is guiding you toward what you hope for. That's faith."

I always picture those big churches with full bands playing and people with their hands in the air when I hear the word "faith." I did a faith fall one time from a table into some other kids' arms, but they dropped me. Maxine's explanation is a little clearer. But what if my house really isn't there? What if it really did burn down? What if what we hope for and act toward is wrong? I try to ignore the anxiety that's testing my faith.

Maxine slides on a pair of sunglasses and pats my shoulder. "Have fun," she says and walks out the door to the picnic table with her bag of books.

Max tosses a couple of buckets, some rubber pants, and some funny-shaped mixing bowls in the side door, then walks around to the driver's seat.

"Ready?" he asks and motions me toward the passenger seat.

For what? *Whatever is next.* "Yes."

We pull out of the RV park and through a bustling little town with a park full of kids, a farmers market, and streets full of shops and shoppers, dog walkers, and strollers.

We drive back toward the mountains we came down from last night, but it's new from the passenger seat with daylight. The road winds beside a river that cuts the valley between the steep rocky mountainside. We drive through a few tunnels.

We talk a little about gold mining and how it was a big deal in this area. Then Max glances my way. "I've been thinking a lot about some of the questions you've been asking," he says.

I don't remember what questions I've asked. I have so many, and I'm not sure I've paid attention to any of the answers he's given. "Which ones?"

"Mainly about all the different perspectives you have and will come across in your search for truth. But also about why the devil would be afraid of fire, which is actually related to how you get rid of him."

I wait for answers, intentionally paying attention, but he's silent. He's just driving with a contented smile.

Finally, we turn around in a town and head back down the same road we came up on. Maybe he's showing me the answers. What could it mean to drive up a mountain just to come back down? How does that relate to perspectives and the search for truth?

"Why did we go up the mountain just to come right back down?" I ask, hoping for clarity.

"Oh, there was no room to turn around on the road," he answers. He slows down, pulls over, and parks on a short but wide rocky shoulder next to the river. He turns off the motor, then goes to the back of the RV.

He hands me a sweatshirt and a pair of the rubber pants with suspenders, then grabs the same gear for himself. We put them on, and Max hands me a bucket and two mixing bowls. But they are not mixing bowls. They're thick, hard, rubber discs that are about five inches deep. They're wide on the outside with a long slope to a small flat circle for a bottom. They have grooves like steps along one side and are smooth the rest of the way around.

Outside the motor home, cars whiz by both ways, and I wonder if they wonder at the beauty or if they're used to it and are annoyed that it slows them down on their way to work. It looks like the beer commercials you see with a clean river dancing down the rocky mountains, but without the beer.

I follow Max to the riverbank and heed his instruction to be careful stepping down the boulders to the water's edge. There are rocks the size of two of me resting in the river as the water passes quickly but not forcefully around them.

"Have you ever panned for gold?" Max asks.

"Nope," I say confidently.

"Are you sure about that?" Max's smile looks like he's up to something. "So what you're going to do is look for the slow spots—behind rocks, around the bend. Where the river slows, the heavier elements drop." His feet are in the water, and he's bending down with the pan on the slow side of a jagged black boulder.

I get in the water too. The silt beneath my rubber feet stirs, and the water sparkles.

"Is that gold in the dirt?" I ask.

"Sure is!" Max says like an excited kid. "We'll take a bucket of it home to pan out, but right now we're looking for little flakes big enough to be proud of. The biggest I've gotten here was about the size of my fingernail." He holds up his pinky. "But the real thrill is in the search."

He teaches me a few methods of panning. Spin the water out of the pan, shake the rocks and sediment, and dig through it with your fingers. I can do this. "Always face the light when you're looking for gold. Go on, try it. Remember: slower water, face the sun, have fun!"

I find a striated boulder ten yards or so downriver and sit on a pink granite rock reaching into the cold water from the edge. The constant *hush* of the river is loud enough to make me quickly forget the passing cars above the bank as the steady flow and changing ripples relax me.

I dip the pan deep into the dirt and swirl it, shake it, and finger through it. Max is already in his own world. It doesn't take me long, either. I don't know what I'm doing, but the repetition is meditative and the cold water keeps me from slipping into a daze. Dip the pan, swirl it, shake it. Dip the pan, swirl it, shake it. Dip the pan . . .

I'm enjoying the motions so much I almost forget I'm looking for gold.

Stretching my back, I'm not sure how much time has passed. Ten minutes? Thirty? I used to be so obsessed with time. Max is upriver a little now, bending down and standing up, sorting sediment, bending down and standing up like a repetitive prayer. He sees me and waves with a wide grin.

I walk carefully into the river toward a bend on the other side. The water should slow down there, I think. I get to the other bank and step around the corner, but someone else is already there. He's in rubber pants over overalls, probably in his midfifties with gray stubble, thick tan skin, and wiry hair stuffed under a tattered straw cowboy hat.

"Howdy," he says with a friendly but almost crazy joy in his eye. He's got a pan in his hand, too, looking where the water slows down.

He looks like he could have been out here for decades. He loves the search. I wonder how much gold he's found. I wonder what he does with it. I decide to leave him be and wade sure-footed through the clear, glistening flow back to a speckled boulder shaped like the rear half of a Volkswagen Bug. It's cut right down the middle. Where's the other half?

I lean against the flat part with my back to Max and my face to the sun, bend down, and scoop up a mix of water, dirt, and rocks. Spinning and sifting, spinning and sifting. Sorting and spilling, sorting and spilling. On what must have been the hundredth scoop, I realize how happy I am. Is it because of the rugged mountains, tall green trees, and the calming rush of the crystalline water? Is it because I don't have to think about where I've been and what's next? I'm able to be where I am, no responsibilities, no fears, no conflict. I'm just panning for gold. But I can't stay here forever like the man around the bend. I'll have to reenter reality soon. I could be back in school next week! But I don't have to be the same person and live the same life I was when I get there. It can be new. *I can be new.* A glitter in my pan catches my eye, and I almost lose it as I jump up in excitement.

It looks like a flake of pollen and stands out bright yellow against the dark silt, reflecting the light as I tilt it toward the sun. I fish around for it, and it sticks to my finger. I shake it off into the second pan I had set on top of the boulder. It's only about a fourth of the size of my pinky nail, but I found gold!

A new fever of energy takes over, and I'm finding flakes every few scoops. Now that I know what I'm looking for, I've modified my swirling and shaking to make the flakes stand out. The sun helps. I could do this all day.

After another immeasurable while, when my arm starts to cramp, I assess my findings. I've got about thirty small flakes like the first one, two the size of my pinky nail, and a few quartz crystals too.

Max is sitting on a boulder out of the water, taking in the scenery. I can't wait to show him. Scooping down a few more one-more-times, a big black rock flips over in my pan and reflects a yellow chunk bigger than my thumbnail. That'll do!

I slosh upriver to Max with a big grin.

"Well? What did you find?" Max asks.

I hand him my pan, proud and waiting for his approval. He laughs a boisterous laugh, leaning back and returning forward. It must be the big one that got him.

"How much do you think it's worth?" I ask.

"Not enough to get rich on," he says, "but we've had a rich experience, haven't we?"

"Yeah, thanks for bringing me out here. Did you find any?"

"A little," he says, not showing it off. Is he embarrassed that I found more than him? I peek into his pan and see some darker flakes and a few small, round dark-gold pebbles.

"Is that gold?" I ask.

"Just a little."

"Why does it look so different from mine?"

He holds a thinking face with a smile. "I don't know how to tell you, but you've panned out a good dose of paint chips."

I don't believe it. "Paint chips? In the river?"

"Every once in a while, the river floods with snow melt and wipes out the highway. That's the yellow paint from the highway stripes. You did a great job of finding it, though!"

But what about the big one stuck on the rock? I flip it over, and sure enough, it's tar and gravel pavement. I'm embarrassed.

"How about I give you ten dollars for your findings?"

I'm disappointed and almost ashamed of my waste of time. "That wouldn't be right. It's not worth that."

Max pushes back. "I think it's the buyer that determines the value. Plus, it makes a great metaphor."

I wait for his metaphor, but he leaves it at that. We fill the buckets with river mud and let it settle while we take off our rubber pants. Then we pour off the water from the tops of the buckets.

"There'll be some gold in here, I'm almost certain," Max says. "I guess it would have helped if I'd shown you what to look for!"

We drive back down the mountain, passing a few more wide shoulder areas with cars parked and people in the river panning and fly fishing.

Max starts putting thoughts into words. "Searching for truth is a lot like panning for gold. I guess first of all, you need to know what truth looks like; otherwise, you'll end up with a collection of yellow road paint." I'm still embarrassed, but listening.

"There are so many philosophies, perspectives, and ideas out there. Some are good, some adequate, some deceptive, and some outright wrong. There is so much of it in the world that the truth can be hard to find. So you've got to search for it, sort it out.

"But you have to know where to search. Just like we did, you have to go where the river slows down. Life goes by so fast, you have to slow it down as much as you can. What is heavy with truth will drop out of the current, and the thoughts with less weight will flow on."

The silence of being alone in the car. Sitting on the river in Livingston. Walking the trails at Dinosaur Monument. Standing in the river panning for gold. Slow it down.

"Once you're in the spot where life slows down, you'll still have some mud to sort through. Learn its properties, sift and sort, hold it to the light. Truth will always reflect the light."

He waits for me to think about it.

"So," I say, "Christians are like gold and the rest of the religions and people who don't believe in Jesus are worthless?"

He makes a face like I said something he wasn't expecting.

"God gave all people worth when He made them. He'll pay ten

dollars for a paint chip of a person easily. Every person is of equal value to God, and He wants to purchase *all* of us back if we'll let Him. But not all *ideas* are equal. We're talking about truth. Christianity is a religion, and even Christians aren't immune to walking around with paint chips thinking they've got gold. Jesus is the light of the world. True ideas will reflect Jesus. Put His words to the test, and you'll reflect Jesus too. Cherish His truths in your heart, separate them from the muck, and others will recognize the value. If the goal is value, gold is the standard."

"But. . ." I don't know what I'm arguing. "It just seems so easy to say Jesus is the answer." Like my Sunday school class.

"It is easy to say," Max agrees. "But it's not so easy to know what you mean by it. We need more people like you who are willing to pan it out."

"Can't you just explain it?"

Max is looking for words as we pull in under a stone arch entry that leads into the quaint, lively downtown.

[Welcome to Golden—Where the West Lives]

Did I stump him?

"So when we get back," Max finally answers, "take my gold and show it to Maxine. Tell her it's yours."

Why would I do that? "But it's not mine," I respond.

"Neither are you."

Huh? "What do you mean?"

"That's my explanation."

"Of what?" I've forgotten what the question was.

"Of Jesus. Truth. Christianity."

"I am not mine?"

"Yep."

Max is enjoying this. I think I'm starting to get it. "I'm God's."

"Yep. What else?"

"My life is not my own anymore. I gave that up at the cross."

He nods. "And now you have something beyond valuable, what He intended from the beginning."

Words from a hymn on that last night in Jackson pop into my mind. "I will cling to that old rugged cross, and exchange it someday for a crown." This is the most valuable I've felt in a long time. Max is grinning, either proud of his metaphor or that I'm catching on.

We hang a right at a light and drive by the police station, city hall, library, history museum, and back by the now-crowded farmers market and family-packed park. Golden is busy with people but not aggressive like Jackson. Or was that just my perception?

We pull into our space, where Maxine is still reading at the picnic table. She doesn't look up until after we've hooked the motor home back up and sit with her.

Her voice is content and loving. "Have you had a nice morning?"

"Yes ma'am."

"It was perfect." Max kisses her forehead. "What did we miss here?"

"Well, you missed a wonderful morning devotional," Maxine answers, "and if I don't get started on lunch soon, you'll miss that too."

Is it already lunchtime? The sun is right above us. Where did time go? Downstream. We were in the slower water.

"Wait a second," Max says as Maxine starts packing her bag full of books again. "I want to show you what we've found." I feel myself blush.

Max hops into the motor home, but instead of bringing out just his real gold, he brings back a green rubber pan with both of our findings mixed together. Maxine inspects our efforts.

"I see you found some paint chips along with your gold," she says. "Reminds me of our first time out here, decades ago." She grins at Max, and he blushes. "Redemption, the first time I brought Max panning for gold, we were out there almost all day. When we finally came back together, he was so cute and proud of his pan full of gold. You should have seen his face when I told him it was all paint chips!"

So Max made the same mistake! I don't feel so dumb now!

"You did the same thing I did?" I laugh a laugh I haven't known in years. Max and Maxine laugh with me.

"And now that they're next to each other," Max says to me, "it's easy to tell them apart, isn't it? We all have to start somewhere!"

I volunteer to help Maxine with lunch, but she says we should make up for missing the devotional time. Devotion. I like the idea, and I'd like to say I'm going to start doing them. It seems like a good way to break the routine of life and start out with a reminder that there is a deeper purpose, that wisdom is a good guide for the search.

Max and I walk over to a bench at the tree line that separates the RV park from the river. It has to be the same river we were panning for gold in. The bench reminds me of the one in Jackson, the way it sits under a tree in front of an opening to the water.

"Let's read Matthew 3:11," Max says, then waits patiently as I pull the Bible out of my backpack and find the verse. It takes a while. Max starts talking.

"This verse is about baptism. Baptism had a big significance to people in Jesus's time, not only as a symbolic cleansing but also as a sign that they were joining the fight for God's good kingdom. John the Baptist was preaching about the kingdom of heaven and stirring up a lot of anticipation. Things were changing. Would you like to read?"

"Sure," I say. "But I'm not a very good reader."

"You only get better with practice. Matthew 3:11," he reminds me.

"'I baptize you with water for repentance. But after me comes one who is more powerful than I, whose sandals I am not worthy to carry. He will baptize you with the Holy Spirit and fire.'"

"Glance ahead. Who is it that is coming after John the Baptist?"

I read the headings. The Baptism of Jesus; Jesus Is Tested in the Wilderness; Jesus Begins to Preach. "Jesus?" I say it in a weird, unsure Sunday school voice.

"Right. John the Baptist recognizes that, while he is a man, Jesus is God in the flesh. John baptized in a human way, with water. How does he say Jesus will baptize?"

I look back. "With the Holy Spirit and fire?"

"Yep. Now hold that thought. So, you know that gold we searched for, found, and sorted out?"

"Yeah?"

"Is it pure? I mean, we worked hard for it. Is everything we brought back pure gold?"

"No." I don't see where he's going.

"You're right. There's only one way to purify gold. Nothing that we did today could do that."

"Then how do you make it pure?" I ask without really thinking about it.

"It has to go through the fire."

"You burn it?" I think about that for a minute. "I don't get it."

"To get rid of impurities in gold, you put it in a crucible and hold it over the fire. As it heats up, it melts, and anything that isn't pure gold will rise to the top. Then you can remove it.

"Well, as you read about Jesus, you'll notice He's always talking about the 'kingdom of God,' or the 'kingdom of heaven.' A lot of people miss the point and think He's talking about the afterlife. Now, there's plenty about heaven in the Bible, but Jesus is talking about His holy kingdom, here on earth right now, that He wants everyone to be a part of. It's a beautiful place to be, where He reigns with peace, love, hope, joy, and pure truth."

"That sounds nice. How do I get there?"

"You have to go through the fire. Just like the gold." Max smirks at his way of setting it up. "We can't take anything with us that would work against that peace, love, hope, joy, and pure truth of God's kingdom. It would burn up in the fire. But the devil—all he has is impurity. All he is, is sin and lies. That's why he would be afraid of fire. And it's why every Christian shouldn't be."

I've always pictured the devil as the strong, red, horned guy with the pitchfork and tail, laughing from his home in the fire. Like he was the god of the fiery furnace. But he's not. He can't go through the fire. It's his prison! All the times Longstoryshort got nervous about fire flash through my head. That eye for smoke and how nervous he was of the caldera below Yellowstone . . .

"Can the devil take human form?" I ask.

Max cocks his head. "Well, I don't know how that all works," he replies humbly. "But I do know that anytime we lie, anytime we accuse, anytime we take part in things that lead to death, we're willingly or unwillingly participating in the devil's schemes."

"So he's inside all of us?"

"In a way. There's an old Native American story about a grandpa and grandson around the campfire. The boy asks his grandpa why there's evil in the world. The old man thinks for a minute and then tells him, 'There are two wolves inside all of us. One is a good wolf, and the other is evil. They fight all the time.' The boy thinks about it and asks the eternal question, 'How do you know which one wins?'"

I've heard this story. "The one that wins is the one you feed, right?" I'm a little proud for finally knowing the answer to something. My mind drifts to the native vs. colonized debate that's been stuck in my thoughts. One side isn't good and the other evil. The people aren't. The metaphor doesn't work for that. But good and evil do exist, and they do fight against each other. Like the two wolves. God versus Satan. Truth versus lies. The Natives and the settlers each had both in them. They couldn't share a motorcycle because the motorcycle was a lie they both believed. Or was it? I don't know. I'm confused again.

"I don't know," I say doubtfully into our river-rushing silence.

"That's okay," Max says. "Humility is the starting point of all good things—not knowing is the beginning of wisdom."

Even that seems too deep for me. Why does this doubt and sadness keep coming over me? I was laughing not more than half an hour ago. I look over at the road, half expecting to see a motorcycle. I don't.

"So how do you make him go away?"

"The devil? You walk through the fire."

He leaves it at that. I put the Bible back in my pack and move over to the river. I find a rock about the size of the one I flipped over on the mountainside in Montana and sit down. I'm not after happiness now. I need something more. Something that doesn't come and go with the wind.

Max lets me mull in my thoughts as I toss pebbles into the water.

"You have a lot going on in your head," he finally says. "Have you ever thought about writing?"

"I have a notebook I've been writing in. It seems to help."

"Every genius keeps a journal, but not everyone who keeps a journal is a genius," Max says automatically like he's quoting something. "Have you ever thought about turning any of it into a book?"

Kerplunk. "No one would be interested in what a teenager thinks."

"You don't think so?"

"I don't have anything to offer the world. Nothing of value, at least."

"You don't think so?" Max repeats.

"Anyway, I wouldn't know how to begin."

"Were you able to pan for gold?"

"For paint chips," I chuckle self-defeatedly.

"Now that you know what gold looks like, would you be able to find it?"

Oh. "Probably."

"There you go! Then you can write a book!"

Wait. What? I don't get it.

"What if you began with how, when, and why you left home, then write out everything that has happened since. Every sight, every thought."

"I've kind of done that already," I say, thinking about sitting on the bench by the river in Sacajawea Park. "But it's not like a book or anything. It's just a bunch of thoughts and times and people and places."

"What else is a book made of?"

"A plot."

"You're living it. A kid on his way home, who somehow ended up with a bloody ear and panned for road paint instead of gold. You're living a story in the making!"

"But how does it end?"

"That's up to you," he says. "It's still being written."

"But who would read a bunch of random thoughts from a kid?"

"I would," Max says earnestly. "But it's not about who would read it and only a little about the writing."

"Then why write?"

"So you can slow down your thoughts. Writing lets you take a pan full of words and shake out what's valuable. The important things reflect the light, and what's muddy can be washed away. But the good stuff happens when you refine it. The more you put it through the fire with the red pen, the more refined it becomes. There is nothing holy that is unrefined. There is nothing refined that isn't holy."

I place the last stone on a stack of flat rocks at my feet and consider it. "Would you help me?"

"Of course!"

"What if I put all that work into it and no one likes it?"

"Then they can take a hammer and nail it to a tree. Is our worth dependent on whether someone likes us or the things we do?"

"I don't know. You were about to give me ten dollars for some yellow paint."

"Never write *for* praise. Write *to* praise. If it has an ounce of truth in it—"

Bang! A door slams nearby, followed by some yelling. Max and I turn our heads and see the drunk man from last night and the crying woman grappling in the space outside their RV.

"I'm going to call the police!" she yells.

"You're not going to do a thing, you stupid woman. You're nothin'!" His hands hold tight to her wrists as she struggles.

Max starts walking quickly toward them. I grab my backpack and follow.

Smack! He hits her, and Max sprints to the situation. The woman falls to the ground, dazed and sobbing.

"Get Maxine," he hollers to me as I stand frozen, watching. "Call the police!"

I can't move. Max is standing in front of the woman on the ground like an ancient wall. The other guy is pacing in front of Max, staring him down. His jaw flexes repeatedly, and his cutoff sleeves reveal tense, tight muscles. His clenched fists bob up and down with his heaving chest. I'm terrified for Max. That guy is younger, drunk, and angry. But Max just stands there, hands on his hips like he's linking arms with invisible angels.

"Call the police, Redemption."

"Get out of my way, old man," the guy roars. "This ain't got nothin' to do with you!"

I shake off the paralyzation and sprint toward the motor home, but Maxine is already walking around the corner with the phone to her ear.

"Call the police, Maxine! Max is in trouble!"

Her eyes get wide and she looks scared, but she immediately hangs up and dials the police. She walks briskly toward me. Together, we rush to the scene to see the angry drunk shove Max aside and grab the woman's arm to drag her up.

Two young country boys walk around the corner to see what the commotion is all about.

"Grab him!" Max hollers from the ground at the young men. Both of them are over six feet tall. The one with a mat of brown hair coming out from under a trucker hat looks like he wrestles hogs for a living, and the other is stocky without being fat, has pale skin, curly red hair, and a long country beard.

They look at each other and grin at the chance to use their strength for good. Why couldn't I have done that?

The drunk man is still yelling. "Get up! Quit causing a scene," he screams at the woman, who is fighting his forcefulness from the ground. Max gets up, but he seems winded from the shove. He leans one arm against the neighboring RV. A few faces move in the window behind him.

The country boys move in, taking the aggressor by surprise. The redhead puts him in an iron-grip bear hug while the other one pries the guy's hand off the woman's arm.

Then he bends down and asks a couple times over her sobs, "Are you okay? Are you okay?"

Max kneels by her side as well, with his hand on her back. "She will be now," he says, "if she wants to be."

A police car pulls in, and two officers approach quickly. It feels like I'm watching a real-life cop show. It's not long before the drunk is in handcuffs, pleading with the uniforms that it's all a big misunderstanding. That she hit him.

An ambulance parks in the middle of the road, and a medic begins tending to the woman. The two officers lead the drunk to the back seat of the squad car. One gets in the driver's seat, and the other comes back with a notepad.

Max hugs Maxine while the country boys give an animated replay of the excitement.

The police car siren blares a short *whoop!* and the policeman with the notepad nods at the driver as he approaches Max.

"I understand you were the first on the scene?"

Max takes a few steps to me, puts his hand on my shoulder, and replies, "We witnessed it all."

"We need a statement from both of you then. We'll send another squad car unless you want to meet us down at the station."

"It's only a few blocks," Max says. "We can walk. I could use the exercise."

They pull away. The woman sits with her head in her hands at the picnic table while the medics talk to her.

Maxine gives me a big hug, then holds on to Max, her head resting on his chest, her eyes closed.

"I wish you wouldn't always rush to save the day," she scolds him lovingly. "He really could have hurt you. You're not as young as you used to be."

"I love you too" is his simple rebuttal.

As we walk from the RV park to the police station, I apologize for not helping.

"I know I'm not supposed to be sorry, but I am. You ran to help like it was nothing. I just stood there. Those other guys helped, and if they didn't show up, you might have really been hurt. Or he might have beat her even more."

"You did do something. You got Maxine to call the police."

"She was coming anyway," I mumble. But I guess a few seconds might have made a difference. "It's just frustrating. I want to be a person who helps. A person who has courage. A person who knows what to do and does it."

"Wanting to be that way is a start," Max encourages. "Plus, you *are* doing something that will make a big difference. You were a witness, and you are going to give your testimony. Sometimes that's even more important than knowing what to do when it's happening. A lot of people wouldn't have the courage to speak up and say what they saw."

Like the people in the window of the other RV.

"Another reason to write your book," Max says.

"What do I tell them?"

"Just what you know. Nothing more, nothing less."

Nothing. It hits me.

I know what I need to do.

At the police station, we sit in a room together, and the same officer with the notepad asks which one of us wants to go first. I volunteer to go first, and one at a time in a cold gray room, he takes our statements. He says they will be used in court if it comes to that, but with our testimony, it's a pretty clear-cut case.

When we've finished, the officer thanks us and walks us back toward the station lobby.

"Max?" I say with a quivering confidence.

"Yes?" he calmly responds as we both stop walking and face each other.

I catch a breath, then look straight into his face. "Thank you for your hospitality."

The police officer stops a few steps in front of us and patiently allows us to have a moment.

"Are you sure?"

"I'm sure. I've got some fire to walk through. Tell Maxine thank you. Tell her I'm going to be a husband to someone like her someday."

"Are you going to be okay?"

A rush of confidence baptizes me, and somehow I know—I'm going to be okay. "The Lord is my shepherd."

"You know where we are if you need us. We'll stick around for a while." He reaches in his back pocket and pulls out a card with his phone number and email on it. "Call if you need anything. Any time. And email me your first draft."

"Okay."

"Give me your word?"

"I give you my word that I'll give you my words."

He thumbs back through the wallet and pulls out a ten-dollar bill. "This is for the gold I bought from you."

"You mean my paint chips?"

"Sometimes recognizing when something isn't gold is just as valuable as the gold itself."

He gives me a hug and says a quick prayer for me, nods to the officer, and walks away.

"Can I talk to you?" I ask the policeman. I manage to keep the quiver inside me from showing in my voice.

We go back to the interview room, and I tell him all about driving away from Dallas in my dad's car. I confess to abandoning the car on the side of the road after the wreck. I own up to using my parents' credit card and it being declined, in case they reported it stolen. I need to take responsibility and face the consequences if I really am in trouble. Or maybe clear up a missing-person case.

"There's more I need to tell you, but first I wanted to own up to anything I might be in trouble for," I conclude.

He leaves the room with my driver's license.

Part of me hopes it's not too bad and he can find me a way home, but my stomach is pretty sure there will be consequences. I'm a little nervous of what they will be. I imagine that when Mom and Dad get the call that I'm okay, happiness will come out on top of the slew of emotions they must be going through. At least I hope it will.

The officer comes back. "You're clear. No missing persons, no criminal complaints, no open cases," he starts. No missing persons? "There was a man arrested for trying to use your credit card in Montana."

"About that," I say, and tell him everything I can remember about the rest of the journey. Meeting Longstoryshort, him putting my declined credit card in the saddlebag of another motorcyclist, changing his license plate before going into Yellowstone. I recount being locked in the garage at Grace's, tell him where the house is, and remember to tell him about the other kids Longstoryshort supposedly helped. My heart aches for them with the clarity hindsight provides.

I describe Ghost—his tattoos, haircut, height, and features. I remember he drives a van and was supposedly passing through Dallas. I tell the officer about the conversation on the other side of the window at the diner in Little America. I can still hear the words, *I'll get him hooked this afternoon, and you can break him.* Everything is so clear looking back. Why wasn't it before?

I relive running away from the diner and Longstoryshort trying to force me back, hitting me, and my fight with him. He might have a bad left eye now under that matte-black helmet.

You're nothing, kid! You don't know anything!

I may be nothing. But I know.

You're weak! You're a coward!

But I'm not going to be.

Your family isn't even going to want you back! You're going to die out here without me.

I shake my head. He was just shouting through the fire. He can't hurt me. I hope what I've shared keeps him from hurting anyone else. I finish up by explaining who Max and Maxine are, and how Max not only saved that woman today, but they saved me as well.

The officer finishes scribbling notes I think only he can read. "Thank you. Would you mind staying here for a moment?"

I don't mind. I feel good. It's not happiness; it's deeper. Like my body knows I've done the right thing. Like I'm not running from anything anymore. And it felt good to tell it all. From leaving school to how I ended up with Max.

I will write it all down. I will refine it. Maybe it can help somebody, even if it's only me.

I flip open the notebook to write, and it lands on the drawing of the pictograph from the Swelter Shelter. The larger character dressed with lines of power and wisdom holding the universe, the smaller character shrugging his shoulders—it's me and Max. And it's not the universe or a solar system, it's a gold pan with nuggets in it. And the fading character with the mask over his head is Longstoryshort. And the floating arm was cut off to prevent the whole body, the whole world from being thrown into hell.

I can't stop the single laugh that escapes me. It seems absolutely silly, but it's all there, and it makes sense. It might just be in my head, but it gives me hope—like I've hit a landmark on an invisible map that overlays the world.

Almost like God is grinning at me now.

After probably half an hour of scribbling notes in my notebook (that probably only I can read), the officer returns with a laptop. He has me look through mugshots and police sketches. There he is. Longstoryshort. Underneath the picture of a sketch, there's a list of aliases. Bacchus, Phaedrus, Screwtape, among others.

"The left eye?" the officer asks. I confirm, and he turns the laptop and types some notes. While he's typing, he asks me more questions and to repeat a couple things. He works a few minutes more, closes the screen, and lets me know that Longstoryshort has been wanted for a long time in connection with a lot of cases. The information I provided might help them track him down.

I didn't see a photo of Ghost though. The officer asks if I would be comfortable describing him to a sketch artist. I do, and a few hours later, the officer and I walk out of the station into late afternoon sunlight. I feel worthy of God's love, courageous and strong.

The world is big and good for a moment, but then the officer asks, "So what's next?"

And the moment pops as I realize I don't know what I'm doing next.

"I don't know." How does the story end? "I have to get home."

His radio beeps and requests an officer. "Be right there," he says into his mic. "Stick around," he says to me before trotting back inside. "We'll figure something out."

How far is Golden from Dallas? Would they even be able to get here without driving all night? I know it's like six hours to Amarillo, and that's still two states away. Why didn't they ever call back? I sit down on a bench outside the station doors, then go back in to call home.

"Mom, Dad, it's me again. I'm at the police station in Golden, Colorado. Please call me back at this number. Everything's okay, but I need you. I'm sorry. For everything."

I wait outside on the bench, writing in my journal, reading more words of Jesus, trying to hum out some tunes from the hymnal Max gave me. I check in a few times to see if they called back. The police don't seem too worried about it, and I try not to be. Some social worker is supposed to come by later. I watch people walk their dogs and kids as the sun crawls across the sky. I practice silence and prayer.

An aggravated voice carries from around the corner. "So can I have my dog back now?" A softer voice answers, and I can't make it out. "I *told* you I'm not a criminal . . . and I am *not* a bum. I was just taking a nap. Since when is that a crime?"

The quiet voice responds, and then a short guy who could be thirty or fifteen stalks around the corner with a full camping pack almost as big as he is on his back. A medium-sized dog trots beside him on a leash. The man's floppy Australian-looking hat hides his eyes, but his face is clean-shaven around a French goatee.

"Jeez!" he says, taking a seat next to me and rubbing the scruff behind the dog's ears. "You'd think a person could take a nap in peace. My dog is still not biting anyone!" he yells around the corner.

"Everyone else has dogs around here. Calling me a bum." He looks at me. "Don't even know what a bum is. Jeez."

246

He doesn't look like a bum to me. Why would they call him that?

He mumbles to himself a moment more, then straightens up. "Terrible way to make an acquaintance; my apologies." He holds out his hand for me to shake. "Hobo Roadrunner," he says. "A pleasure to meet you."

EPILOGUE

I don't know what made me think it was a good idea to leave the police station and hop a train with Hobo Roadrunner, but I did. I'm sure if I'd gotten hold of Mom or Dad, I wouldn't have done it. I can't justify it with logic, but here I am in a park in Raton, New Mexico, waiting out the sunlight for the next leg. I'm going to make it home. I know I am.

I can't wait to surprise Mom and Dad, covered in coal dust and smiling a big white smile. They'll know how hard I worked to make it back. I'll get a job to get my dad a new car, help around the house to show I appreciate being part of the family, and finish out school with the best grades I can muster. I don't need to go out with my friends, and I don't need a phone to distract me or a girlfriend to keep me from feeling alone.

I used to think life was so boring, that there was never anything to do. But there are stories unfolding all around us, characters worth meeting, worlds worth discovering—and worlds worth avoiding.

Who even knew there was an underground culture of train hoppers and traveling workers? They even have an annual convention and an official code of ethics!

There is so much going on in the world I had no idea existed. I feel like when I get home, the problem is going to be that there will be too many things to do instead of too few.

I'm taking Max's advice and filling my story pan with words that

I can shake out and refine. I still don't know if Longstoryshort was actually the devil, but I am fully convinced he has embraced the evil that's inside him. It still seems unbelievable that kidnapping and trafficking are real, and that I was so close to it. I don't think that part has sunk in completely.

Why is it real? *Why* does it exist? I can only think that it comes down to people being overpowered and controlled by their animal urges, to a point where they no longer view other people as humans but as a means to an end. And they're willing to pay, to harm, and to lose their own souls in the process to get it.

But how do we stop it? Is it really a part of the machine that can't be removed? Or do we ignore it because doing that would also mean we'd have to address and remove something within ourselves? I can't help but think again of Mike asking for advice on how to approach lust, sex, and porn with his kid. The raging urges are real. The access to porn is quick, easy, and anonymous. Sex is not only available, it's expected and even celebrated.

Laws are already on the books, so how would more laws fix it? Or would it just become more underground? And that still doesn't answer what to do about lust. Could you enforce mandatory cold showers? Do you take arms and wage a war, or is it a war we have to fight inside first?

I think West was onto something. What's the difference between humans and animals? he asked. Humans have the ability to choose something better.

What would I tell Mike's kids? I'd tell them that those urges are normal and expected. I'd tell them that feeding the urges, though, only makes them grow. And there's a point where the need to feed the urge overpowers the ability to deny it. It can take you over. Isn't knowing that the starting point? The place it begins? I'd tell them that it's a fight worth fighting, and that there *can* be victory. But there can be defeat. Longstoryshort was a kid once too.

I picture Max saying, "Take it through the fire."

It's not too far a stretch from being teenagers having weekend parties and using alcohol as a temporary getaway to somehow ending up like Mike, Lewis, and Joe, drinking every night instead of being responsible adults making the world a better place. It's going to be our turn next, and we're just playing out the world that's been handed down to us. And that world has all types of evil. It's up to us to make it better, but to make the world better, we're going to have to acknowledge and address the evil that's inside us first.

I went to hobo church this morning, and the thing that stood out was how the minister told all of us grimy and wandering people that it doesn't have to be this way. There are resources out there to help, he said, but we have to want the help enough to use it. And not just to enable a lost lifestyle, but to help leave it. I didn't get the impression that many of the hobos thought they were lost. He said the hardest thing to accept is that we need change, and the next hardest thing is to make the sacrifices needed to begin it.

"It takes sacrifice," he said. "The devil hates sacrifice."

As for me, I don't want anyone else to be harmed by the world I came so close to being sucked into. I can't do much more than walk through the fire myself. That might be like a ripple in the river that is quickly swallowed up, but there really are resources out there that are making a difference.

I asked one hobo (he didn't want me to share his name) about the safety of women and kids in hobo world. He referenced back to the same Hobo Code of Ethics that Roadrunner told me about. He quoted rule number thirteen from memory: "Do not allow other hobos to molest children; expose all molesters to authorities—they are the worst garbage to infest any society." He also said he'd heard of hobo molesters and rapists being thrown under trains.

Maybe they have it more together than the rest of us. You never know by the looks of people. They also mostly all have phones. Some even have YouTube channels and chronicle their journeys. He said bluntly that porn is a problem everywhere and confessed his past addiction to it. He told me about a bunch of resources out there, like one called fightthenewdrug.org, where you don't have to be affected to learn how to help. He said he chose the hobo life to be free, but brought all his chains with him. He wants to reenter society at some point as a completely free man and help others get there too. I told him about Moses because that's what it reminded me of. He shared some of his beef jerky.

The sky is clear, and I'm hopping a train tonight. If everything goes right, I'll be home late tomorrow.

Monday evening, somewhere outside Lubbock, Texas.
Forget everything. Forget it all.

I lost Roadrunner at the railyard, running from the police, but not before I finally got through to Mom on his phone. Dad is in jail. "You're just like him," she screamed. "Don't come home!"

So now, I'm ducking a sandstorm in an abandoned house some-where south of Lubbock.

What do I do now?

God, where are You?

Order Information

To order additional copies of this book, please visit
www.redemption-press.com.
Also available on Amazon.com and BarnesandNoble.com
or by calling toll-free 1-844-2REDEEM.

CPSIA information can be obtained
at www.ICGtesting.com
Printed in the USA
BVHW081636151221
624016BV00009B/984